● ● ● ● ● ●

She sent Donna a copy of the finished video, and then she called her friend.

"Hello?"

"I'm done. Check your email."

Donna called back ten minutes later.

"*Oh my God, Shayla*! That's crazy!"

"Crazy good or crazy bad?"

"Crazy *good*!" Donna exclaimed. "I can't, oh my God... I can't believe you got him to admit so much stuff."

"I didn't have to do much."

"In the car," Donna said, "when he started talking about Millie, I don't think I ever hated him so much."

Shayla nodded. "That was pretty bad."

"And when he pulled his dick out..." Donna laughed. "Girl, he was looking good, don't get me wrong. But I almost threw up."

"So, you like it?" Shayla asked. "Is there anything you want me to change?"

"No," Donna said quickly. "It's perfect the way it is. When did, how'd you do that? When'd you learn to make videos like that?"

"I took some classes."

"Those cameras in your car," Donna said. "Where'd you get those? How much did all of that stuff cost?"

"It was expensive," Shayla admitted. "But I only had to buy it once. It's worth it to me."

"What about when he, you know, touched between your legs? I'm glad your face was blacked out, because I know you was about to scream."

Shayla didn't respond to that. Donna didn't understand the complexities of her perverted mind.

"Can you send me Joseph's email address?" she asked.

"Why?"

"I told you, I have to give him a chance to come clean. I'll send the video to him first and let him sweat for a while. If he doesn't confess, I'll send it to the rest of the church."

● ● ● ● ● ●

HARLOT

KEITH THOMAS WALKER

KEITHWALKERBOOKS, INC
This is a UMS production

KEITH THOMAS WALKER

KEITHWALKERBOOKS

Publishing Company
KeithWalkerBooks, Inc.
P.O. Box 690
Allen, TX 75013

For information write
KeithWalkerBooks, Inc.
P.O. Box 690
Allen, TX 75013

ISBN-13 DIGIT: 978-1-7320624-7-4
ISBN-10 DIGIT: 1732062471
Library of Congress Control Number: 2020901985
Manufactured in the United States of America

Second Edition

Visit us at www.keithwalkerbooks.com

MORE BOOKS BY KEITH THOMAS WALKER

Fixin' Tyrone
How to Kill Your Husband
A Good Dude
Riding the Corporate Ladder
The Finley Sisters' Oath of Romance
Blow by Blow
Jewell and the Dapper Dan
Harlot
Plan C (And More KWB Shorts)
Dripping Chocolate
The Realest Ever
Jackson Memorial
Sleeping With the Strangler
Life After
Blood for Isaiah
Brick House
Brick House 2
One on One
Brick House 3
Jackson Memorial 2
Backslide
Threesome
Backslide 2
Threesome 2
Election Day

NOVELLAS

Might be Bi Part One
Harder
Primal Part One
The Realest Christmas Ever

Hotline Fling

POETRY COLLECTION

Poor Righteous Poet

FINLEY HIGH SERIES

Prom Night at Finley High
Fast Girls at Finley High
Bullies at Finley High

Visit keithwalkerbooks.com for information about these and upcoming titles from KeithWalkerBooks

ACKNOWLEDGMENTS

Of course I would like to thank God, first and foremost, for giving me the creativity and drive to pursue my dreams and the understanding that I am nothing without Him. I would like to thank my beautiful wife and my mother for always pushing me to be the best I can be. I would like to thank Janae Hafford for being the best advisor, supporter and little sister a brother could ever have.

I would also like to thank (in no particular order) Beulah Neveu, Deloris Harper, Denise Fizer, Michele Halsey Hallahan, Priscilla C. Johnson, Kim Tanner, Tia Kelly, Edwina Putney, Melissa Carter, Cathy Atchison, Lanita Irvin, Ramona Weathersbee, Cynthia Antoinette Taylor, Jason Owens, Ramona Brown, Johnathan Royal, Sharon Blount, BRAB Book Club, and Uncle Steven Thomas, one love. I'd like to thank everyone who purchased and enjoyed one of my books. Everything I do has always been to please you. I know there are folks who mean the world to me that I'm failing to mention. I apologize ahead of time. Rest assured I'm grateful for everything you've done for me!

8

CHAPTER ONE
CHURCH SUNDAY

For as long as she could remember, Shayla Humphries loved Sunday mornings. This was the day God gave us for rest, a day for worship and for family. Sunday was a day for collard greens and black-eyed peas and pot roast with potatoes and carrots or a succulent Butterball ham. Sunday was a day for giving and for good will towards your fellow man.

Shayla considered these things as she listened to the voice messages saved on cellphone #3. She kept up with this phone by remembering the last four digits of the number, which, coincidentally, were 3666.

According to her father, 666 was an evil number, the number of the beast who would come in the end days. The beast would torture and horrify anyone who was left behind after the rapture. Shayla believed in the rapture. She knew the anti-Christ was real as well, but she didn't think there was anything particularly *evil* about cellphone #3.

Then again, some of the messages she got last night were anything but Christian:

"You a nasty wench! A demon spawn. You think you can come up in here and mess up what me and my husband got? Girl, you ain't messed up nothing! I see you for who you is, and so does Allen. You ain't did nothing but make yourself look like a slut! And if I ever see your ass again, Lord have mercy. My man's staying right here with me, so poof, be gone. Dumb ass whore!"

Shayla grinned and shook her head. She pressed seven to delete the crazed woman's rant. The next voicemail on her phone was from Allen himself. She rolled to her side and closed her eyes as she listened to this one:

"Hey, hey, Crystal. I – I'm sorry but I had to give my wife your phone number. She's, she say she's gonna call you. I'm, I mean, she, she probably is gonna call you. I didn't wanna give her the number, but she wouldn't let it go. She went through all my shit. I'm sorry. I'm, I'm really sorry. I still want, to, to see you. I wanna be with you, Crystal. Send me a message, if you can. I, I really wanna hear from you. And, I'm sorry about my wife. She's, I think she's gonna call you..."

That message made Shayla sick to her stomach, but her twisted grin remained. She knew she should leave well-enough alone, but it upset her that Allen's wife still wasn't getting the picture. Some wives will always blame the other woman. Even if they find evidence of multiple affairs, it's always the other woman's fault.

Allen's wife thought he was as pure as the driven snow. In her mind, every time he left the house, voluptuous vixens accosted him and threw him to the ground and raped him. They *forced him* to take them to nice restaurants. They made him go to the jewelry store and buy them nice things – things Allen would never even consider purchasing for his wife.

These scandalous women were the problem. They were evil and wretched. Some of them were real-live witches. They casted spells that made good husbands commit adultery.

Shayla frowned. She sighed. She opened her eyes long enough to dial Allen's home number. It was clear she was going to have to dispose of cellphone #3 today, so why not burn all of her bridges?

His wife Betty answered after two rings.

"Hello?"

"Hi," Shayla said. "Is, may I speak to Allen?"

Pause.

"Who is this?"

"This is Crystal – Oh my God. Did I, I meant to call his cellphone..."

"*Crystal?*" Another pause, this one longer. Betty's breaths came hot and hard. "Girl, I *know* you ain't calling my house." Her voice was low now. Low and mean.

Shayla scratched behind her ear and then held out her hand so she could examine her fingernails. She needed a manicure, but it could wait a few more days.

"Who is this, his wife?" she asked.

Betty exhaled loudly, mostly through her nose.

"Ain't no need for you to be calling me," Shayla said, "talking all crazy. Me and Allen gon' be together – no matter what you say. You might as well get used to it, 'cause whenever he ain't right in your face, he prolly licking on me. When he get home and kiss you, I know you can smell it. You like the way I taste, don't you? That's why you still with him, 'cause you like it."

Betty was so infuriated, she couldn't speak right away. "Listen here, you little nappy-headed–"

"Why don't we share him?" Shayla offered. "I don't mind sharing. Matter of fact, you can have him most of the time. I just want him one day a week, maybe two."

"He don't want you, whore!"

"Why he put hickeys on my thighs then?" Shayla wondered. "Why he spend your car payment on a bracelet for me? I don't wanna argue with you, lady. Let's just agree to disagree." She laughed. "We gon' share Allen. We doing it anyway, so you might as well get with the program."

"Allen!" The woman barely moved the phone away from her face before yelling. "Get your ass in here right now! I got your *whore* on the phone! How the hell you let her call our house?!"

"*Daaaang*," Shayla said. "Ain't you going to church today, Mrs. Archer? You know, God don't like ugly."

"You gon' get yours," the woman growled. "I swear before God, you gon' get yours!"

Her voice was so menacing, Shayla felt a chill roll down her spine.

"Tell Allen I'm sorry for calling his house. Tell him we can meet up at our usual spot later."

"Allen, get your ass in here *now*!!"

Shayla disconnected, and then she turned cellphone #3 off for good. It was a cheap, prepaid gadget she got from Walmart. She paid cash and never had to register it before use. She had absolutely no fear of repercussions.

She was slightly disappointed Allen's wife chose to stay, but she didn't feel bad about her role in their marital dysfunction.

Hell, their marriage was a sham way before she ever hit the scene. She tossed the phone to the floor and rolled to her other side, hoping to catch a few more Z's before she had to get up and get ready for church herself.

She was in a good mood. She loved church Sundays. It was a perfect day for rest and relaxation, good food and good friends and peace towards your fellow man.

Donna called at nine a.m. sharp. Shayla was up by then. She stepped out of the shower and rushed to dry herself but didn't make it in time. She put on a black robe and found her real phone (cellphone #1) on the nightstand. She returned to the bathroom and called her friend back as she opened the medicine cabinet and removed her deodorant and other essentials.

"Shayla?"

"Yeah, what's up?"

"You woke?" Donna asked.

"I just got out the shower."

"You still coming?"

"Yes, I'm coming. I told you I'd be there."

"I know," Donna said. "I was just checking. I'm, never mind."

"Are you nervous?"

"Yeah, a little."

"I thought you weren't coming," Shayla said.

"I know," Donna replied. "But I thought about it, and I think it will look suspicious, if I'm not there today, you know?"

"It's not like you think," Shayla said. She flinched a little from the coolness of her antiperspirant. "Nobody's gonna know you had anything to do with it, unless you tell them yourself."

"I'm not telling nobody," Donna assured her.

"I'm sure you won't," Shayla said. "And don't forget you don't know me. I won't say anything if I run into you, and you shouldn't speak to me either. Don't even look at me. You don't want them people coming after you when it's over."

"I know."

"For real," Shayla insisted. "I done seen it get real ugly, a couple of times. Some of the same people praying for you every Sunday will slash your tires if they find out you had something to do with it. They'll kick off they shoes and fight you right there in the church house. I seen it happen."

"I'm not telling *nobody*," Donna said in a hushed voice.

She was spooked now, and that was good. She needed to understand there were serious consequences to what they were doing. Shayla never had to see those people again, but Donna lived on the same street as some of them.

"Thanks again for doing this," Donna said. "If there was any other way..."

"If you wanna back out, tell me now," Shayla said. "'Cause it might get ugly."

"No, I don't wanna back out," Donna said. "He deserves it. You'll, you'll see when you get there."

"Alright, well let me get off this phone so I can get dressed."

"Service starts at ten."

"I don't want to be on time," Shayla said.

Shayla was tall for a girl, standing nearly five feet eleven barefoot. If she was thinner, she would've had the perfect build for high fashion modeling, but God blessed her with shapely breasts and wide hips that couldn't squeeze into most outfits from the Marc Jacobs collection.

But she had the perfect build for urban wear. She could rock a pair of jeans like nobody's business, and all the men found it hard to stay on task when she wore a pair of tight, black slacks to work.

Her skin was brown like Cognac. Her lips were full. Her eyes were small, but her lashes were long; they added depth and volume to her dark brown orbs. She usually wore her shoulder-length hair in a bun or ponytail. Today it was straight and layered with no bangs.

She put on lipstick and mascara and then slipped into a pink bra and panties set. She put her robe back on and left her bedroom for the first time that morning. She heard gospel music coming from her sister's room two doors down. Carla had her door open, but Shayla stopped at Lisa's room first. She knocked softly and then pushed the door open when she heard her friend say, "Come on in."

Lisa was 34, the same age as Shayla. They were best friends in high school and were still inseparable. They got their first apartment together during their last year of college. Three years later, they were both still hopelessly single, so they upgraded to a rent house. Shayla's little sister, Carla, begged to move in with them when she dropped out of TCU. Shayla and Lisa welcomed her with open arms.

A lot of their friends assumed there was constant friction in the household – with three grown women under one roof, but there were surprisingly few catfights. Everyone had their own life to live, and the roommates were never stupid enough to go after the same man.

Lisa was still in bed, cuddled up with a Zane novel. She looked up at Shayla briefly, and her eyes quickly returned to a steamy love scene.

"What's up?"

"Nothing," Shayla said. "I see you're up bright and early, reading your bible."

"It is a *good book*," Lisa said and snickered. She lie on her stomach with her legs bent behind her. Her colorful toe socks kicked the air casually. Lisa was attractive, but she was Shayla's opposite in many ways. She was half a foot shorter and a lot smaller. She could still fit into a size zero.

Lisa's skin was fair like coffee with two dashes of milk. She had short hair and large eyes and a wide smile that could barely contain a perfect set of choppers that were a little too big for her face. Everyone who loved her commented on how beautiful Lisa's smile was. Her opponents loved to call her "Big Mouth," which was mean, but not as bad as "Crocodile;" the moniker she endured in the third grade.

"What you getting dressed for?" Lisa asked, noticing Shayla's makeup.

"I'm going to church today. You're coming with me, right?"

"Hell no."

"Come on."

Lisa rolled her eyes. "I don't wanna."

"Do it for Jesus."

"He never did nothing for me."

Shayla chuckled. "It's a new church."

"Where at?"

"Alvarado."

Lisa's frown intensified. "Hell no, Shay! I don't wanna go to no *Alvarado!*"

"Come on," Shayla said. "You can bring your book with you and pretend it's a bible."

"Those country-ass churches are the worst."

"I'll take you to lunch afterwards."

"Why you going?" Lisa asked. "Who's acting a fool over there?"

"Joseph Youngblood, the head usher."

"An *usher*? Come on, man. That's not even worth it."

"It's worth it to my friend," Shayla said. "She says he's real blatant. I wanna see for myself."

"How many times are you going?" Lisa wondered. "I'll go today, but that's it. I don't like those hick towns. They make me feel like I'm stuck in *Children of the Corn*. I be waiting for Malachi to show up with his eyes glowing and shit."

Shayla laughed. "It won't be that bad."

"They probably got a blind organ player," Lisa guessed. "And at least one choir member with *special needs* – and *he* sings the loudest."

"Girl, stop," Shayla said, laughing. She turned and exited the room. "We're leaving in forty minutes."

"*I still don't wanna go,*" Lisa grumbled. She threw a pillow that bounced off the doorframe.

Shayla continued down the hallway until she reached her sister's room. Carla had her television tuned in to gospel music. She emerged from the closet in her typical Sunday morning gear: a knee length skirt, an unflattering blouse, skin-tone stockings and black pumps. She had her hair pulled back in a ponytail.

She looked her sister up and down and frowned. "Good morning."

"Good morning," Shayla replied. "What's that look for?"

"What are you getting dressed for?" Carla wondered. She went to her dresser and checked her hair in the large mirror affixed to it. She didn't wear makeup, but she found a pair of gold earrings that suited her.

"I'm going to church," Shayla said. She took a seat on her sister's bed and reached for Carla's bible. She opened it and flipped through the *real* good book, not surprised to see her sister's scribbles on nearly every page.

"Going to church where?" Carla asked, still looking at her mirror.

"Alvarado," Shayla said. "Beth Eden, off 67."

Carla secured her earrings and turned to face her big sister. "What are you going over there for?"

"Same old, same old," Shayla replied.

"You gonna sleep with him?" Carla asked.

"I don't do that anymore. At least I try not to."

"Who told you about this one?" Carla asked. She leaned with her butt against the dresser. She folded her arms over her stomach and looked down at her sister.

Shayla put the bible down and rose to her feet. Subconsciously, she didn't like to be in a position of inferiority. "Donna."

"Who's Donna?"

"One of my sorority sisters. I don't think you know her."

"She called you out of the blue and said you had to come to her church to take care of their problem? Couldn't *nooobody* else do it?"

"She knows I've done it before," Shayla explained. "She asked if I could check him out. And I talk to her all the time. It's not out of the blue." She chuckled.

Carla shook her head and turned back to her mirror.

"You gotta trip *every* time?" Shayla wondered.

"I just don't see why you can't come with me to Daddy's church, if you're going to church anyway..."

"You know I'm not going to Daddy's church."

Carla turned back to her. "It's not like you really going to church anyway, Shay. Your body may be there, but your head's somewhere totally different. You starting to act like Lisa. Do you even believe in God anymore?"

Shayla laughed, but her sister was serious.

"Of course I believe in God. I believe in Jesus and Moses too."

"It's not funny."

"Okay, it's not funny." Shayla straightened her face. "But what this guy's doing at Beth Eden isn't funny either. He's got a wife and six kids. *Six kids*, Carla. His wife's fat, and he thinks he's the smoothest thing alive. Everybody at the church knows what's going on – *except* his wife."

"Why can't somebody else tell her?"

"They tried," Shayla insisted. "But they never have enough proof. He keeps talking his way out of it. Even the pastor told some of the women to leave him alone and stop spreading rumors. After that, this dude got even more bold. It's disgusting, Carla. You should hear the way Donna tells it."

"And you're *drawn* to it," Carla said knowingly. "You don't just wanna help them, you wanna get all in the mix. You love it. You can't get enough."

Shayla opened her mouth and then closed it because her sister was dead on.

"Well, at least I do something about it," she said at length, "instead of just watching and talking behind people's back, like everybody else does."

"You think God respects what you do?" Carla jabbed. "Two wrongs don't make a right."

"I think it's too early to argue with you," Shayla said, shaking her head. "I mean, damn, girl. Can't I say good morning to you without getting this speech?"

Carla loosened up. She smiled out of the corner of her mouth. "Good morning, Shay."

"Good morning!" Shayla said. "Is Jimmy going to church with you?"

Her sister's smile intensified. Her boyfriend of two years was a bright spot in her life. "Yeah, he'll be here in a minute."

"How's it going with you born-again virgins?" Shayla asked. "Still standing strong?"

"We be having temptations," Carla admitted. "But we haven't done nothing."

"If I was you, I would've ran off to Vegas by now to hurry up and get the marriage over with."

"I ain't gon' lie, I do feel like that sometimes. But we only got three months to go. We can make it."

Shayla shook her head. When Carla and Jimmy first met, they were humping like rabbits. Shayla expected a niece or a nephew to be conceived any minute. But Carla started taking Jimmy to church with her, and somehow their father convinced them to become "born-again" virgins and abstain until they were properly married.

Carla surprised everyone by accepting the challenge with minimal heartache. Shayla was surprised to hear Jimmy went along with it as well. It had been seven months since the last time he got his rocks off (with a girl in the room).

"I need to finish getting ready," Shayla said and headed for the door. "Tell Daddy I said 'Hi'."

"I'm sure he'd like it more if you told him yourself."

Shayla kept walking. No way was she getting dragged into that fight again.

"Just tell him," she said. "You know, if I could go *one week* without arguing with you on Sunday morning, I'd take a purity pledge my damned self."

"Really?" Carla's face lit up. "That would be cool, Shay! I got these books you can check out, and..." she trailed off, and her expression changed. "You not gon' take no purity pledge."

Shayla looked back and laughed. "No, I'm not. But have fun with yours."

"I am having fun," Carla snapped.

"That's great," Shayla said. "Enjoy yourself."

"I *do* enjoy myself."

"Could both of y'all shut the hell up?" Lisa yelled into the hallway. "I'm trying to masturbate in here!"

Carla's eyes flashed open wide. She brought a hand over her mouth and backed into her room.

Shayla laughed and continued down the hallway with her eyes averted, not daring to see if Lisa was telling the truth or not.

CHAPTER TWO
MODUS OPERANDI

Jimmy showed up ten minutes later and escorted Carla to her father's church on the north side of town. Shayla and Lisa left the house together shortly afterwards.

Shayla drove her Acura because it was filled with surveillance equipment. She didn't think Mr. Joseph Youngblood would shed his sheep's clothing on their first encounter, but it's best to be prepared.

For morning service, Shayla wore a gray skirt that ran out of fabric two inches above her knees. Her blouse had the sleeves rolled midway up her forearms. Her black pumps had two-inch heels. Overall, she was appropriate for church, but she was aware of the subtleties that caught a man's eye. Her long legs were eye-catching. Her skirt wasn't skintight, but it was by no means loose fitting. Her ass was a definite onion, and men were inextricably drawn to her child-bearing hips.

She kept the top three buttons of her blouse open, exposing a good deal of chocolate cleavage and a hint of her lace bra – but only if she bent over (which a girl can't help but do every now and then, can she?).

"I got a call from Allen's wife today," Shayla said when they got on the freeway.

Lisa looked up from her novel. "Who's Allen?"

"The deacon at Mt Pleasant, in Plano."

"His wife called you?" Lisa wasn't too shocked.

"Allen called me too. He's been calling. He said he had to give his wife my number. But he still wants to be with me."

Lisa shook her head with a smirk. "I thought you were done with them."

"I am."

"Do they always call back after you put their shit out there?"

"Yeah. Usually it's to curse me out. But every now and then one of them gets stuck on stupid."

"You told me you didn't sleep with Allen."

"I didn't," Shayla confirmed.

"So, what'd he say when he called?"

"He said he was sorry, but he had to give his wife my number. He said she was going to call me – but he still wants to be with me."

Lisa chuckled. "What'd his wife say?"

"This bitch is stuck on stupid too," Shayla said with a frown. "She said her and Allen are staying together and he doesn't want me. Basically I'm the only reason they don't have a happy home."

"Damn..." Lisa rubbed her forehead. "I won't never understand women like that."

"I told her me and Allen are still messing around, and we not gon' stop."

Lisa cracked up.

"You wouldn't believe how hot she was," Shayla said. "She almost lost *all* her religion. I had to tell her, "*Mrs. Archer, ain't you going to church this morning?*"

"No, you didn't."

Shayla nodded. "I did. I told her just like that. I told her I don't care if she stays with Allen: We can share him."

Lisa's grin was big and toothy, kind of like a crocodile. "So I guess you're throwing that phone away."

"I was gonna throw it away anyway."

"And, was that a success or not?" Lisa asked. This was a question she posed plenty of times.

"Well..." Shayla tapped the steering wheel. "I exposed him to everyone at church, so they're always gonna look at him funny. His wife is too scared to leave, but she's on his ass now. I don't think she's ever gonna give him any peace.

"No matter what he's doing, she's gonna think he's somewhere with me. I think either he'll change and stop fooling around, or there will be so much stress, one of them will split. But the most important thing is he got demoted at church. He's not a deacon anymore, just a regular Joe."

"He can be a regular Joe and still cheat," Lisa said.

"I don't care about regular Joes," Shayla said. "They're not the ones behind the pulpit, lying to everybody every Sunday."

"I dig it," Lisa said, but Shayla knew that couldn't be true.

The only way Lisa could truly understand her friend's motives was if Shayla divulged all her secrets. And in all the time she and Lisa had known each other, that had never happened.

At a quarter till eleven, Shayla and Lisa arrived at Beth Eden. The parking lot was nearly full. The church was medium size. The grounds had been manicured recently. When they stepped inside, Lisa noticed the foyer was clean and well decorated.

"This looks nice," she told Shayla. "This an all-black church?"

"Mostly," Shayla said.

"There weren't any tractors in the parking lot," Lisa noted.

"I knew you'd like that," Shayla said with a chuckle.

The girls entered the sanctuary through a large, wooden door. Luckily it didn't squeak, because the pastor was in the midst of a light-hearted sermon. He was an older gentleman, over sixty, with a bald head and a thick pair of glasses that had a brown tint. He didn't look up from his notes or acknowledge the late arrivals.

There were nearly 100 parishioners receiving to the pastor's message. Before Shayla could pick a spot, a young man, no more than fourteen, approached and spoke quietly.

"There's some seats over here."

The boy wore black slacks with a short-sleeved, red golf shirt. Shayla looked around and saw four other teens with the same outfit. The young men stood stiffly near doorways and at the ends of the back two pews. They appeared to be a professional group of ushers. She wanted to know where their leader was.

As if summoned by her mind alone, a tall gentleman advanced from the left. He had on the same colors as his crew, but his red shirt was a long-sleeved button down. He wore a black tie and a black jacket. He was roughly Shayla's height with dark brown skin and short hair that was perfectly cropped. He had quick eyes and a large, somewhat European nose. He smiled at the ladies and looked Shayla up and down, in a not-so-Christian way, she thought. She knew his name before he opened his mouth.

"Hi, I'm Joseph," he whispered. "Are you ladies new to the church?"

"Hi," Shayla whispered back. "We're, um–"

"I'll take care of them," Joseph said to the teenager who was still standing there.

The boy backed away obediently and returned to his post.

Joseph smiled at the women one at a time. He had a slight gap between his front teeth, but he was still handsome. His fragrance was pleasant, and even while whispering, Shayla could tell he had a deep, commanding voice.

"I'm sorry we're late," she said. "This is our first time here."

"That's alright." Joseph wasn't tall enough to look down on her, but he kept his head lowered as he spoke. His eyes darted like a snake's tongue. Breasts – lips – breasts – eyes – breasts – breasts – lips – hair – eyes. "Y'all don't mind sitting in the back, do you?" he asked.

"No," Shayla said. She gave him a friendly smile. "That's fine."

"Okay, right this way." He led them ten feet to a half-empty pew. "Here you go."

The usher held out one arm and touched both of the girls with his other hand as they passed. Lisa got her touch on the arm. Shayla got her touch on the small of the back. Joseph Youngblood grinned like a jack-o-lantern.

The best friends sat at the end of the pew rather than scoot down to be closer to strangers.

"Thank you," Shayla told her new main objective. Her smile was just as sinful as his. "Thank you very much."

The service proceeded like any other. Shayla had been to church so many times, she didn't think there was any new information available, just new ways to tell it. Lisa couldn't give a rat's ass about religion, so she found the pastor's sermon as dull as an economics class.

Shayla's focus was on the head usher, and it didn't take long to see his focus was the two beauties God blessed them with this morning. The head usher didn't have a particular post like his underlings, so he moved about on his own accord. He never disturbed the service, but he took the pastor a fresh glass of water midway through the sermon. The rest of the time he was standing somewhere behind Shayla and Lisa.

He didn't have anything pressing to discuss with them, but he found cause to approach them *three times* before the pastor gave his altar call. The first time Joseph wanted to bring them New Visitor cards to fill out. Shayla signed her name as Vicki Williams. She gave them the number for cellphone #4 and left the address blank. Lisa indicated her name was Patricia Holman. She penned the number of another cellphone Shayla stopped using long ago.

Joseph stopped by the second time to ask if they were done with their cards. Shayla noticed the head usher made fewer attempts to conceal his glances at her perky bosoms. He reached over her to collect Lisa's card, rather than wait for her to pass it to Shayla.

On his third stop, he leaned close to Shayla's ear and told her, "Don't hurry off after the service. I'd like to take y'all to meet the pastor."

He was so close, his breaths made her ear tingle. Goosebumps sprouted on her arms. She was trying to play it cool, but if he was going to be this wide-open with it, she figured she might as well get started too. She batted her eyes and gave him a tender smile.

"Okay. We'll wait right here for you, Joseph. Don't forget about me."

The usher's eyes widened for a moment, like he got kicked in the stomach. He recovered quickly. His grin returned. "I'm not gon' forget about you, Sister Vicki." Before he walked away, he was bold enough to add, "Y'all shole look nice this morning."

"Thank you," Shayla replied. "Are you..." She gestured for him to lean closer.

He obliged.

She put a hand on his shoulder and drew him nearer still. When his face was so close to her cleavage, he could concentrate on nothing else, she asked him, "Are you married?"

Her warm lips brushed his ear. Joseph started to sweat, and Shayla knew she had just created one of those dreaded church house *boners*. The usher looked around anxiously with his mouth ajar. Shayla almost laughed in his face. She knew what he was thinking. If they were anywhere else in the world, he would've said, *Ummm*, or *Well, kinda*, or *It's complicated*, or simply *No, Ma'am*. But everyone in the building knew he was married. Plus his wedding band was as clear as day.

"I am," he whispered, grudgingly. "But..."

She couldn't believe he had the gall to add a "*But!*" She waited to see what wizardry he had up his sleeve.

He looked around and apparently realized this might be the reason some of the women at the church spread such awful rumors about him.

"We'll, um, we'll talk after church," he whispered and returned to his post, for good this time.

"That motherfucker ain't even *trying* to be slick," Lisa muttered when he was gone.

"I know," Shayla said, but she didn't tell her friend how much this cat and mouse game was turning her on. "He a wild boy."

The pastor's altar call was a farce. He said he knew *somebody* in the church was in need of deliverance. Somebody was going through something, and they were slipping away from

God's sweet grace, and they should not be too embarrassed to come up front so he could lead them through the Lord's Prayer. He said everything would be forgiven, if they would simply step forward and lay their burdens at the altar.

Shayla knew there were liars, thieves, pervs and sneaks sprinkled throughout the congregation like seeds in a watermelon, but no one raised their hand. No one burst into tears and lurched down the aisle like the miserable wretch they were.

"Maybe he should set up a booth in the lobby," Lisa joked, "so people can confess anonymously, like the Catholics."

"If they do, I would figure out a way to plant a camera in it," Shayla said. "That would be the best reality show *ever*."

The service ended with praise and worship, which was an activity even Lisa could get into. This was also the time when some of the flock felt comfortable enough to turn and check out the newcomers in the back. So many eyes settled on Lisa and Shayla, they felt like a museum exhibit. Most faces offered friendly smiles, but Shayla counted at least three ugly ducklings who couldn't conceal their envy. She noticed several men who had to work hard to keep their eyes in their head.

Quite a few people stopped to greet the city girls on their way out. Shayla thought everyone was polite and welcoming. She saw her friend Donna heading to the children's chapel to retrieve her two girls. As instructed, Donna didn't speak to her sorority sister.

"So, what do we do now?" Lisa asked as the crowd started to thin out. "I'm hungry than a motherf–"

"Hey, Vicki."

Shayla turned, not surprised to see the freaky usher was back. Mr. Youngblood had regained the composure he lost earlier. He stood proud and confident. His smile was gracious and professional.

"So, you came back for us."

"The pastor would like to meet you now," he replied. "He's waiting up front."

"Alright," Shayla said. "We're ready." She grabbed her bible, and they followed him to the first pew.

The pastor was standing with a sharply dressed man on his right and a doting woman on his left. The woman was roughly the same age as the pastor. Shayla could tell this was his wife.

"We got two new visitors today, Pastor," Joseph announced. "They really wanted to meet you."

Lisa coughed loudly with a fist over her mouth. Only Shayla thought her cough sounded like, "*Liar!*"

"Bless your heart," the pastor's wife told her.

The pastor reached to shake their hands. "How you sisters doing today?"

"We're fine," Shayla said. "I enjoyed your message."

"Thank you, young lady."

"This is Vicki," Joseph said and touched Shayla briefly on her shoulder. "And this is her friend Patricia."

"Where y'all from?" the pastor's wife inquired. "You don't live down here, do you?"

"I'm from Houston," Shayla lied. "Patricia lives in Cleburne. I'm on my way home, from a work trip in Pampa. I stopped to visit with my girl last night, and I figured I should go to church today, before I hit the road again. I asked around, and a couple of people told me to check you guys out."

"What kind of work took you to Pampa?" the pastor inquired.

"I'm a sales consultant," Shayla said, "for a pharmaceutical company. There's not too much going on in Pampa, but if they've got at least one doctor's office, that's enough to send me on a road trip."

The small crowd chuckled politely. Shayla didn't feel uncomfortable about lying to a pastor, in church, on Sunday, while standing in front of a huge crucifix mounted on the reverend's podium. She lied in church plenty of times. God had yet to strike her down for it.

"It doesn't sound like you'll be back here anytime soon," the gentleman standing next to the pastor deduced.

"No," Shayla agreed. "I just wanted to get my word for the day, before I move on."

Joseph Youngblood nodded.

"This is my son," the pastor said, referring to the sharp-dressed man. "He's going to take over the church one day. Sure would like to get more folks in here for him."

"What about you, Patricia?" the pastor's son asked Lisa. "Think you might come back to see us next week?"

Lisa coughed again and snickered. Shayla laughed too.

"Now you're barking up the wrong tree," Shayla said. "Patricia *never* goes to church. I had to bribe her with lunch to get her to come with me today."

"You should reconsider," the pastor's son told Lisa. "The Lord's got something for everybody. You don't wanna miss out on your blessing."

"No, I'm good," Lisa said.

"What do you–"

Thankfully, another woman approached before the pastor's son started evangelizing.

"How y'all doing?" the newcomer asked. She was a large woman with a baby in her arms and an older child hanging onto her clothing. She wore a floral print dress that was old and drab, but it helped conceal unwanted layers of cellulite. She got her hair done recently. Shayla thought her rosy cheeks were adorable. Overall, she thought the woman was beautiful.

"We're fine," Lisa said.

"Are y'all coming back next weekend?"

"Naw, baby," Joseph said. "They was just telling the pastor that they's only passing through."

The head usher spoke with a twinge of attitude. It was clear he was uncomfortable in the heavy woman's presence. To Joseph, she was like a big, nasty wart on his mouth. No matter how he tried to keep her hidden, she always popped up again – usually at the most inconvenient times.

"Aww, that's a shame," the woman said. "We sure would like to have you as members." She looked Shayla up and down and chuckled. "Gal, you shouldn't come to church with your blouse open like that. You'll have all these mens in the flesh." She laughed. Both of her chins jiggled. "Won't *nobody* pay attention to the Lord's word!"

Joseph brought a hand to his temple and rubbed softly.

The pastor's wife laughed too.

"She's alright, Millie. You leave these folks alone."

"I'm just kidding," Millie said and patted Shayla on the shoulder. "You know God don't care what you wearing, so long as you come to Him. That's the important thing."

"Amen," Shayla said.

The boy holding on to Millie's dress let go and latched on to his pa instead.

"Daddy, I'm hungry."

He looked so cute and hopeless, everyone laughed. Everyone except for Joseph. He looked like he was trying to will himself to disappear.

"You have a beautiful family," Shayla told him.

"Yeah," Joseph said. "Err, um. Thank, thank you, Miss Vicki..."

Donna called twenty minutes after Lisa and Shayla left the church. They were pulling into the parking lot at P.F. Chang's.

"So, how'd it go?"

"It went fine," Shayla told her. "He's a dog, everything you said he was."

"Did he make a move?" Donna wanted to know.

"Not yet. He was sizing me up. You should've seen how he looked when his wife walked up to us." She laughed.

Donna was too anxious to find humor in this. "So, what happens now? How does this work?"

"I wait for him to call," Shayla said. "I set everything up. I told him we weren't coming back to the church, and I gave him my number on the New Visitor card. If he is what you say he is, he'll call."

"What, what if he doesn't? Are you going to call him?"

"I don't have his number."

"I can get it," Donna offered. "We have a directory."

Shayla shook her head. "Me going after him is not the same, Donna. That's like..."

"Entrapment," Lisa offered.

"Yeah entrapment," Shayla said. "*Anybody* might cheat if a bad bitch like me stalked them."

"You ain't that bad," Lisa said.

"I'm badder than you!"

Donna was not amused. "But you are gonna get him, aren't you?"

"If he doesn't call me, I'll figure something else out," Shayla offered. "But he's gonna call."

"How you know?"

"Because he's a dog," Shayla said. "And all dogs are the same: They shit on the floor, eat their own vomit, and they can't think straight when it's some new pussy in the neighborhood. I know what I'm doing, girl. Trust me."

"Alright," Donna said. "I trust you."

Shayla could tell she really didn't, but that didn't matter because she was right, as always.

When she and Lisa returned to their home in Overbrook Meadows, just two hours after they last saw Joseph and his portly wife, she got a call on cellphone#4. Shayla activated a call recording app and then leaned back in her swivel chair before answering.

"Hello?"

"Hell, hello? Can, may I speak to Vicki?"

"This is she."

"Hi. This is Joseph." *Woof Woof!* "From Beth Eden..."

CHAPTER THREE
THE PREACHER'S DAUGHTER

Shayla laughed. "I knew you was gon' call."

"Huh?"

"I said I knew you was gon' call."

"What you mean?"

"You ain't no good." Her smile was wide and evil.

"What, I don't understand what you're saying," Joseph said.

"You don't understand what I'm saying?"

"No. You just..."

"Okay. We can do it your way."

"Do what my way?"

"Come on, Joseph. I gotta head back to Houston today. You don't have time to play around. If I'm wrong about you, tell me why you're calling."

"I, uh... The pastor, I was calling on his behalf."

Shayla rolled her eyes. "Mmm hmm."

"We, uh... We was wondering if there was something, maybe something we could do to get you to come back to Beth Eden, sometimes..."

"Really?"

"Um, yeah. We're trying to build-up our membership."

"So, what would you suggest? I live in Houston. You want me to drive four and a half hours every Sunday so I can go to your church? I'll have to leave my house at five-thirty a.m. You know what, better make that *five*, in case there's traffic. I'd have to wake up at least an hour before that to get ready..." she calculated. "Is that what you want, Mr. Joseph? Do you know how many perfectly good churches there are in Houston? The one I go to is only five minutes from my house."

"I, uh, I guess I can see what you're saying."

"I already told you I live in Houston," she reminded him. "Don't act like this is brand new news. Why don't you tell me why you *really* called?"

He took a deep breath and summoned his courage. "I just, you know, wanted to invite you to dinner, to go over some of the things our church has to offer."

Shayla shook her head. "Why should I go to dinner with you when we already decided it's not feasible for me to go to your church?"

"I, um…"

"Are you gonna bring your wife with you? Is Millie coming to dinner with us?"

There was a pause. She knew he didn't like her knowing his wife's name.

"Probably not. She, uh, she has to stay with the kids."

"What did I do to give you the impression that I'm a patient woman?"

"You, um… Huh?"

"I'll rephrase," she offered. "If I did something to give you the impression that I'm a patient woman, then I apologize. 'Cause I'm not a patient woman, Joseph. I don't like beating around the bush. Either tell me why you called, or hang up the phone. Are you a boy or a man?"

He cleared his throat. "I'm a man."

"Then act like it."

"I wanna see you."

"Good. And what about Millie?"

He swallowed roughly. "I wanna see you without her around."

"But that's your wife. And I'm single. You wanna see a fine, single woman by yourself?"

Joseph was a country boy, not smart enough to suspect a trap. "Yeah."

"Do you want to see me to talk about *church*?" she asked. "'Cause we already talked about church."

"No. I don't wanna talk about church."

"What do you wanna talk about?"

"Uh, you know..."

"Tell me."

"I'm digging you," he revealed. "I think you're beautiful. I wanna see you again, before you leave for Houston."

Shayla thought she had enough dirt for this portion of her exposé, but it never hurt to have more. "Did your dick get hard at church?" she asked.

He chuckled. "A little."

"Is that what you wanna talk about, how I make your dick hard?"

Joseph breathed heavily into the phone. Shayla knew exactly what was going on: His head was about to *explode*. His mind couldn't accept that a beautiful, voluptuous woman fell into his lap like this. Not only was Vicki fine as hell, but she liked to talk dirty. *And,* if that wasn't enough to make him have a stroke, she seemed interested in his indecent proposal. This was the scenario of his dreams. If only it could always be this easy.

"We can talk about anything you want," he said at length.

"Alright. I'm down," she said. "Where do you wanna take me for dinner?"

Joseph thought they'd reached the point where they could bypass the meal and go straight to a motel room, but no. Vicki was the kind of ho who liked to be wined and dined, like any other woman.

"Where you at?" he asked.

"I'm still in Cleburne."

"There's an Applebee's on Main."

She frowned. She thought she was worth more than a forty-dollar dinner bill, but it was her own fault for including *Cleburne* in her cover story. Applebee's was probably the fanciest restaurant in the sleepy town.

"That's fine," she said. "How about six o'clock?" It was a little after two now.

"That's cool with me," Joseph said.

"I'll wait for you in the lobby," Shayla said. "See you later, Mr. Usher man."

"Alright. I'll see you at six."

She disconnected and checked to confirm the app recorded the call. Back in the day, this would've been the end of it. She got Joseph to acknowledge he was Millie's husband, and he wanted to meet a young, single woman without his wife around. As a bonus (or *boner*), she even got him to admit she gave him an erection at church.

That was probably enough to cook the head usher's goose, but she had been doing this for over ten years. She was like a prosecutor now. She didn't want *enough* evidence. She wanted mountains upon mountains.

She had to meet with him to seal the deal. That could be dangerous, but she loved the thrill of the hunt. She loved when men put their hands all over her. In the old days, she loved sleeping with the men she destroyed, like a black widow.

She stopped doing that only because her little sister made such a big deal about it.

She put on a skin-tight dress and left the house at 5:15. She made it to Cleburne thirty minutes later and had time to scout the Applebee's before Joseph got there. She wanted to bring Mr. Youngblood back to her car after they ate, so her parking spot was crucial. She had to find a place that was secluded enough for him to feel comfortable kissing her, but *not* isolated enough for him to think they could hop in the backseat and fog up the windows.

She picked an area that was on the side but not right next to the building. There were no restaurant windows directly in front of her, but there was a steady flow of traffic behind her. She went inside to wait for her date. He walked through the entrance at five minutes till six.

Mr. Youngblood had on the same outfit he wore to church that day, minus the tie. That was an immediate turn off. It was safe to assume he hadn't bathed. She had already decided to avoid intercourse, and this reinforced her decision.

Then again, the head usher was a fine man. Shayla preferred dark skin over high yellow brothers. She thought Joseph looked like a chocolate bon bon. Plus he had a nice build. His bulging chest and shoulders offered a hint of how stacked the rest of his body was. His twelve and a half inch shoes made Shayla wonder what his Sunday morning erection looked like. The way he devoured her with his eyes made her nipples stiffen.

She stood and offered a dainty hand. "Hello, Joseph."

The usher didn't take his wedding ring off for this tryst. He took her small hand in his and shook it softly. "Vicki."

He looked her up and down, his eyes narrowing by degrees. Shayla's dress was dark red. It had a scoop neckline that showed off oodles and oodles of cleavage. Her hourglass figure was on full display. She knew Joseph wanted to see how well the dress accentuated her ass, so she made him wait. Rather than approach the hostess, she waited for her date to go ahead of her.

"Uh, a table for two," he said.

"Right this way, sir."

"I can't believe you didn't bring Millie with you," Shayla teased as they followed the hostess through the restaurant.

Joseph looked her in the eyes and grinned. "Millie who?"

Shayla didn't work on evidence-gathering while they ate. She had two hidden cameras on her purse, but it's sometimes awkward to keep your hand bag on the table during dinner.

Instead she enjoyed her meal, and she enjoyed the silly lovers' game they played. She never gave Joseph casual glances. Each time they locked eyes, hers had fire and desire burning behind her pupils. She reached to touch his hand several times. She adjusted her bra twice at the table, supposedly because it was new, and *"This damned thing doesn't fit right."* During one adjustment, she flashed a good deal of areola, and Joseph's eyes became as big as silver dollars.

He waved at their waitress. "Check please."

When they got up to leave, Shayla led the way this time. Joseph followed like a zombie, his eyes glued to her tail feathers.

It was seven o'clock when they got outside. They sun was starting to set, but they still had forty minutes of daylight. Before Joseph could suggest something stupid, Shayla asked if he wanted to sit in her car and talk. She could tell he would've preferred if she followed him to a motel, but he understood that *talking* and *taking her out to eat* are sometimes a prerequisite.

They climbed into Shayla's Acura, and she put the key in the ignition and turned the radio on. She turned the music down and pushed a button on the radio to change the station. But the station didn't change, because the button she pushed was actually to turn on her surveillance equipment. On the left side of the dash, a faint green light came on inside the air-conditioning vent. The cameras were rolling; it was show time.

Joseph didn't notice anything out of the ordinary, because his brain was still stuck on the beautiful areola he glimpsed inside the restaurant. He wanted to suck Vicki's titty so badly his mouth watered.

She turned to him and gave him a disarming smile before she got down to the business of ruining his life.

"Thank you for dinner," she said. It was important to establish she wasn't a prostitute.

"That's alright," Joseph replied.

"Didn't you wear that shirt to church today?" she asked. Her intention was not to embarrass him. She wanted the audience to know she had been to Beth Eden, and this adultery started at the church.

"This, uh, this a different shirt," Joseph lied. "I got more than one red shirt in my closet."

She smiled. "I'm still tripping on you having a hard dick at church..." She already mentioned this during their phone call, but it was so damning, she had to bring it up again.

He smiled. "The way you had your mouth on my ear, anybody would've got hard."

Shayla didn't like that answer. She needed to appear to be the victim, rather than the aggressor. She planned to delete that comment when she did her edits.

"So, are you sure about this?" she asked. "You're the head usher at your church. You can get in a lot of trouble."

"Don't nobody know where I'm at," Joseph said.

"What about your wife? I know you had to tell her *something*."

"She don't be all in my business like that."

"Why they call her Millie?" she wondered. "Is that her real name, or a nick name?"

"It's a nick-name," Joseph said. "I don't know where she got it from. It fit her though. Don't she look like a *Millie*?"

Shayla laughed. "I don't know what a Millie is supposed to look like."

"When I hear *Millie*," Joseph said, "I think of some fat, nasty heifer."

She didn't expect that, but she loved it.

"Why you marry her, if you don't like big women?"

"She wasn't that fat when I met her," Joseph explained.

Shayla chuckled. "That doesn't mean you have to stay married. You're the one who keeps getting her pregnant. How many kids y'all got anyway?"

He frowned. "Man, I don't wanna talk about that shit."

"That's cool. I'm just trying to figure out why you're here with me. It looks like you have a nice family."

"If it was so nice, I *wouldn't* be here with you," Joseph agreed. "My wife don't take care of herself no more. She disgusting. I don't even wanna look at her half the time. I love my kids, but them motherfuckers get on my nerves too. I wanna leave, but we got a nice house and cars and shit. So I dip out every now and then, whenever I feel like I'm about to go crazy. When I get back home, I'm happy. I can put up with Millie and them for another month."

Shayla laughed again. "Is that what you're doing now, dipping out?"

"You don't want nothing long-term either," he replied. "You going back to Houston."

"You're right," Shayla said. "I don't know when I'll be back this way."

"Then we both doing the same thing."

Shayla narrowed her eyes, but otherwise didn't show how much his comment disgusted her. She and Joseph were *nothing* alike. He was cheating on his wife and talking bad about his children, dishonoring a vow he made to God. She, on the other hand, was single with no kids. She was free to come and go and fool around with whomever she pleased.

But that was immaterial. She wasn't sent to be his guidance counselor. She was there to destroy him. She felt she had all of the preliminary evidence she needed. The next step was to acquire indisputable video proof of Joseph's adultery.

She adjusted her bra again and waited for his eyes to return to hers.

"What now?" she asked.

"Can I kiss you?"

She nodded and he quickly leaned towards her. She closed her eyes when their lips touched, and a smoldering fire erupted in her belly. Within a second, his tongue slipped inside her mouth, and his hand made its way to her breasts.

The trouble started long ago.

Shayla's mother was the middle child of a small, Christian family. Irene was fair-skinned, with big, brown eyes and long, dark hair. When she met Shayla's father, Benjamin was a recovering addict, working at the Union Gospel Mission in Overbrook Meadows' homeless district. Irene's church went to the shelter to help feed the needy one lonely Christmas Eve, and she found herself working alongside Benjamin in a well-organized assembly line.

It was his task to deposit a ladle of green beans on each plate as the homeless men, women and children shuffled by. Irene added ham and a golden-brown dinner roll. The young Christians talked and smiled a lot during the night, and when it was time for Irene's church to leave, they exchanged numbers.

Their courtship was not easy, given Benjamin's background and Irene's straight-laced upbringing. Benny spent many hours trying to convince her father that he was a changed man. He already did a lot of good in the community, but his ultimate goal was to open his own outreach church. He wanted to help addicts become productive citizens and parents again.

Few thought he'd pull it off, but Irene believed in him. They were married in 1986, and sure enough Benny opened his church the same year. He called it Victory in Christ Outreach. Within a month, Pastor Benny had four recovering addicts under his care.

Shayla and Carla were born four years apart. It wasn't easy growing up as "pastor's daughters." It was even more complicated because Benny didn't have a regular church. Everyone in his congregation was either recovering from drugs or the relative of one of the addicts in the "men's home," where the fallen angels had to live for at least six months.

Sometimes the men would sneak out at night and get high, and Pastor Benny had to kick them out of the program. Sometimes they came to the men's home with the sole purpose of stealing. Shayla learned at an early age that she should never leave her purse unattended – especially at church.

Despite these annoyances, she had a good upbringing. There was plenty of love in her home, and her mother was always there for her. That all changed in the fall of '97. Irene began to have terrible headaches that were so bad she couldn't sleep through the night. An emergency room visit led to follow up appointments with a neurologist and then an oncologist. Finally she was diagnosed with a malignant brain tumor. All Shayla knew at the time was Mommy was sick and her head hurt all the time.

Irene had her first brain surgery when Shayla was twelve. Her headaches went away for a while, but they were back within a couple of months. After Irene's second surgery, the doctors told Pastor Benny they couldn't remove all traces of her deadly tumor. It would grow back, and when it did, it would be considered inoperable.

No one told Shayla her mother was going to die, but she turned thirteen that year, and she had a good idea. She saw her mother's pain and her seizures, which occurred at least once a day. Even Carla knew Mama wasn't getting better.

Eventually Irene couldn't get out of bed anymore, and she was admitted to the hospice unit at Jackson Memorial. There was nothing they could do for her except keep her comfortable. She had an endless supply of morphine to make her transition to the other world as painless as possible.

It was around this time that thirteen-year-old Shayla experienced the most tragic and mind-blowing event of her young life. It's rare that an adult can pinpoint the exact moment when their world changed forever, but Shayla never had trouble pinpointing hers. It was February 14th, Valentine's Day. The year was 1999. The weather outside was cool enough for a jacket but not a heavy coat.

Shayla was in a foul mood that day because she did not get a Valentine's card from the boy she liked at school. Rodney gave his pretty, red envelope to a curly-hair girl named Nicole. Shayla wanted to talk to her mom about her first heartbreak when she got home, but she couldn't. Her mother was at the hospital. Her condition had deteriorated to the point where, on some days, she didn't remember she had two beautiful daughters.

Shayla couldn't talk to her father about her heartache either, because this was a Wednesday night, a church night, and the pastor was busy finishing up his message.

Benny dragged both of his daughters to church that day. Shayla would never forget how upset she was about the whole situation. She wondered why no one would be honest about her mother not coming home. She wondered why her father cared more about drug addicts than his own family. She wondered why she had to go to church three times a week, *every* week. She knew this wasn't the norm. Her friends at school were only forced to go on Sundays. Some didn't have to go *at all*.

When they returned to the house at nine-thirty, Carla went straight to sleep, but Shayla found dreamland elusive. Pastor Benny brought one of his secretaries home with them. They were in the living room discussing a rally planned for the following weekend. Shayla couldn't hear much of what they were saying, but she heard enough to know their banter was light-hearted, with a good deal of laughter sprinkled in. Shayla became angry, thinking it was not right for her father to have a good time with another woman, while her mom was sick in the hospital.

She wanted to go in there and tell them to, "*Knock it off!*" But she was just a kid, and even though her father hadn't spanked her in years, she knew he would take a belt to her backside if she disrespected him like that. She fell asleep with tears in her eyes.

She woke up three hours later. That was odd because this was a school night, and she was very tired. Even more peculiar were the new sounds Shayla heard through her thin bedroom walls. She knew her dad's secretary was still there because most of the sounds she heard were feminine.

But that didn't make sense, because it was too late for the secretary to still be there, and the sounds Shayla heard was not the talking she heard earlier. They were *humping* sounds – the kind of sounds couples make in R-rated movies. Shayla sat up in the darkness and frowned. The noises were discreet, but she knew she was not mistaken. Her heart thundered as she threw back the sheets and crept quietly from her bed.

At thirteen, Shayla knew what sex was. She'd seen plenty of animal sex on the Discovery Channel and caught a few glimpses of soft porn on late night TV. But when she crept down the hallway and pushed her father's bedroom door open, just a little, everything she thought she knew about sex was blown out of the window.

What Shayla saw that night was similar to the sex she saw on the Discovery Channel, but it was also one hundred percent different, because that wasn't some baboon's red ass pumping in the middle of her parents' bed. That was her father's big, black ass, and that was the first time Shayla had ever seen it. At that moment, ninety-nine percent of her being wanted to run back to bed and forget she saw *anything*, but one percent of Shayla's mind compelled her to stay there and watch a little longer.

Somehow the minority won out.

Pastor Benny was not completely nude. He still had on his tee-shirt and his socks. The woman on the bed with him wasn't fully nude either. She had on all of her clothes, except her skirt was pushed up around her waist, and her panties were pulled down past her knees. They dangled on one of her legs like a slutty ankle bracelet.

Another thing Shayla found strange was the woman wasn't lying on her back. She was on her hands and knees, and she had her rump exposed. Shayla looked closer and saw she was actually on her *elbows* and knees. Her face was pressed into the pillows. Shayla knew she was trying to muffle the sounds of their sinful act.

Shayla's eyes bulged. She was both disgusted and amazed. She watched her father grip the woman's ass and pull her hips to him at a quickening pace. She heard their thighs slapping together. She heard the woman's moans of pleasure increase in length and volume.

Pastor Benny told her to be quiet. He was sweating. The woman gripped the sheets like she was in pain, but Shayla knew she liked it. She knew this because the woman didn't just lean forward and wait for her lover's thrusts. The secretary threw her ass back at him, as fast as she could, so that the impact of his plunges was much deeper.

Shayla began to cry. She knew this wasn't right. She knew what her father was doing was evil. Incredibly sinful. She knew that if her mother was here, Irene would scream and cry and possibly attack the other woman. Irene might make Pastor Benny pack his things and leave the house, and in a couple of months, they would go to court and get a DIVORCE.

Even if Irene didn't catch them, Shayla couldn't believe her father would do this while her mother was literally *dying* at the hospital. She found it hard to breathe. She felt like she got kicked in the stomach, like someone reached into her chest and ripped her soul in two. The heartache she felt at school yesterday was nothing compared to this new pain. This was a hundred, no, a thousand times worse.

In that instant, Shayla hated her father and his lustful secretary. She wanted to run in there, with tears streaming down her face. In her mind's eye, she saw herself walk right up to the bed and point an accusatory finger between her father's eyes and tell him, *"You're a liar! You're a cheater! You're going to hell, Daddy! You're going straight to hell!"*

Her legs itched to get moving, but at the height of her disgust, betrayal and sorrow, she found that she couldn't look away.

Pastor Benny's pumps were already faster than a locomotive, but he found the stamina to go faster, and deeper. His secretary howled like a dog in heat, and her head shot up from the pillow. She looked back at the pastor with her lips set in a sneer.

Her face was moist with sweat. Mascara ran from her eyes in jagged lines. She was animalistic. Hideous.

"You finna cum?" she breathed.

Pastor Benny nodded stiffly, unable to speak.

"Wait, I wanna, I wanna taste it," the secretary announced. She pulled away from him, and Shayla was unfortunate enough to see her father's penis. She saw that it was big and hard and stiff. It glistened with the juices of their transgression. She watched as it bounced slightly with each of her father's heartbeats.

Her face grew warm with shame as the secretary spun around on the mattress and grabbed hold of Pastor Benny's manhood with both hands. She put it in her mouth – which made Shayla's eyes grow even wider, but at the same time, she was no longer revolted by their lovemaking.

On the contrary, Shayla stared in wide-eyed fascination. She wiped the tears from her face so she could get a better look. The secretary's neck whipped back and forth as she sucked, and Pastor Benny's body began to tremble. He grabbed hold of the woman's head and looked up to the ceiling, but the secretary took his dick out of her mouth and said, "No. I want you to watch."

Pastor Benny looked down at her, and the secretary began to stroke his manhood again. Shayla knew she should go back to her room, but a force beyond her understanding compelled her to inch closer to the gap in the door to get a better look. Her mouth hung open. Her eyes strained to take in as much as they could.

Pastor Benny spoke once more when he climaxed. He said the word, "*Jesus.*" Shayla would never forget that, because as he spoke, a white liquid squirted from his penis. His secretary gobbled it up like it was honey. She licked and sucked and kissed and slurped, and suddenly Shayla realized she wasn't mad at her father anymore.

And she knew that was bad.

And she knew she was bad too, because instead of being concerned about her mother, she was hypnotized by what she was witnessing. She couldn't wait until she was old enough to experience the same ecstasy the secretary felt. She wanted to bend over and expose her rump for a man. She salivated at the thought of what her lover's white honey might taste like.

She knew her thoughts were horrible. And when she crept back to her bedroom, she knew her mind was demented. She cried and thought about God and her mother. And when the sun finally came, she wouldn't dare talk about any of the things that happened the night before.

She wouldn't tell her father what she saw, and she wouldn't tell her sister, and even if her mom was healthy enough to understand, she wouldn't tell Irene either, because it wasn't just Pastor Benny who sinned that night. Shayla knew she was a sinner too. She was just as bad as the secretary, with her mascara running and white honey all over her mouth.

Twenty-one years later, Shayla continued to have misgivings, when it came to sex. She knew it wasn't right for head usher Joseph Youngblood to put his hand between her legs, but his hand was warm, and his touch was soft, and his fingers felt good on her labia. She spread her thighs for him, and Joseph slipped his fingers under her panties. He grunted when he felt how wet she was.

He sucked her neck and his middle finger slid smoothly into her juice box. Shayla gasped and thrust her hips forward, urging him to probe deeper. She didn't want to have sex with this man, but she would do it, just as she didn't want to feel guilty when she masturbated, but she did that countless times during her adolescent years.

Joseph spoiled the deal himself by being overzealous. He whispered something that sounded like, "*Goddamn!*" and then abruptly backed away. "This shit's starting to hurt," he said as he tore his pants open and let his dragon free.

Shayla looked down at his manhood, and her heart skipped a beat. Joseph was as hard as a steel pipe. His dick shot up a good eight inches from his body. And it was fat, too. This was the kind of dick Shayla could go to town on. She wanted to stroke it and suck it until his white honey came out. She wanted to yank her panties off and climb on top of him and ride him like the black stallion he was.

She might have done all of these things (and more) if a car didn't park behind them at that exact moment, reminding her where she was and what she was supposed to be doing.

Joseph saw the way she was staring at his dick and grinned. He was unprepared for what came next.

"Uh, what are you doing?" Shayla asked.

"Huh?"

"Why you pull your dick out?"

His bottom lip hung dumbly. "What you mean?"

"We're in the parking lot at Applebee's. And it's not even dark outside. You can't be pulling that thing out like that."

"I, I thought we was–"

"I'm a freak," Shayla admitted, "but, damn. I still have *some* standards. Put your dick up, man. Act like you got some sense."

Joseph put his soldier away obediently. "Alright."

"You wanna get a room?" she asked.

He nodded. "Yeah. For sure."

"Follow me in your car," she instructed.

"Alright, cool." Joseph fastened his belt and tried to adjust his boner so it wouldn't show when he got out of the car. "Which way you going?"

"South on 35," Shayla said. "I still gotta make my way to Houston when we get through."

His smile was big and stupid. "Alright. Lemme get my car."

"Hurry up, before I change my mind," Shayla said. She licked her lips, and Joseph shot his load of pre-cum.

"I'ma wear that ass out," he promised.

"Talk is cheap," Shayla said. "Hurry up and get your car."

Joseph opened the door and climbed out of the SUV. Shayla started her Acura and put it in reverse before he was a few feet away. Joseph looked back in time to see her put the car in drive and speed out of the parking lot. She went west on HWY 67 and then jumped on I-35 going north.

He called her on cellphone#4.

"Yeah?"

"What you doing, girl? I don't even know what way you went."

"I'm going home," she told him. "You need to go home too. If you tell your wife and your pastor what you did, I won't expose you."

"What? Hell is you talking about, girl?"

"Go home and make love to your *wife*," she suggested. "Tell her you love her. Tell her you're sorry."

"What?"

She hung up on him. She kept her thumb pressed on the power button until the device prompted her to Power Off or Restart. She chose the first option.

CHAPTER FOUR
THE EXPOSÉ OF JOSEPH YOUNGBLOOD

When she was a sophomore in college, Shayla dated a policeman named Roderick Owens. She met him during a routine traffic stop. Roderick claimed she was going 42 in a 35 mph zone. Shayla was almost positive she never pushed her speedometer over 40, but she didn't have to do too much arguing on the side of the road. Officer Owens melted when Shayla flashed her award-winning smile, and he put away his ticket book when she agreed to go out with him.

Shayla thought dating a cop would be fun, but Roderick turned out to be a big stick in the mud. He had an awesome body. Everyone thought he was handsome, but Shayla thought he was stale and corny. He wouldn't even wear his police uniform to bed, even though she asked several times.

Just when she was ready to give Officer Peabody the boot, Roderick got promoted, and Shayla was intrigued with his new assignment. Overbrook Meadows had a big auto theft problem. To combat it, the police department developed a task force which would bring bait cars to the city for the first time.

Roderick said it would be like the *Bait Car* television show: The police would stage an incident and leave a fully functional vehicle on the side of the road in a high-crime area. A car thief, noticing the keys were inside, would think it was his lucky day. He'd hop inside and go for a joy ride (or head to the chop-shop if he was a professional). What the thief didn't know was he was being monitored the whole time.

The bait cars were wired for video and sound. They even had night vision cameras, so the operation could run twenty-four hours a day. Once the theft was fully in progress, the police would follow him and shut the bait car down by remote.

Roderick said he would be in charge of the new task force, and Shayla couldn't hide her excitement. This was what she always needed: A bait car. Not to catch thieves, but to catch freaky deacons with their hand in the cookie jar. If she could get equipment like that installed in her car, she could take her vendetta to a new level. The possibilities were endless.

So she dated Roderick a full month past the day she planned to leave him. He didn't know anything about the surveillance apparatus, but after a little prodding, he gave Shayla the number for the company that did the installation. She called Spy Ville, and (for a hefty fee) they agreed to provide her with the same set-up the task force had – minus the remote to shut down her car's engine.

After she got what she wanted from Roderick, she kicked his boring ass to the curb. But he didn't give up without a fight. He sat in her passenger seat crying, begging her to give him another chance. She recorded his pleas with her brand new system, and she and Lisa made fun of him later that night when she downloaded the video to her laptop.

When she returned from Cleburne, Shayla opened her trunk and pulled up the floor panel to expose her spare tire. Next to the spare was a small CPU, no bigger than the average bible. She pushed a button on the side of the computer, and a disc popped out of the CD drive. She took it inside and got started on the download.

She had two missed calls from Donna on her real phone, cellphone#1. She returned the call while she rendered the video.

"I'm starting to think you don't trust me at all."

"Is everything, how'd it go?"

"It went fine," Shayla said. "I'm done."

"You're done?"

"Yep. Just got home."

"Wha, what happened?"

"He acted a damned fool. I got him with his pants down. A lot of incriminating evidence. It's open and shut. There's no way he can get out of this."

"You, are you sure you have enough? Girl, he's real sneaky."

"I got him with his *pants down*," Shayla reiterated. "*Literally*. Ain't no way he can talk his way out of it, when he's sitting there with his dick in his hand."

Donna gasped. "What? You, you got a picture of his *dick*?"

"Not a picture. A *video*. Get with the times, grasshopper."

Donna chuckled nervously. "What, what it look like?"

"His dick?" Shayla asked with a grin.

"I'm, I mean... Somebody said it was real big... I don't, I mean, I really don't care, but..."

"He can do porn," Shayla assured her. "I was half a second from jumping on him my damn self. He's a no-good bastard, but he is fine."

"You didn't have sex with him?"

"I don't do that anymore."

"What, what are you gonna do with the video?"

"I'm gonna edit it and put a little movie together," Shayla said. "I'll send it to you when I'm done, and you can check it out, let me know if you think anything's missing."

"And then what?"

"And then I'll send it to Joseph. I'll tell him to come clean, or I'm going to expose him."

"He ain't gon' do nothing but lie to you," Donna predicted.

"I always give them a chance," Shayla explained.

"I don't wanna give him a chance. He done had too many chances."

"I'm sorry," Shayla said. "That's the way I roll."

Donna sighed. "Alright. When are you gonna be done editing it?"

"Gimme a couple of hours."

Lisa appeared in the doorway when Shayla got off the phone.

"What's this I hear about porno dicks?"

Shayla laughed. "The head usher. Girl, that nigga's packing."

"You done?" Lisa took a seat on the bed and looked over Shayla's shoulder.

"I haven't started editing. But yeah, I'm done with Joseph. I don't think it could've went any better. I got this fool to call his wife fat and *everything*. He even said his kids get on his nerves."

Lisa grinned.

"And then he pulled his dick out at Applebee's," Shayla reported.

"Nuh uhn!"

"Yes, he did, girl."

"In the restaurant?"

"No!" Shayla said with a chuckle. "In the parking lot. In my car."

"So, you got it on tape?"

"And you know this."

"It was big?"

"Big and long and fat."

"You didn't do nothing?" Lisa asked.

Shayla knew her friend had a freaky streak of her own. Six years ago, Shayla took down a deacon at Mt Pleasant in Saginaw. The set up was the same as Joseph's, except Shayla was unmercifully attracted to caramel-coated Brother Brown. When she got him in her car, the deacon's kisses were tantalizing, and his hands were like electric eels; slithering and titillating every place he touched.

Shayla couldn't stop herself from ripping his pants open and giving him a blow job. When she gave Lisa a copy of the video, her friend stayed in her room for the rest of the night. Shayla didn't chastise her for masturbating with the footage, but she did tell her, "You nasty," when Lisa wanted to return to Deacon Brown's church the following Sunday.

"I didn't even touch it," Shayla said as Joseph Youngblood's video finished rendering. "I wanted to, but I knew I wouldn't be able to stop until we were buck-nekkid at a motel."

"You haven't had a video like that in a long time," Lisa noticed. "I would've liked to see something like that..."

Shayla turned and frowned at her. "You know, most people couldn't watch a video of their best friend having sex."

"Why?"

"It's kinda weird, don't you think?"

"I don't think it's weird," Lisa said. "I've seen all your videos, and I never *once* fantasized about you."

"I didn't say that."

"I'm not gay."

"I know you're not."

"But if one night I did want to, you know, cuddle with you in your bed, in our panties, there's nothing wrong with that."

Shayla gave her friend a look.

Lisa laughed. "I'm just kidding, Shayla! Jeez, can't anyone take a joke anymore?"

With Lisa watching, Shayla created the exposé for Joseph Youngblood. She started with a black screen and Silk's "Freak Me" song playing softly in the background. The music volume came up slowly, and Shayla inserted the words "HEAD USHER JOSEPH YOUNGBLOOD" in big, red letters. A second later she dropped Joseph's name and replaced it with "IS A LIAR!" and then "IS AN ADULTEROR!" and finally "IS A FREAK!"

Lisa thought that was an awesome opening. Shayla was just getting started. She faded to black again, and then inserted a picture of an old-time house phone. She added the sound of a standard ring for two beats. She then inserted the first phone conversation she had with Joseph. That call was perfect, so she let it play through in its entirety.

Lisa's eyes lit up when Joseph finally admitted that, ""I'm digging you. I think you're beautiful. I wanna see you again, before you leave for Houston." She shook her head in disappointment when Shayla asked him "Did your dick get hard at church?" and Joseph said, "A little."

"What?" Shayla asked her friend. "You don't like it?"

"I do," Lisa said. She was lying on the bed now, with her head propped on the heels of her hands. "I'm just wondering why he didn't suspect anything. 'Cause as I'm listening to this, I can see *exactly* what you're trying to get him to say."

"People don't think like that unless they have a reason to," Shayla said. "Nobody expects someone to record their conversations."

"I guess," Lisa said. "But I still think he's dumb."

"Oh, he's definitely dumb," Shayla agreed. "That always makes it easier," she said with a smirk.

After the phone call, Shayla faded to black and introduced the big, red letters again: "LATER THAT DAY…"

She inserted the video from her car at that point. She planned to delete a portion of the scene, but she let it play all the way through first, to make sure there wasn't anything else she should take out.

Lisa was startled when Joseph started talking bad about his kids and his Millie. She jumped off the bed and got closer to the computer when the head usher pulled his dick out.

"Oh my damn."

"I know," Shayla said. She shifted in her swivel chair, her panties unexpectedly becoming moist.

"I would've hit that," Lisa muttered.

"Don't think it wasn't hard to walk away."

"So why didn't–" Lisa abruptly started laughing when Shayla told him to act like he had some sense and put his dick up. "No, you didn't!"

"I don't know if you could see the headlights," Shayla said, "but somebody parked right behind us. And this fool's sitting there with his dick out."

Lisa chuckled. "It's hard to believe how in control you are. It's like, whatever you wanted him to do, he did it."

"Men get stupid over pussy. Next time you bring a man home, tell him to stand on one foot for ten seconds, or you're not giving him none."

"I can't do that," Lisa exclaimed, her grin big and toothy.

"Yes, you can. Try it. You'd be surprised how much power you have."

Lisa shook her head and returned to the bed to watch her friend complete the video.

After Joseph got out of her car, Shayla faded to black one last time. Her next message was in the same font she used earlier, but she changed the letters to white, rather than red.

"JOSEPH YOUNGBLOOD, YOU HAVE SINNED."

"SEEK FORGIVENESS,"

"FROM THE LORD AND YOUR WIFE."

"REPENT AND SIN NO MORE!"

Lisa thought that was a great ending. Shayla's video was six and a half minutes long.

"Is that it?"

"Hell no," Shayla said. "You know I gotta hide my face..."

Shayla rewound the video to when she and Joseph were in the car. She used editing software to create a black rectangle that was roughly the size of her head. She programmed it to obscure her face, wherever her head moved. When she was done, she played the car scene again. Everything was the same, except she was now an anonymous hoochie with a black box for a head. You couldn't even see her hairstyle most of the time.

"It's good you started doing that," Lisa said.

"I know," Shayla agreed, but she spoke with a tinge of regret. She'd been obscuring her face in similar scenes for five years, but she didn't think to do this with her first exposés. There were exactly *four* dirty videos out in the world somewhere with her beautiful face fully intact.

The worst thing about that was Shayla was a lot freakier back then. In two of her worst videos, not only could you see her face, but she went down on one pastor and let another one take her from behind. The odds of those videos resurfacing were slim, but she couldn't rule it out completely.

She sent Donna a copy of the finished video, and then she called her friend.

"Hello?"

"I'm done. Check your email."

Donna called back ten minutes later.

"*Oh my God, Shayla!* That's crazy!"

"Crazy good or crazy bad?"

"Crazy *good!*" Donna exclaimed. "I can't, oh my God... I can't believe you got him to admit so much stuff."

"I didn't have to do much."

"In the car," Donna said, "when he started talking about Millie, I don't think I ever hated him so much."

Shayla nodded. "That was pretty bad."

"And when he pulled his dick out..." Donna laughed. "Girl, he was looking good, don't get me wrong. But I almost threw up."

"So, you like it?" Shayla asked. "Is there anything you want me to change?"

"No," Donna said quickly. "It's perfect the way it is. When did, how'd you do that? When'd you learn to make videos like that?"

"I took some classes."

"Those cameras in your car," Donna said. "Where'd you get those? How much did all of that stuff cost?"

"It was expensive," Shayla admitted. "But I only had to buy it once. It's worth it to me."

"What about when he, you know, touched between your legs? I'm glad your face was blacked out, because I know you was about to scream."

Shayla didn't respond to that. Donna didn't understand the complexities of her perverted mind.

"Can you send me Joseph's email address?" she asked.

"Why?"

"I told you, I have to give him a chance to come clean. I'll send the video to him first and let him sweat for a while. If he doesn't confess, I'll send it to the rest of the church."

"I think you should send it to the whole church *right now*," Donna said. "Don't give him a chance to confess."

"Everybody deserves a chance."

"Alright," Donna conceded. "I'll send it to you. Thanks again, Shayla. For real..."

"No prob."

Shayla checked her email a few minutes later and opened the message from Donna. Joseph's address was jyoungblood132@gmail.com.

She composed a short message to the head usher:

"Did you go home and make love to your wife like I told you to? Your time is running out, Joseph. You must confess. Repent. Turn away from you evil ways. You have 24 hours."

She attached his video and sent the message from BLACKWIDOW11544.

When she turned off her computer, it was after ten. This had been a long Sunday. She took a shower and climbed into bed thinking about the dick she passed up and the stupid usher who was connected to it. She wondered what the odds were that Joseph would do the right thing. Probably slim to none, but tomorrow she'd know for sure.

On Monday night, she checked the voicemail on cellphone#4. She had four new messages. One was from the former praise and worship leader at Mt Hebron in Euless. He wanted to remind Trina (Shayla's name for that job) that he might be going to hell, but she was going to hell too. And when they met in the fiery kingdom, Lucifer would let him have his way with her forbidden fruit.

Shayla thought he was a fool for leaving the message, but that guy was old news.

The next three messages were from Joseph. She listened to them with an array of emotions, ranging from excitement to pity and finally a vindictive kind of anger that ensured there'd be nothing but trouble ahead. In his first message, Joseph was fearful and apologetic. In the second one, his temper started to get the best of him. Shayla chose to save his third message, because Joseph's frustration brought out his true colors:

"Bitch, what the fuck is you, some kind of detective? Why don't you answer your motherfucking phone? If I'm a ho, you a ho too, 'cause you was down with all that shit. How the hell you gon' record me and threaten me with some dumb shit? Who the fuck is you?! What do you want? I ain't got no money, so if that's what you looking for, you wasting your time. Why don't you call me, so we can talk about this?"

*He huffed and puffed. "You know what? You a shiesty ass bitch, and whatever you trying to do ain't gon' work! You the one that was on me! You called me! **You** wanted to go to that restaurant. You got this tape looking like I'm the one who was wrong, when I didn't even do nothing! All I did was, I just... Goddamn, I can't stand you, bitch! If I ever see you again, I swear to God I'ma cut yo motherfucking throat!"*

Gee willickers, Batman! Shayla thought, and then she laughed. She connected her cellphone to the computer and downloaded the threatening voicemail. She pulled up the final draft of Joseph's exposé and created one last scene. She called it "THE AFTERMATH." She added Joseph's rant, because the people at Beth Eden needed to know their head usher wasn't just a womanizer. He was also a foul-mouth thug who might be capable of violence.

Donna called after Wednesday night service with predictable news.

"That nigga ain't did *nothing!*"

"What you mean?" Shayla asked.

"He's still the head usher!" Donna reported. "He's still telling those boys what to do, and his wife is walking around looking stupid. She don't know *nothing*! Pastor don't know nothing either."

"I knew he wasn't gon' confess. He called me yesterday."

"What he say?"

"You'll see," Shayla said. "I added it to the end of his video. You said you had a church directory?"

"Yeah," Donna said. "I got everybody's number."

"I need emails."

"How many you want?"

"As many as you can get. I definitely need all the church leaders. And the gossips."

"LaTrisha Paige," Donna said right away. "She got the biggest mouth in the church. If you get it to her, she'll forward it to everybody she can think of."

"Good," Shayla said. "Gimme everything you got."

She waited thirty minutes and checked her email. Sure enough, Donna sent dozens of contacts. Her friend didn't write a name next to most of them, but a few important ones had additional info. Shayla saw one email was for "Pastor's wife." There was one for "Deacon Murphy" and "LaTrisha Paige."

Shayla composed a simple message from her BLACKWIDOW account. It read: "Joseph Youngblood is a wolf in sheep's clothing. He is an adulterer. I have proof. Check the attachment."

She sent the video to all the contacts Donna gave her, and then she undressed and took a hot shower. As the steam filled her bathroom and the warm spray soothed her skin, she couldn't help but wonder what the pastor's wife would think if she watched the video. Maybe someone would warn her ahead of time. Or maybe she always wanted to see the head usher's dick.

Shayla chuckled and told herself, not for the first time, *You know, you really need to talk to somebody about your issues...*

On Sunday afternoon, Donna called with good news for the first time.

"Oh my God, Shayla."

"What?"

"You did it."

"Tell me more."

"The whole church is jacked up," Donna reported. "Everybody is talking about your video! The pastor couldn't even give a sermon. He just talked about how demons were attacking the church, and everybody needed to stick together."

"What about Joseph?"

"He was crying like a lil' bitch," Donna said with a chuckle. "For the whole service, he was down on his knees, bawling at the altar. His wife was crying too, but she wouldn't go nowhere near him. The pastor told everybody to come down and pray for Joseph, but only two people did it. I never seen nothing like it. Everybody had their arms folded over their chests, and they was like, '*Uhn uhn. I ain't praying for that freak.*'"

Shayla laughed. "So, he's not the head usher anymore?"

"The pastor didn't say that for sure," Donna said. "But he did say we're gonna have some changes in the church leadership. He said Satan was attacking us from the outside, but we have Satan on the *inside* too, and he wasn't gon' stand for it."

Shayla liked that. It wasn't always clear if her exposés were successful. Sometimes a wife won't leave for months after they learn the truth about their husband. And pastors had to be the most forgiving people in the world. Shayla hated when they said stuff like, "Well, Brother So-in-So may have had a weak moment, but we are bound *by the law of God* to forgive this man..."

There was a chance that might happen at Beth Eden, but so far it sounded like their pastor recognized a snake when he saw one. He made Joseph grovel during Sunday service, and he promised there would be changes in the leadership. Shayla believed she'd accomplished her mission.

As for the folks who thought *she* was the one being used by the devil, they should open their eyes and see how the world really worked. The notion that only Satan did terrible things was preposterous. What about the story of Job or all the first-born Egyptians who were killed because Pharaoh was stubborn?

Sometimes *God* works in mysterious and horrific ways too.

CHAPTER FIVE
THE FREE MAN

The next morning Shayla had the most wonderful dream. She was up in heaven, standing at the pearly gates with Saint Peter. There was a long line of men waiting to get in. One by one, they stepped up to the gate and tried to convince Saint Peter they were honest, Christian men. They talked about how involved they were with their church. Some of them were deacons and even pastors.

But Saint Peter didn't care to hear anything they had to say. He listened politely and then he turned to Shayla. Without speaking, he asked her to cast the deciding vote.

She looked each man in the eye, and each time she recognized him. These men were all perverts and freaks. They turned away from the love of their wives and sinned with members of their congregation. Some of them used drugs and slept with prostitutes.

Shayla wore a look of contempt for every one of them.

She sneered and bared her teeth. She stepped forward and ripped their shirts open, revealing three bold, red sixes that were branded on their chests. She told them that they did not belong in heaven because God was not their father. Their father was the devil, and they had been doing their father's will during their time on earth.

"Now go!" she ordered, and a fiery, smoke-filled pit opened beneath their feet.

The men were banished to hell one at a time, but this was a never-ending battle. The line of sinners stretched for miles, as far as the eye could see.

Shayla turned back to Peter after she cast judgment on each man, and the saint smiled at her and nodded his approval.

And Shayla was happy.

And it was good.

She woke up at 4:38 am.

She still had over an hour of rest before her alarm clock was set to go off. She rolled onto her side without opening her eyes. Her elbow bumped a warm body. This was such a rarity, she opened one eye to see if he was real. She smiled. Freeman lie with his back to her. Shayla stole the blanket from him while they slept, leaving him with just a sheet draped over his lower body.

Freeman's upper body was beautiful enough to take a picture, especially his back. Shayla liked her men dark like black cherry cola. Freeman was a ball player in college. Years later, he still took care of his body religiously. She tagged along once when he went to run the bleachers at Farrington Field. Shayla thought she could hang, but she was exhausted after twenty minutes. She took a seat and watched him complete the workout by himself.

Up and down, up and down he ran, his sinewy legs flexing rhythmically, his tennis shoes barely touching each step. When he finally called it a day, his body was drenched with sweat. His tank top clung to his frame like butter on a biscuit.

Shayla didn't like dirty boys, but when he approached and gave her a hug, she didn't mind his sweat. She ran her hands from his waist to his chest and pushed him against a cool, concrete wall. She groped him unabashedly while they made out.

No one saw them, but Freeman laughed and told her she was too aggressive. Shayla blew it off. She knew he liked that about her. All men did. That's why they kept calling. They kept coming back. Freeman, for instance, was given his walking papers six months ago. Yet here he was.

She traced a finger down his spine and looked at the clock again. 4:39. She considered letting him sleep, but it wasn't like they were married. He only spent the night once, maybe twice a month, depending on her mood. She knew he wouldn't mind her twilight advances.

She scooted closer until her breasts pressed against his powerful back. She kissed him on the neck, and the ends of his cornrows tickled her nose. She wrapped an arm around his torso and inhaled his essence. She caressed his stomach and his chest, and her fingers slid down into his boxers.

Morning wood. There was nothing like it.

She grinned in the darkness.

He chuckled. "Sometimes I wonder if you even need me to be awake."

"*Somebody's* awake," she purred. She wrapped her hand around his hardening member and stroked tenderly. "Good morning."

"Morning," he muttered.

"Boy, I ain't talking to *you*."

Freeman Collier was once the head of the youth ministry at Mt Sinai in Overbrook Meadows. He was young and vibrant and never too busy to push the kids on the swing or hop on the merry-go-round when he got it going super fast. He was a middle school teacher during the week, which made him especially adept with his Sunday school duties. He always impressed upon his students the importance of working out and staying in shape.

It was probably the latter that did him in.

No man at Mt. Sinai was as fine and hallelujah sexy as Mr. Collier. He didn't help the situation by being a notorious horn-dog. The parents of some of the Sunday school kids flirted with him when they came to retrieve their little ones after church. If said parent was wearing a tight skirt that showed off a plump booty that God just so happened to bless her with, Freeman couldn't help but flirt back.

Everyone knew Freeman was married, but they couldn't understand why a man with his physical and mental attributes was satisfied with a woman like *Naomi Collier*. That girl was skinny and shapeless, and you'd be hard-pressed to find someone as boring. She and Freeman had two kids. Remarkably, she didn't sprout an ass during either pregnancy. Naomi also had a sharp nose and pointy chin that made her look like a chicken. People called her "chicken head" long before Project Pat popularized the moniker.

But Freeman stayed with his wife. Well, he did for three and a half years. Things started to unravel when a pretty, young thing named Larissa Cole hit the scene.

Larissa had recently returned to Overbrook Meadows after her no-good husband broke her heart while stationed in Japan. Larissa followed her army hubby around the globe for five long years. There was no telling how long he'd been sleeping around during that time. He finally slipped up and got a Japanese woman pregnant. Larissa booked a flight home before the urine was dry on the pregnancy test.

Six months later, she was doing her best at starting over. She had a new job, a new home, a new car and a new church at Mt. Sinai. The final piece of the puzzle was a new man. She thought she found one when she met a chocolaty youth minister. Freeman didn't wear a ring, and he responded to all her advances. He even touched her ass once when they hugged – and this was on church property.

When Larissa discovered Freeman was in fact married, and his wife went to the very same church as them, she nearly blew a fuse. In the old days she would've brushed the dirt off her shoulders and gone about her business. But the wounds from her husband's betrayal were fresh. Plus she didn't want her sons looking up to an unrighteous brother. She thought church should be the *one* place where you can find a positive role model.

She called an old friend from high school who she heard would help expose sneaky bastards who somehow made it to leadership positions in their church. Shayla said she'd be happy to take the assignment.

The first time she went to Mt. Sinai, she knew it would be an easy job. Shayla didn't have a child with her, but Freeman didn't protest when she walked into the children's chapel.

"Excuse me," she said. "I thought I was headed for the bathroom..."

"Uh, no," Freeman said. He wore black slacks with an olive button-down and black tie. His hair was long. He wore it braided to his skull. His eyes were curious, his eyebrows bushy. A neat goatee framed his soft lips.

"It's actually this way," he said. He led her to the restroom while thirty nosey kids looked on with smiles on their faces.

Shayla wore a dark skirt to church that morning. Her blouse was sleeveless with not too much cleavage showing. But her skirt was tight and short and a slit up the backside made it look even smaller. Freeman fell in love with her ass at first sight.

"You, uh, you can use that one down on the left," he said and pointed. "But that's more of a children's restroom. There aren't any adult bathrooms in this building." He knitted his eyebrows but didn't ask what she was doing there in the first place.

"Oh," Shayla said and feigned embarrassment. "I'm so turned around. This is my first time at this church."

He smiled. He had nice teeth. Overall, he reminded her of a young Michael Vick.

"This is a big place," he agreed.

"What's your name?" she asked and gave him a sexy once-over. "I think I might want to go in there and see what you're teaching. Are you a pastor?"

"Uh, no," he said with a grin. "I'm over the youth ministry."

"If I had Sunday school teachers like you when I was little, I'da had my black ass at church *every* Sunday," Shayla said.

Freeman laughed rather than take offense to her language.

"I don't know if I'll be back here though," she continued. "The pastor in the big building is boring me to sleep."

"I'm sorry to hear that." Finally he asked, "Do you have any kids? Did you bring them to church with you today?"

Shayla shook her head. "Never married. No kids. How about you?"

"I have a boy and a girl."

She noticed he didn't mention a *wife*. Her eyes narrowed. "I wouldn't normally do this, but I don't think I'm gonna see you again..." She pulled her cellphone from her purse. "Can I have your number? I wanna call you sometimes, if that's alright. My name's Crystal, by the way."

Freeman didn't miss a beat. "Sure." He took her phone and punched in the number. He waited until she was about to put her phone away before adding, "But I'm married. Is, that okay?"

"You're married?"

"It's complicated."

She chuckled. "It's okay with me, but what about your wife?"

"I don't tell her about every phone call I get."

Shayla shook her head and smiled. "I promise not to say anything either, Mister..."

"Collier," he said. "Freeman Collier."

She left the children's chapel and headed straight for the parking lot rather than return to the main building to hear the rest of the pastor's sermon. She got in her car smiling, thinking this had to be one of her easiest jobs. The fool didn't even try to lie or hide his intentions. It was like he wanted to get caught.

She called him a couple of hours after church, and he agreed to meet her at a restaurant that evening. They dined on sushi, and then she lured him to her Acura for some after-dinner smooching. By the time she put the youth minister out of her car, Shayla had enough evidence to bury him three times over. But she waited for him to get into his own vehicle and follow her to a hotel room.

She didn't record any of the action in their suite, but she wished she had. Freeman wasn't just built like a gold medal champion, he performed like one too. He licked her from her toes to her earlobes, and his stroke game left her breathless.

The loving was so good, Shayla felt bad about having to expose him. Rather than send him an ominous video like

Joseph's, she called him and tried to persuade him to do the right thing.

"Baby, you need to tell your wife what's going on. You need to tell your pastor too. You gotta step down from your leadership duties at the church. If you're just a regular church member cheating on your wife, I don't have a problem with it. But you know it's wrong to do this kind of stuff when all of those kids look up to you."

Shayla figured he was too nice a guy to curse her out, and she was right. But she didn't expect what came next. The youth minister began to pant and sniffle, and much to her surprise, he started to cry.

"You, you're right, Crystal."

Shayla raised an eyebrow. "Yeah?..."

"I'm gonna step down from my position at Mt. Sinai," Freeman said. "And I'm gonna leave my wife. I know it's wrong. I shouldn't stay with her if she doesn't satisfy all my needs."

Shayla picked her jaw up off the floor and asked, "Why'd you marry her, if you feel like that?"

"It used to be different," he explained. "When I first met her, I was new in Christ. I had just started going to the church, and they asked if I could teach Sunday school, you know, since I'm a teacher." He sniffled. "And then I met Naomi, and, I don't know... Back then I was looking more with God's eyes than with my real ones.

"I didn't care that she was skinny and, you know, kinda funny looking. She's a good woman on the inside, and that was all that mattered. We got married, and then we had kids, and, I don't know what happened to me. Pastor says my 'old man' is rising up. But I don't think it's my *old man*. I think it's who I am. I love your personality, and I've always liked women with curves. I think God wants me to have a woman I'm attracted to.

"You know..." He sighed. "I'm glad I met you. It's like, I wanted to get caught, so it would all be over, one way or the other."

Shayla didn't know what to think of him at that point. Her assumption was he was lying his ass off, but a week later she got a call from her friend Larissa.

"It worked," Larissa reported. "Freeman stepped down."

"He what?"

"He's not the youth minister anymore," Larissa reported. "I heard from Patrice that he went and talked to the pastor on Wednesday night. He said he didn't want to be in leadership anymore, and he was gonna divorce his wife."

Shayla's eyes were wide. "Who's Patrice?"

"She's the church secretary. Freeman wasn't at church today, but his wife and kids was there. She looked a mess. I didn't want to ask her what happened, but my friend Shaquika asked her, and she said Naomi said Freeman had left her."

Shayla shook her head in confusion. "Damn, girl. Your church has more gossips than a bingo hall."

"Gossiping's better than *cheating*," Larissa said. "Anyway, I just wanted to tell you thanks. I'm glad we don't have to deal with that no punk no more."

But that wasn't entirely true. Freeman called Shayla a couple of months after their tryst. He wanted her to know he left his wife, and she had been served with divorce papers. He was officially and legally separated.

Shayla wondered why that was her business, and he said, "I did this for you, Crystal. I'm a free man now." He chuckled at his own pun. "I was hoping me and you still have a chance to be together."

At that point, Shayla felt like she was the one whose life was turned upside down. Freeman did everything she told him to, but she never told him to do it for *her*.

She didn't want a boyfriend – especially not some freaky-sneaky who committed adultery Lord knew how many times. But she was glad he came clean, and she was flattered he did it for her. Plus she couldn't forget their night of passion at the Holiday Inn. She decided it wouldn't hurt to date him – but first she had to do some house cleaning of her own.

"Um, well first of all, my name's not Crystal..."

That was six months ago. Shayla wouldn't say she and Freeman had been in a "relationship" since then, but she had to admit they had *something* going on. She never told him what her true motives were when she met him, and she didn't tell him she continued to expose scandalous church leaders.

As far as he was concerned, Shayla was somewhat of a savior. She gave him the push and enticement he needed to leave his unfulfilling situation at home. He thought divorcing his wife would make Shayla trust and possibly fall in love with him. But because of the way they met, she didn't think she could ever fully trust him.

But that didn't mean they couldn't have sex.

With a few strokes, she had him rock hard.

He looked back at her. "So, I guess you're feeling amorous."

"What?" Shayla sat up with a start and looked around wildly. "Who, who said that? Who's in here?" Her eyes settled on Freeman's face. "Oh. Hey, baby. Didn't realize you were still here."

He grinned. "Very funny."

"I'm just kidding." She lie back and rolled away from him. "I'm alright."

He rolled towards her and wrapped an arm around her midsection. He kissed the back of her head. "What do you mean you're alright?"

"I'm cool," she said. "We don't have to do nothing."

He ran a large hand from her thigh to her ribcage and back down again. His touch sent tingles through her chest. She was completely nude. She didn't normally sleep in the buff, but she didn't have the energy to put on a pair of panties after they made love last night.

He scooted closer until his chest pressed against her spine. He pushed his hips forward, and his manhood poked between her thighs. Shayla's eyes were closed, her lips parted. Her smile was devilish.

He sat up on one elbow. He continued to caress her with his free hand. He kissed behind her ear and fondled her breasts. He caressed her belly and continued south until he encountered her eager kitty. He nibbled her earlobe and licked and sucked the side of her neck.

"Cut it out," she grumbled.

"You started it." He stood on his knees and pulled the blanket away. He admired her nudity for a moment before rolling her onto her stomach.

"Too sleepy," she muttered, but she didn't resist his advances.

Freeman straddled her legs and massaged her shoulders with his big, manly hands. Just when she started to enjoy it, his fingers slid down to her hips. He squeezed her ass and chuckled as he gave the right cheek a hearty smack.

"Ouch! Boy, you'd better quit."

"Get up then."

"Get up for what."

"You want me to beg?"

"Kinda."

"I ain't too proud." He pulled her hips towards him. "Come," he said. "Bring that ass over here."

Shayla quit her silly game. She brought her knees forward and pushed her ass back until she was in the proper doggy style position. She kept her head low and planted her forearms on the mattress.

Freeman rubbed her ass tenderly and fondled her clit. Shayla didn't feel wet, but once he worked two fingers past her labia, he found she was nice and slick.

"You got another rubber?" she asked him.

Freeman got off the bed without complaining. He found his jeans on the floor and came back with the contraceptive. Shayla waited anxiously while he tore the wrapper open with his teeth. She reached back and guided him in, to make sure he really put the condom on.

Freeman's dick was bigger than average. He always encountered opposition with the first attempt of insertion. The pain was not immediately pleasant. Shayla took a deep breath and blew the hot air into her pillow. She gripped the sheets and squeezed her eyes closed as he slowly worked his hips.

Just when she was ready to send him to the bathroom for lubrication, he got the head in. She inhaled sharply and shuddered. He backed out a little to get more of her moisture on the shaft, and then he entered again, slowly. This time he didn't stop until he was balls deep in her love. He backed out again.

Shayla moaned softly and looked back at him.

Freeman pulled her closer and started working his hips with a steady rhythm.

Shayla faced forward and blew out another moan. This one was laced with more pleasure than pain.

She let him take a shower first. She dozed off while she waited for him to get out. Freeman sat on the bed and woke her when he was fully dressed and ready to leave. He placed a tender hand on her cheek and kissed her forehead. She smiled before she opened her eyes.

"Awww. Aren't you sweet."

"Do you know what today is?" he asked. His voice was deep. He spoke softly and affectionately, but Shayla's smile slipped away. She hoped he wouldn't say something stupid like *It's our anniversary.*

She shook her head. "No."

"Today's the five-month anniversary of my divorce being finalized."

She frowned, hoping she wasn't expected to give him a gift or anything.

"It's been six months since I stopped sleeping around," he went on. "You've been the only woman in my life since then..."

She couldn't say the same for him, so she didn't say anything at all.

"Last month I asked you to be my woman," Freeman said.

Shayla shuddered inwardly. She wished he'd just leave. She wanted to roll away from him and pull the covers over her head.

"You told me you couldn't do that," he recalled. "You said that because of the way we met, you didn't trust me."

She waited. If he already had the answer, what was this conversation about?

"So, I gave you some time," he said. "I waited, and I fell in love with you and only you. We've been together for four months. So, I have to ask, hasn't it been long enough, Shayla? Haven't I proven myself to you? I'm happy with what we have, but I want more of you. You know that. Don't you want more of me?"

She sighed. She wasn't upset with him for asking these questions. As a man, it was only natural for him to want to claim her. And he was right about the past four months. He did everything he could to prove she meant the world to him.

All of her girlfriends thought Freeman was a good catch. He had the perfect body, the perfect skin. He was smart and sweet.

The only thing he ever did wrong, that Shayla was aware of, was cheat on his boring, unattractive wife. She felt she should forgive him. Freeman was nothing like her father. Unfortunately, she still saw her father in every man she snared in her black widow's web.

She shook her head. She opened her mouth to speak, but he got up and left the room before she could get the words out.

CHAPTER SIX
ALAINA MCGHEE

Shayla's sister was the first to leave the house that morning. Carla worked 7am-7pm as a PCT on Jackson Memorial's trauma unit.

Lisa and Shayla left the house together at 7:30. They were both employed at Midwest Media, a downtown advertising firm. Shayla worked as a marketing consultant for three years before she got Lisa a job in Human Resources.

Lisa drove this morning, while Shayla sat contemplative in the passenger seat.

"Freeman asked me to be his girl again," she said at length.

"What time did he leave?" Lisa asked. "I didn't see him when I got up."

"About six o'clock."

"Why does he leave so early?" Lisa wondered. "Why can't we all have a big, family breakfast?"

Shayla grinned. "That would be something, huh?"

"Can he cook?"

"I don't know," Shayla said. She frowned. "Did you hear what I said? Freeman wants to be in a relationship."

"I heard you."

"You don't think that's worthy of commenting on?"

"You two should be in a relationship."

"I can't."

"Which is why I didn't want to comment on it."

"That's kinda wrong."

"It's not wrong for me to choose not to argue with a tree stump."

"You calling me a tree stump?"

"Pretty much. I won't get anywhere talking to you about Freeman."

Shayla returned her attention to the morning traffic.

"Has your reason changed?" Lisa asked. "You still don't trust him?"

"It's not that," Shayla replied. "I trust him. I know he hasn't been with anyone but me."

Lisa nodded. "Mmm hmm."

"I don't think he'd cheat if we were in a relationship."

"Then it's not his problem, it's yours," Lisa noticed. "If I was him, I'd move on. He's wasting his time."

"But I don't want him to go," Shayla said honestly.

"You know, if you forgive your father, you can probably find a way to forgive Freeman too."

Shayla shook her head. "I can't forgive my dad unless I tell him what I know."

"That was a long time ago. You should be able to talk to him about it by now."

Lisa only knew that Shayla found out about her father's adultery. Shayla never told her she caught Pastor Benny in the act, because that wasn't the only problem. She still believed her unnatural fascination in the midst of the sin made her an accomplice.

"When are you gonna see a counselor?" Lisa wondered. "Everything you do, at those churches, is because of your dad's one, little affair. I know it hurt, but don't you think you're taking it too far?"

"Maybe if you believed in God you'd understand," Shayla said, growing irritated. "When you're a pastor, it's not *one little affair*. It's a *very big deal*. When you have a church and a congregation that believes in you... They give you money every service to keep the church going, but they're also paying for your house and your car and your food, clothes for you and your family. If God supposedly called you to be the one to lead a group of people, then *no*, you can't act like everybody else. You're special. If you don't want to be special, then you need to sit with the regular folks.

"My daddy wasn't just a preacher, Lisa. He was my whole world. And it's not *one little affair* when my mama's in the hospital with a nasty glob of cancer eating her brain out. There's nothing insignificant about that."

Lisa heard this argument before. She didn't back down. "Fine, Shayla. If that's the reason you give for your *hobby*, that's great. More power to you. But Freeman doesn't deserve to be stuck in limbo. He left his wife and kids for you. He got a divorce and stepped down from his position at church. What more do you want?"

"*I don't know*," Shayla growled.

"That's why you have to go to counseling."

Shayla rolled her eyes. She was sick of coming back to this conclusion.

"You're the one who's acting like a tree stump."

Lisa grinned. "But you know I'm right..."

"You're *something*," Shayla said. She was upset, but her friend's toothy smile helped her let it go. She didn't always like Lisa's honesty, but it was good to get a no-bullshit assessment every now and then.

Midwest Media employed more than 2,000 people. By ten o'clock, they were all fully engaged in their specific duties. On the sixth floor, Shayla and her team were finishing up an ad campaign for Johnson Pharmaceuticals when another manager paid them a visit. Patricia Moresby supervised a crew two floors down.

"Having fun?" she asked.

Patricia was tall and attractive, one of the friendlier people in the building.

"We're making progress," Shayla told her. "What's up?"

"Just stopping by to introduce a new hire. Her name's Alaina McGhee. Alaina, these are some of the marketing consultants."

Patricia stepped aside to allow Alaina room to peek inside the boardroom, and Shayla's heart stopped cold. A chill ran through every bone in her body. As she struggled to breathe,

Shayla (not for the first time) was glad she had dark skin. Thanks to her melanin, no one saw the blood rush from her face.

The new hire was a short woman. Her hair was styled in a bun. Alaina had skin the color of caramel, big lips with a coat of red lipstick. She was overweight, but not unattractively so.

Shayla fought hard to keep her eyes from bugging. Just when she was able to take a breath, Alaina scanned the people in the room, and the two women locked eyes. Alaina's smile fell. She couldn't hide her look of shock any more than Shayla could. Then she looked away, at Robert and Stephanie, but her eyes came back to Shayla.

"That's Lynda..." Patricia was saying. "That's Jesse on the end, and Robert, and Trisha, and Shayla..."

"Nice to meet y'all," Alaina said.

Shayla's face was burning now. She was sure she'd broken out in a sweat. She looked away. The women locked eyes again, and Alaina looked away.

The introduction lasted no more than twenty seconds, but to Shayla, it felt like an eternity.

"We'll see you guys later," Patricia said as she backed out of the room. "I got a few more people I want to introduce her to."

"Nice to meet y'all," Alaina said again, a lot less cheery this time, Shayla noticed. The new hire turned and followed her manager down the hallway.

When she was sure they were gone, Shayla looked up and took a deep breath. She had goose bumps on her arms and neck. She wiped her brow, and sure enough, her forehead was dotted with sweat. She thought she might throw up. If she even looked at a toilet at that moment, her breakfast would come up for sure. None of her colleagues noticed something was amiss.

Alaina McGhee.

Shayla didn't know the woman's name during their first encounter, but now she knew she'd never forget it.

The group broke up at eleven-thirty. As soon as she got back to her office, Shayla called her friend downstairs.

"Human Resources. This is Lisa."

"Did you forget to tell me about the new hire?"

"What are you talking about?"

"*Alaina McGhee,*" Shayla hissed. "Patricia brought her by, says she's the new girl in advertising."

Lisa thought for a second. "Short, black lady? A lotta lipstick? A little chubby?"

"That's the one." Shayla's stomach rolled. She tasted acid in the back of her throat.

"What about her?" Lisa asked. "What's the problem?"

"You didn't recognize her?"

"No."

"First United in Mesquite," Shayla prompted.

"I don't remember her," Lisa said, "or that church."

"How could you not remember *Pastor McGhee*?" Shayla wondered. "Tall, light-skinned dude. He bought me that tennis bracelet, the one you wore to the Christmas party last year..."

"The guy with the new Mustang?" Lisa asked. "With the big wheels?"

"That's him," Shayla said, happy to hear some recognition.

Pastor McGhee's exposé ended fifteen months ago. The first time she and Lisa attended his church, they saw the pretty Mustang with gleaming 22-inch rims parked in a spot reserved for the pastor. Lisa said that was exactly what she didn't like about church: It was bad enough the pastors live high on the hog off money they collected from their poor congregation. But some of them didn't have the decency to keep it on the down low.

Shayla strung Pastor McGhee along for weeks because he was constantly buying her gifts, hoping he'd one day offer her something special enough to pry her beautiful legs open. He was not successful. When Shayla grew tired of his advances, she sent his exposé video to most of the members of his church. Last she heard, he had been ousted.

"Alaina McGhee is Pastor McGhee's wife," she told Lisa.

"Uh uhn."

"Girl, why would I say it if it wasn't true?"

"You recognized her?"

"*Yes,*" Shayla said, near exasperation.

"She recognized you too?"

"She did. But I don't know how. I blocked my face in that video. And we only went to their church twice."

"Yeah, but it was a small church," Lisa recalled. "They don't do nothing but gossip in those little churches. Every eye was on us the moment we walked through the doors, especially with that outfit you had on."

Shayla didn't remember what she wore to First United, but it was always something borderline-inappropriate.

"Just because she recognizes you, doesn't mean she knows you're the one who slept with her husband," Lisa offered.

"I didn't sleep with him," Shayla reminded her.

"I know. But your video made it look like you did."

"What if she *does* know it was me in the video?" Shayla wondered.

"Don't bother what-iffing yourself to death," Lisa advised her. "You might as well assume everything you think is true: She remembers you from church, and she knows you're the girl in the video."

"I don't wanna assume *that*! Why, how could you let this happen?"

"Why you blaming *me*?"

"You work in *Human Resources*. Basically, you hired her."

Lisa laughed. "I didn't hire her, Shay. I just push papers. Patricia Moresby hired her."

"You did her screening," Shayla pouted. "You took the picture for her ID card and everything."

"Shayla, I didn't remember the girl. I still don't, not really. What do you think's gonna happen?"

"I don't know. Damn." She sighed. "What the hell is she doing in Overbrook Meadows anyway? Mesquite is damn near 50 miles away."

"It's obviously a coincidence," Lisa said. "Why are you so worried? What do you think she's gonna do?"

"There's only three ways this can go," Shayla surmised. "Either she'll attack me, or she'll start telling people stuff about me, or she won't do nothing at all."

"And you win either way," Lisa said. "If she attacks you, she gets fired. If she starts spreading rumors, she gets fired. And if she does nothing, then there's no problem."

"I still have to see her every day," Shayla whined. "That *is* a problem."

"How often do you see people from her department?" Lisa wondered.

Shayla shook her head. "Not that much, but still…"

"I don't know why you're so surprised. Texas is big, but it ain't *that* damn big. You should've known you'd run into someone you messed over sooner or later."

Shayla frowned. "That's your solution? Get over it, because it was bound to happen?"

"No, that's not a solution, Shay. You don't need to come up with a solution until she makes a move. Don't get bent out of shape over what might be nothing. Just go on about your business."

That was good advice, but Shayla didn't think she could take it. How do you go on about your business when your new coworker knows you're the whore who slept with her husband? For all Shayla knew, she might have caused Alaina's marriage to end.

"Where you going for lunch?" she asked.

"Chick-Fil-A," Lisa said. "You want something?"

"I'm not that hungry, but I could eat some waffle fries."

"Are you okay?" Lisa asked. "You don't sound too good."

"The wages of sin is death," Shayla said. "So anything that doesn't kill me, I'm pretty sure I can handle."

"That's the spirit. And if shit does hit the fan, remember: You've been here for five years. They'll fire Alaina way before they fire you."

Shayla tried to find solace in that, but she couldn't. Her work persona was completely separate from the flirty girl she portrayed at the churches she visited. She worked hard to build a solid reputation at her job. She'd prefer the shit not hit the fan at all.

"Call me when you get back with the fries," she told Lisa. "I'll come down and get them."

CHAPTER SEVEN
PASTOR BENNY

Lisa and Shayla were still talking about Alaina when they got home. Shayla tried to cut the conversation short before they went inside, but her best bud didn't have a clue.

"If you're still worried about it, I can probably find some way to get her fired."

"No, I don't want to do that," Shayla said. "Not right now, at least."

She followed her friend into the kitchen. They found her sister at the sink washing dishes. Carla had on a white tee shirt with the teal scrub pants she had to wear to work at the hospital. She dried her hands and turned to face her roommates.

"How was your day?"

"It was fine," Shayla said.

She continued down the hallway, but Carla asked, "Who y'all trying to get fired?"

"Oops," Lisa said.

Shayla stopped and rolled her eyes. "Nobody," she called over her shoulder. "We was just kidding."

Carla grinned. "How come you don't never talk to me no more. I like kidding around too."

Shayla shook her head. She went back to the kitchen and took a seat at the table.

"Today I ran into someone from my past," she explained. "She's the wife of a pastor I exposed. Or, at least she *was* his wife. They might have broke up."

Carla's eyes widened. She sat across from her big sister with her mouth open.

"She works with you?"

"Not directly. She works in a different department. Lisa's the one who hired her."

"I didn't hire *nobody*," Lisa said. She backed out of the refrigerator with leftover spaghetti.

"She remembers you?" Carla asked her sister.

"She looked like she did," Shayla said. "But I don't know if she remembers me from going to her church, or if she knows I'm the one who got her husband in trouble."

Carla shook her head. "You can't fire her."

"I don't want to fire her," Shayla said. "She doesn't work for me anyway. We were just trying to figure out what my options are."

"Maybe you shouldn't have messed with her husband," Carla ventured.

"And *that's* why I didn't want to tell you about it," Shayla said and got up from the table.

"Wait." Carla grabbed her arm. "We can still talk about it."

Shayla sat back down reluctantly.

"Just because I don't agree with you doesn't mean we can't have a conversation," Carla said.

"It's not about you agreeing with me," Shayla replied. "It's about you telling me I wouldn't have these problems if I wouldn't have done this or that. You never want to help. You just condemn."

Carla flinched as if Shayla slapped her. "I do want to help. I love you. I wish we were closer."

"*Awww*," Lisa said as she set the timer on the microwave.

Shayla sighed. "I'm sorry. I didn't mean it like that. I want us to be closer too. But sometimes you get on one of your holy-roller trips, and it can be kind of – overbearing."

"It's not a *holy-roller trip*," Carla said with a grin. "It's the way Daddy raised us. Anyway, I stopped hating on the way you live your life."

"You did?"

"Yeah," Carla said. "No matter what you do, at the end of the day, you're still my big sister."

Shayla grinned. "I appreciate that."

"But you're right," Carla said. "I can't offer you any advice for this problem, 'cause I do think you shouldn't have done what you did in the first place…"

Shayla laughed. Lisa did too.

"But I want you to feel like you can talk to me about it," Carla continued.

"Alright," Shayla said. "Will do." She stood again and stretched her back. "I can't wait to get out of these clothes. I'm wearing a robe for the rest of the night."

"No, you're not," Carla said. "We're having dinner at Daddy's, remember?"

Shayla put a hand over her face and rubbed her eyes. "Are you serious?"

"*Yes,*" Carla said. "You're still going, aren't you?"

Hell no, Shayla thought. The last thing she needed after a day like this was a dose of *Pastor Benny*.

"You gotta go," Carla said, reading her expression. "You hardly ever come with me to Daddy's house. Melinda's making us enchiladas. She already called to make sure we were still coming."

Shayla looked her sister in the eyes and forced a smile. "Alright. I'll go – if Lisa goes too."

Both girls turned to Lisa, who had a string of pasta hanging from her mouth. She slurped it down quickly. "I'll go for the enchiladas. But your daddy better not try to convert me again. I never ask him to *stop* believing in Jesus. Why can't he get off my case?"

Pastor Benny Humphries lived on the southwest side of town. Shayla liked growing up there, but as she got older, she began to look at her father's decisions with a critical eye.

Pastor Benny's church, for example, was on the north side, near the homeless shelters. Her father said he chose that area because he wanted to be close to the people he was most interested in reaching, the downtrodden, the drug addicts and alcoholics. But when it came to raising his own family, Benny wanted to provide his girls with a safe, beautiful environment, which was why he chose a two-story house on the "good" side of town.

Shayla thought that was a great thing for her father to do, if his intentions were pure. But what if they weren't? What if Pastor Benny was another shiesty hustler, taking from the poor, so he could live lavishly in a castle far away from his lowly subjects?

Another thing that ruffled her feathers was her father's choice for a second wife. When their mother died, Pastor Benny waited exactly eight months before he started dating a beautiful Latina named Melinda. Not only did Melinda have more curves than a slinky, but she was only 28 at the time. The good pastor was 43.

Again, there was nothing fundamentally wrong with him marrying a young, voluptuous woman. But Shayla thought religious men like her dad were supposed to see everyone's *inner* beauty – not be awed by their outer shell. Plus Shayla witnessed her father's sinful sex acts first hand, so she knew he was corrupted by a lust demon.

Carla, on the other hand, never found fault in their father's decisions. The way she saw it, Pastor Benny worked hard at his church. He changed the lives of addicts who would've otherwise ended up in the penitentiary or the graveyard. So he deserved a nice house, just as much as a fireman or policeman did.

As far as Melinda, Carla believed God always knows what's good for you, and He will find a way to fulfill your desires if you are pure at heart. Their father was obedient to God's will, so he deserved to have an amazingly beautiful woman by his side.

Shayla used to tell her sister, "You think Daddy can do no wrong."

Carla always shot back, "You think he can do no *right*."

For the sake of their relationship, the sisters agreed to disagree. This was a trend they'd been following since their mother died, and they were quite good at it by now.

Melinda greeted them at the door. She had a happy homemaker apron tied around her waist and an oven mitt on one hand. She pulled the mitt off and reached to embrace her stepdaughters.

"Carla! Shayla!" She hugged them one at a time and then stepped back to admire them.

"You ladies look so much beautiful every time I see you!"

"Thank you," Shayla said.

"You look pretty too," Carla said. She smiled with genuine enthusiasm.

Shayla thought Carla had an easier time accepting their new mom because she was only ten when their father remarried. Shayla was fourteen, and she had a lot of contempt for this *hussy* who, try all she wanted, could never take their mother's place. It didn't help that Shayla was only fourteen years younger than her father's new bride.

Melinda had long, jet black hair that flowed midway down her back. Her eyes were big and beautiful. Her nose was perfect, her lips full. Her breasts were perky, and her smile was dazzling. She was the only woman Shayla knew who could walk out of the house with no makeup and still be ready for a photoshoot.

"And how are you?" Melinda asked Lisa. She gave Shayla's friend a side-to-side hug that was just as loving.

"I'm great," Lisa said. She sniffed the air and smiled warmly. "Something smells really good."

"Mi enchiladas," Melinda said. She had a strong accent that sounded awesome when she spoke Spanish. "Come. Your father, he waiting for you in the dining room."

She turned and led the way, and Shayla girded herself for what was sometimes an uncomfortable encounter. Pastor Benny rose from his seat at the head of the table and grinned broadly as his daughters entered the room.

"Well, I'll be. Ain't this a sight for sore eyes..."

Benjamin Humphries was a tall man. He wasn't muscular, but he wasn't fat either. Shayla thought he was in great shape for sixty-three. His hair was short and salt and peppery. He had a big nose and dark, rich skin like a melted Hershey's.

The pastor had large hands and feet. His voice was deep and authoritative. He wore a thin moustache and large glasses. Looking at him now, it was hard to believe he was once a shriveled up dopefiend with more holes in his veins than potholes on Rosedale Avenue. Shayla couldn't picture her father robbing a convenience store with his hand stuffed in his jacket pocket, his fingers pointed to look like the barrel of a gun, but once upon a time, he did exactly that.

Pastor Benny approached Shayla first, because he hadn't seen her in well over a month. He couldn't help but treat her like the prodigal son each time they met.

"How you doing, baby?" He wrapped her up in a full body hug.

"I'm fine," Shayla said. She kept her arms to her sides, but she appreciated the affection. She closed her eyes for a second and inhaled his cologne, loving the warmth and security he provided her. When she was a child, this embrace was always the safest place to be. To this day, she still felt small and needy when she was with her father.

He kissed her on the cheek as they separated. "I'm glad you could make it, Shay."

"Me too," she said, and she meant it.

Melinda's dinner was awesome, as usual. She made her enchiladas from scratch. Her rice and beans were restaurant quality.

Shayla always got a little emotional when they had a family dinner at her father's house, because everything reminded her of her mother. The dining room was the same. Melinda had prepared her meal in the same kitchen Irene once created memories on Sunday afternoons.

But Shayla was older now. She knew it wasn't right to resent Melinda *just because*. She didn't think she would ever truly love her stepmother, but she was happy her father had found someone to share the rest of his life with.

And as far as life partners go, Shayla didn't think her father could've made a better choice. Not only was Melinda exotic and beautiful, but her love for Pastor Benny was true. You could see it in her eyes whenever she watched the pastor as he spoke.

After supper, everyone was stuffed. Melinda cleared the table and brought coffee and cheesecake. Shayla found herself having a good time, but she should've known the good pastor was buttering her up for what had become a common plea.

"So, what are you doing this Sunday?" he asked after a few bites of his dessert.

"Huh?" Shayla looked up from her plate with a confused expression.

"This Sunday," her father repeated, "between the hours of ten am and twelve pm. Do you have any plans?"

"Ummm..."

Lisa snickered. "Didn't you say you were gonna feed homeless orphans that morning?" she offered.

Carla thought that was hilarious. Shayla did too. Pastor Benny chuckled and then narrowed his eyes at Lisa.

"Young lady, you know I would love for you to come to church too. I believe God has a powerful assignment for you. It could be as beautiful as the conversion of Paul."

"You think I can be as great as Paul the Apostle?" Lisa asked.

"I think your stories are similar," Pastor Benny agreed.

Lisa offered a big, toothy grin. "How are our stories similar? Paul of Tarsus, formerly known as Saul, was a persecutor of Christians before his conversion. I never persecuted anyone."

"I see you know your bible," the pastor said.

"My grandmother used to read me all kinds of funny stories at bedtime," Lisa quipped. "One day she read about a big, bad wolf. The next day it was a big, bad god. I like the wolf story better, because at least it had a happy ending."

Carla's jaw dropped. Shayla wanted to laugh. Pastor Benny was somewhere in between, but it was hard to knock him off balance.

"If you like happy endings, you should know that the *only* way to have a happy ending when you breathe your last breath – or when I breathe mine – is to accept Jesus Christ as your Lord and savior. Do you–"

Shayla's cellphone rang. She was glad for the interruption. She knew it was rude to take the call at dinnertime, but she thought it was just as rude for her father to threaten Lisa with fire and brimstones every time they met. She dug her phone from her purse and turned away from the table.

"Excuse me, y'all. Hello?"

"Hey, Shay. It's Janet. You busy?"

"No." She looked back to her family and told them, "I have to take this," before she got up and headed for the living room. "What's up?" she asked her friend when she was alone.

"I was wondering when you're coming to my church?" Janet's voice was low and breathy. She was always soft-spoken, but Shayla could hear pain and even misery in her tone.

"You alright?" she asked.

"I'm okay, just sitting here watching some old family videos."

Shayla shook her head. Her heart sank, even though she never met Janet's recently deceased sister. She wondered how long she would wait before she watched family videos if Carla or Lisa suddenly passed away. She figured she'd give it at least a decade. Janet's sister Beverly had been dead for only four months.

"I'm, I'm not sure," Shayla replied. Truth be told, she didn't want to go to Janet's place of worship. The Hill was a mega church in Denton. Shayla didn't like to operate at large churches, because it was too hard to get close to the authority figures. You could go every week for a month and never get any one on one time with the pastor.

"You're still coming, aren't you?" Janet asked. She was primed for disappointment. Shayla didn't have the heart to contribute to her friend's sorrow.

"Yes, I'm coming. How about this Sunday?"

"That, that would be great," Janet said. Her mood brightened a little. "I really appreciate it, Shay."

"But I can't promise it'll work," she said. "I don't operate too well at those big churches."

"That's fine. If you can't get him, it's okay. Just, so long as you try..."

Shayla sighed. She liked helping people out, but this exposé was different. Usually her friends wanted her to bring down powerful men for selfish and even spiteful reasons. Janet was the first one who ever came to Shayla with a genuine cause for alarm. According to her, the pastor of The Hill may have blood on his hands.

"Alright, I'll give you a call later this week," Shayla said and cut the call short.

She returned to the dining room. Thankfully Pastor Benny wasn't still trying to convert Lisa. Melinda was finishing up a story about how awesome her and Pastor Benny's cruise was last summer. Shayla took her seat and listened with a friendly smile on her face.

"Alright, so you're coming to our church this weekend, right?" Pastor Benny asked when his wife was done speaking.

"I'm sorry, I can't," Shayla said. "That was a friend of mine who invited me to *her* church this Sunday."

Lisa and Carla gave Shayla knowing looks, but neither of them said anything.

Pastor Benny couldn't hide his disappointment. "You know you hurt my feelings, right? I know about these churches you've been going to, Shay. What I can't understand is why you're running all over the state trying to find a church home when you already got one. You've always had one."

"I told you, I'm looking for something new," Shayla replied. "I love you, Daddy. You know that. But, no offense, I've been listening to you all my life. *Clean your room. Pay your tithes. Wash the dishes. Love thy neighbor.* Everything you tell me to do is good, but I can't be a freethinker at your church. I feel like whatever you say *has* to be right, because you're my dad.

"At other churches, I can learn at my own pace. I get to hear the message in a different voice, from a different face, a different angle. I think it's a good thing, to listen to different pastors." She looked at Carla. "Would you want to go through all four years of high school with just *one* teacher?"

She should've known her sister wouldn't have her back.

"Daddy switches up his teaching style. Sometimes he lets the assistant pastor give the message," Carla said.

Shayla grinned. "Of course Daddy's little girl feels that way."

"You're *both* Daddy's little girls," Pastor Benny said with a smile.

"No, she's the *little*, little girl," Shayla said. "The baby always hangs on the longest."

"It's not a matter of holding on to me," the pastor replied. "I want you to come to my church for selfish reasons. But you're right: It doesn't matter where you get the word, so long as you do get spiritually fed. I love you, Shayla. If you believe your quest is helping your relationship with God, that's good enough for me."

"I love you too, Daddy," she replied with a smile, though a great wave of guilt made her chest hurt.

"Amen!" Lisa said and everyone laughed.

CHAPTER EIGHT
THE HILL

The next morning, Shayla couldn't get the new hire Alaina McGhee off her mind as she got ready for work. She knew there would be a confrontation today. Over the past twenty-four hours, she had a lot of time to consider her quagmire, and Alaina had time to think about it too.

Their drama could be as mild as a phone call or as major as a beat down. If Alaina was a hood chick, Shayla might run into a gang of angry black women in the parking lot when she got off work. The group would include one big mama who already had her shoes off and another battle-scarred beast with purple extensions and a razor blade concealed in her mouth.

Shayla was *fairly* certain it wouldn't go down like that, but she'd be foolish to rule it out completely. What she knew for sure was something was going to happen, and she was pretty sure it would happen today.

When she got to the office, she spent the next few hours waiting for all sorts of hell to break loose. She was afraid to leave her desk, because she didn't want to run into Alaina in the hallway. She risked a trip to the breakroom at lunchtime and ate a cold sandwich, rather than tag along when Lisa recommended going to Olive Garden.

By five-thirty she hadn't received any ominous calls or emails, and Shayla wondered if she was driving herself crazy.

On Wednesday she wore pumps to work instead of the heels that looked better with her outfit. Her thinking was heels would put her at a disadvantage, if she had to throw down.

But Shayla didn't see Alaina on that day either.

On Thursday morning she convinced herself to forget about it. Of course that was the day she ran into her nemesis on the elevator as soon as she got to the office. There were three other people in the confined space when Alaina jumped on at the last second. A large man stepped to the right to give her room, and Alaina told him "Thank you." The new hire looked at her watch and wiped her brow, and with a great heave of her shoulders, she exhaled a grateful, "Whoo. Made it."

Shayla took a step back and to the left. Her heart hammered.

"What floor?" the big man asked.

"Four," Alaina said.

Shayla took another step, and her heel encountered the back wall. There was nowhere to run. She was trapped.

When the elevator started moving, she left her stomach on the ground floor. The sense of vertigo was so overpowering, her knees were weak. She hated feeling like this. Ever since she started her exposés, she was always a predator. Everyone else was the prey.

After a few seconds, the elevator stopped on the fourth floor. Alaina turned and gave Shayla a quick once over before she got off.

"Your name's *Shayla Humphries*, right?"

She didn't want to answer. This had to be a trap. She straightened her posture and tried to sound confident. "Yes."

Alaina nodded and got off the elevator without another word. Shayla watched in confusion as the doors closed. When the elevator stopped again on the sixth floor, she rushed to her office and called her friend.

"Human Resources, this is Lisa."

"I just saw her," Shayla breathed.

"Who? Alaina?"

"Yeah. We were on the elevator together."

"Did she say anything?"

"Yes. She said, '*Your name's Shayla Humphries, right?*'"

Lisa thought for a second. "She asked you your name?"

"No. She already knew my name. She wanted to confirm it."

"Why?"

"How the hell should I know? Why this bitch asking my name?"

Lisa chuckled.

"I'm serious," Shayla said. "This shit's getting on my nerves. Who the hell asks you your name and then walks off?"

"She's just messing with your head," Lisa offered. "Like, you know how if you go somewhere, and one of the employees is being rude, you'll say, '*What's your name,*' you know, like with an attitude. Even if you don't file a complaint, for the rest of the day, they'll think you got them in trouble."

Lisa's explanation sounded plausible, and Shayla needed something to grasp onto.

"You think she's just messing with me?"

"It's obvious she already got under your skin."

Shayla sneered. "I'ma go give her a piece of my mind."

"Mmmm, *okay*. Let's see: You go to her church, make out with her husband – and record it... You expose her husband, possibly ruin their marriage, and then you go give her a piece of your mind when she gets a job. That's real classy, Shayla."

Shayla laughed.

"I thought we were gonna wait for her to make a move."

"She did–"

"Her asking your name is *not* making a move," Lisa said.

Shayla sighed. "I just want to know what her intentions are. If she would come right out and call me a bitch, I'd feel a lot better."

"Oh, is that all? Well, I'm getting busy down here, so I'll talk to you later, *bitch*."

Shayla shook her head with a grin.

Lisa hung up before she could formulate a response.

Shayla didn't run into Alaina again on Friday, and, all things considered, she didn't think she had too much to worry about. In one full week on the job, she only saw the new hire once, and that was on the elevator. All Alaina did on that day was ask her name.

To further help Shayla get her mind off things, she went to the movies with Freeman after work. He was feeling so amorous, she missed the second half of the show. Freeman kissed her neck in the back of the darkened theatre, and he sucked her lips, and he didn't protest when she unzipped his pants and covertly gripped his manhood like a stick shift.

He took her to his apartment afterwards, and she had his pants down to his knees a few moments after he locked the door. She backed him into the wall and pressed her body against his. She sucked his tongue while she stroked his erection. She dropped to her knees before he was fully hard, because this was the only time she could deep throat him.

Freeman sighed pleasantly as he looked down at her. She cupped his balls as she sucked, leaving a coat of saliva along his shaft. She looked up at him, because she knew he liked to see her eyes while she pleased him. Her eyes were seductive. His were dreamy.

She backed away and then took him all the way in until her nose brushed his pubic hair. His mouth fell open. He grew two more inches in her mouth. Shayla hummed softly and worked her head like a hammer. She stroked his meat and concentrated her mouth and tongue action on his fat head.

She felt him pulsating a moment before he reached and placed both hands on her head. With his fingers on the back of her neck, he pumped his hips slowly, urging her to take him deeper, and deeper. She gave it her best shot. She flicked her tongue as he jabbed her tonsils. She watched his face and waited for her fix like a heroin junkie. Her mouth salivated at the thought of his ecstasy. When his breaths quickened, Shayla sucked harder in anticipation.

"Oh. *Oh*..." was all he could manage.

Freeman was a big man, and he always had big ejaculations because sometimes she made him go a whole week without sex. She felt his explosion with her hand before he erupted in her mouth. The stream of semen didn't merely spurt from his dick. It shot out with enough force to send it three feet across the room, but she made sure none of it was wasted on his soft, beige carpet.

With her lips tightly sealed, she sucked like she had a thick milkshake and a regular size straw. Before her mouth could fill, she swallowed and continued sucking. When she was sure she had all of it, she parted her lips and licked the semen lingering at the tip. She squeezed his dick and milked it until the last of his essence came forward. She licked him clean, her eyes locked on his the whole time.

He took a staggering step back and leaned on the wall for support. His dick jumped in her mouth. She backed away then. She knew he needed a few minutes to recover, but Freeman grabbed hold of his dick and stroked it slowly. Shayla was always turned on by a man jacking-off in front of her. She couldn't look away.

"Take your panties off," he ordered, still massaging his meat.

She stood and yanked her G-string off quickly. She stepped out of the undergarment without taking her heels off. She reached to unzip her skirt, but he pushed her towards the couch. She didn't know where he was leading her, but there's something about a man pushing you around with one hand while stroking himself with the other that makes you obedient.

"Turn around," he said.

She did as she was told.

He pulled her skirt up from behind and urged her forward until her thighs encountered the arm of the sofa. He pushed her shoulders down, and she supported herself with two hands on the soft cushions. He eased in behind her and moved her feet apart with his size twelve loafers.

Shayla felt like she was about to get dicked down by a police officer. And she liked that a lot. She closed her eyes and almost let him penetrate her without a condom. At the last moment she had to remind herself that the sex may be good, but it wasn't worth having his baby.

"You got a rubber?" she asked.

A part of her hoped he'd tell her *"Shut the fuck up, bitch."* But in all the time she'd known him, Freeman never disrespected her in the least. He went to his room to find the contraceptive while Shayla became so aroused, she felt her juices on her inner thighs.

When Freeman returned, he was still as hard as a cinderblock.

There was no need for lube on this night.

On Sunday morning, Carla left for church first because she had to help set up for a picnic they were having after services. Shayla and Lisa left together a few minutes later. Their destination was The Hill. Lisa brought a new steamy novel, but she preferred to talk when they were on the road.

"Has Freeman asked to be exclusive again?"

Shayla shook her head. "No. I got a feeling he's gonna leave me, sometime soon."

"Why you say that?"

"Because we have so much fun together." Shayla smiled, thinking about Friday night. "Everything's perfect..."

Lisa frowned. "Usually if someone's gonna leave you, they don't do it because everything is perfect."

"It's perfect for *me*," Shayla clarified. "It won't be perfect for him unless we're a couple. I got a feeling he wants to get married."

"He said tha-"

Shayla cut her friend off. "You know who does need to hurry up and get married?"

"Carla and Jimmy?" Lisa guessed.

"Damn skippy. Did you see the way he was staring at her ass this morning?"

"Carla knows it too. Her dresses are getting tighter every week."

"I think she's waiting for him to breakdown and ask for sex first. That way it doesn't have to be her who gave in."

"That sounds like something she would do. Both of y'all Humphries girls are sneaky."

"We get it from our daddy," Shayla said and regretted it immediately. She'd been trying to take it easy on her dear, old pa. She was only aware of her father cheating one time. For all she knew, that was his only affair. It wasn't right to judge him for a twenty-year-old sin.

"Speaking of big sneaks," Lisa said, "do you want to tell me why we're going to The Hill?"

"Pastor Jefferson Tate."

"You're going after the big cheese," Lisa noticed.

"For sure."

"What'd he do?"

"You know it's always about cheating when I get called in," Shayla said. "This time we also got a *death*."

"Ooh, *murder*," Lisa said. Her eyes lit up. "I likey."

"Not murder," Shayla said. "Suicide."

"That's still good."

"No, it's not. The dead girl is my friend Janet's sister. Her name's Beverly. I never met her."

"Who's Janet?"

"Janet Sessions. She went to college with us. I took a couple of classes with her my senior year."

"Skinny girl, with micro-braids?"

"That's her," Shayla said with a nod. "She says her family has never been too close, but she and Beverly were best friends. Beverly went to church at The Hill. One day she told Janet she had a *big* secret, and she had to swear not to tell anyone."

Lisa nodded.

"The secret was," Shayla continued, "Beverly was having an affair with Pastor Tate. Beverly told Janet that she and the pastor had been seeing each other for three months, and she was in love. She said the pastor loved her too, and he was gonna leave his wife and run away with her."

"Run away from all of his power at church?" Lisa said skeptically.

"Janet told her it was a bad idea. But she never saw Beverly so happy. Pastor Tate gave her a lot of nice gifts, and he sent flowers to her job. It was hard for him to get away from his wife, but he made time for her at least once a week."

"Time for a candlelit dinner or time for sex?"

"Both. They always had sex, but Janet says the pastor wined and dined her too. Beverly never had a man like him."

"What'd she do, start asking for more of his time?" Lisa guessed.

"You already know. Beverly kept pestering the pastor to leave his wife, and finally he broke down and told her he couldn't do it."

"For the kids..." Lisa said with a slight sneer.

"Exactamundo."

"She killed herself for that?"

"She tried," Shayla said. "Or maybe the first time was just to get his attention. All Janet knows for sure is she got a call from her sister one night, and Beverly told her she was gonna take a bottle of pills. Janet called 911, and the police found Beverly unconscious at her house. They took her to the hospital and managed to save her."

Lisa was confused. "I thought–"

"I'm getting to it," Shayla said. "There weren't a lot of people at the hospital with Beverly, 'cause, like I told you, their family is not really close. Most of the folks who showed up were from the church. And guess who had the nerve to bring his black ass down there?"

"The pastor?"

"He prayed at her bedside like he didn't have nothing to do with what was going on with her. Janet said she'd never been so disgusted. But Beverly wanted him there, so it wasn't nothing she could do about it."

Lisa shook her head. "That's messed up."

"It gets worse. After Beverly made it out of the hospital, I guess Pastor Tate decided she was too much of a screwball, so he broke it off with her."

"And she killed herself?"

"Yes, but not until she found out he already had two more girlfriends. He messed with one girl's head enough to make her attempt suicide, but he wouldn't stop having affairs. Beverly took *two* bottles of pills the second time. They had her funeral at The Hill, and you know Pastor Tate gave the eulogy."

Lisa looked like she was going to be sick.

"After that, nothing has changed at the church," Shayla said. "Janet doesn't know if he's still sleeping around, but you know he is. And nobody knows anything. He got Beverly's blood on his hands, and he's telling everyone else how to live their lives. His congregation loves and respects him. So Janet wants me to expose him. She wants everyone to know his secrets. She wants him to hurt like he made her sister hurt. If I can get him to step down – or maybe get the church to oust him, Janet will feel like at least *some* justice was served."

After a few beats, Lisa said, "You always give such convincing arguments. Even I'm starting to believe you're the only person in the world who can make this right."

"The sad part about that is, I probably am…"

The Hill was the biggest church in Denton. Located at the intersection of Locus and Windsor, it occupied 15 acres of what had to be the most beautiful hills in the county. The central building was four times the size of a high school auditorium. The surrounding buildings were all new. Many had glass fronts. The parking lot was big enough for a couple thousand vehicles. Luckily they offered valet parking. Shayla pulled up to the main entrance, and she and Lisa got out and stretched their arms and backs.

"I'm not late, am I?" Shayla asked a burly brother who rushed to take her keys.

"Yes, ma'am. But it's alright. If you go with Brother Charles, he'll take you inside to find a seat."

Shayla looked around and noticed four more valets, all wearing red vests. The ushers wore all black. A bald-headed man with big, shiny shoes approached with a warm smile.

"Right this way, ladies."

Shayla and Lisa had been to quite a few large churches in their time, but only the Potter's House in Dallas could compare to the glitz and glamour at The Hill. Lisa spent most of her time taking mental inventory of the numerous extravagances that wouldn't get the parishioners one inch closer to God. Shayla admired the beauty with a less cynical eye. She'd been to orchestra halls that weren't as stunning.

She and Lisa were seated towards the middle of one of the back rows. From there, they had a good view of the alter and the multitude of well-dressed Christians who flocked to this place each week to hear a good word. The man currently behind the podium wore a charcoal suit with a maroon shirt. Shayla could tell by his physical description he was the one she was sent to take down.

Pastor Jefferson Tate was handsome with smooth, light brown skin. He was fifty years old, but his short hair wasn't completely gray. He was clean-shaven with laugh lines around his eyes. He was soft-spoken but confident enough to give power to each one of his words. The booming speakers wired to his microphone didn't hurt any.

The pastor leaned on the podium and smiled warmly at his congregation as he told a joke about how Isaac might have responded when his father was on the verge of sacrificing him. The crowd responded well to him. They laughed pleasantly. They hung on each one of his words. Shayla saw motherly love in some of their eyes. Some watched the pastor with admiration. Others were clearly awed.

Shayla didn't know what to think. She liked the pastor's easygoing style, and there was no denying he was a good preacher. He was educated and cultured. Pastor Tate was a millionaire, many times over, but he didn't have an air of superiority. He seemed down to earth. He was like your favorite uncle or the coolest dad in the neighborhood. Shayla thought he was as lovable as Barack Obama.

She watched him for thirty minutes and tried to find an inkling of dishonesty or a twinge of perversion. But for the life of her, she didn't get any bad vibes from this man.

That was just as well, because by the time the pastor concluded his sermon, she decided her mission was damn near impossible. There were too many people in the upper echelon of this church. Before she could get any one-on-one time with the pastor, she would have to go through an usher, a gang of deacons, the assistant pastor... Hell, maybe even the treasurer.

She felt so bad about her chances, she didn't bother to fill out a New Visitor card or attempt to speak with the pastor before they left. She headed for the valet with Lisa in tow, and they tried to formulate a plan.

"I think you should meet him now," Lisa said. "We drove all the way out here."

Shayla nibbled her bottom lip. "I'm not feeling this place. Sometimes I get good vibes. Sometimes I don't. I don't want to waste time with this if it's not gonna work."

"You knew it was gonna be hard to get close to him before we got here," Lisa said.

"I know. But I don't think I can take him down – even if I do get a video made. You can tell these people love him to death. When they have blind faith like that, they won't believe anything bad about him, no matter how much evidence I get."

Lisa grinned. "Yeah, like how we have indisputable proof that we evolved from apes, but some people refuse to believe it."

"Ah, a creationism joke," Shayla said with a chuckle.

"A creationism joke," her friend agreed.

Lisa opened her mouth to say something else, but at that moment Shayla heard a voice behind them that didn't sound Christian at all.

"*Good Gawd!*"

The girls turned and were surprised to see a smartly dressed man approaching with a sinful look in his eyes. The parking lot was filled with people heading for their vehicles, but it appeared no one else heard his outburst.

Shayla placed a hand on her hip. "Excuse me."

"I'm sorry. I didn't mean to offend," he said, shaking his head. "But you girls have definitely been *blessed*! I don't think I'm worthy enough to even *look* at you."

The stranger was of average height and build. He was light-skinned, which was not a turn-on for Shayla, but he was strikingly handsome. He had medium-length hair that looked naturally curly. His eyes were a light shade of brown. He wore a moustache that was perfectly trimmed. His suit wasn't new, but it was clean. The bible he toted was well-worn.

"Can I ask your name?" he said to Shayla.

"I'm Carrie." She picked the first name that came to mind. Right away she thought it was a bad choice, because there aren't too many blacks named *Carrie*, but the stranger's smile remained.

"Carrie, Carrie, you are so very beautiful," he said.

She couldn't help but smile. "Are you serious?"

"About you being beautiful or about me hitting on you at church. Either way, *yes, Lord*! I'm one hundred percent serious."

Shayla thought his wordplay was borderline blasphemous, but he intrigued her.

"What's your name?" she asked.

"I'm Marcus. Marcus Campbell." He had pretty lips and nice teeth. Shayla liked his eyes, and she even liked his approach. Sometimes confidence can take you further than money.

"Nice to meet you, I think..." she said. She wore a red skirt with a white blouse that day. Her blouse only exposed a modest amount of cleavage. She knew it was her plump derrière he was attracted to. Most black men can give or take a titty, but an ass like hers was like striking gold.

"Is this your first time here," he asked. "I think I would remember if I saw you before."

"Would you, now?"

"Aww hell yeah. I could never forget you."

Shayla was flattered, but she knew she shouldn't be. Any man who approached a woman like this at church had to be bad news. But who wasn't bad news these days? She checked his ring finger and was a little disappointed to see there was no wedding band.

"Yes, this is our first day," she said. "But I don't think we're coming back."

"What? Why not?" His eyes grew large with fright.

Shayla giggled. "We live too far away. We came today because we've been hearing this place is the bomb, but now that I've been here, I can see it's not all that."

"What? Yes it is the bomb!" Marcus said. "You can't decide after only one day."

"Why do you want us to come back?"

"Well, you don't have to come back, if you give me your number. I'm worried I'll never see you again."

"You are very bold."

"I treat every opportunity like it's my only one," he replied.

"I don't think I should give you my number."

He was undeterred. "Well, can you at least try to come back next Sunday? Or you can come to one of the functions during the week. We have singles fellowship on Tuesday nights. Can you come to that? The pastor teaches the class hisself."

Shayla's eyes brightened. "Pastor Tate?"

Marcus nodded. "Yeah. It's like, one of the only times you can get to know him."

Shayla couldn't believe her fortunes. She was ready to throw in the towel, but Marcus gave her renewed hope. "I think I'll come to the singles fellowship."

"That would be great. It starts at seven. Do you want to give me your number, so I can call and remind you?"

She chuckled. She touched his cheek affectionately. "You're cute."

His jaw dropped. He reached to touch his face after she withdrew her hand.

"Wow. She touched me..."

Shayla shook her head, still grinning. Before he could say anything else, a valet pulled up with her Acura. He hopped out and left the door open. "Here you go, Ma'am." He walked away quickly.

"I'll see you Tuesday, Marcus," Shayla said as she and Lisa got into her car.

"Alright, Carrie. I'll be here, for sure."

"What a creep," Lisa said when she closed her door.

"Why you say that? I liked him."

"What kind of weirdo tries to hook up at church?"

"I don't know if you noticed, but I try to hook up with somebody every time I go to church."

"Oh yeah," Lisa said. "You're a creep too. You guys are perfect for each other."

CHAPTER NINE
SINGLES NIGHT

On Tuesday, Shayla got a call at work a few minutes before her shift was over. It was Freeman, affectionately known as the *anomaly*. She knew their relationship was approaching a crossroads, but she didn't know which way they would go.

"This is Shayla."

"Hey, baby. What you doing?"

"About to get the hell out of here," she said as she organized a few folders on her desk.

"Can I see you tonight?"

"Sure, what you got in mind?"

"How late can you stay out?"

"Oh shit, you know what – I can't go out tonight. I have something to do."

"Like what?"

"I'm going to church."

"Church? On a Tuesday?"

"Yeah, it's uh…" She almost told him she was going to singles fellowship at The Hill, but she sensed that might be the straw that broke the camel's back. "It's a bible study."

"You…"

She could almost hear him frowning.

"You're going to a bible study?" he asked.

"I'm not busy tomorrow," she offered.

"Have, have you given any thought to what we talked about?"

She took a deep breath and blew it out quietly.

Freeman, I think we need to talk.

I don't think this is working out.
It's not you, it's me.
You're too good for me.
You should find someone else, someone who will treat you right.

There were many ways to say it, but she couldn't bring herself to break it off. The worst part was she didn't know what she was waiting for. If she wasn't able to get over his adultery in the past six months, what made her think she could get over it in the future?

But she held on, because deep down she thought there was a spark of hope. If she could summon the strength to face her demons, she could go to counseling. Her counselor would teach her how to forgive her father, and she could forgive Freeman too.

And they could live happily ever after.

If only–

"I'm not waiting on you forever," he said.

She didn't know how to respond.

"You got a good man right here," he continued. "Yeah, I cheated on my wife. But I left her, and I'm doing right by you. Nobody's perfect, Shayla. No man on this earth is without sin. You, you don't have the right to judge me."

"I'm not judging you."

"Whatever you want to call it," he spat. "You're casting stones. Do you really think I would cheat on you if we were in a relationship? Do you honestly believe that?"

"No."

"Then what is it? Tell me what the problem is."

She could hear the pain in his voice. "I, I can't."

"I won't wait much longer," he promised. "I don't want to lose you. But if you don't want to be in a relationship, you were never mine to begin with."

He hung up on her, and she wasn't offended. Hanging up on people is just another way of running away from your problems. And running was something she was comfortable with.

Her mood remained introspective ten minutes later when she and Lisa exited the building together. Things worsened when they approached her Acura in the parking lot. There was a folded sheet of paper under Shayla's windshield wiper. She unlocked her car and removed the paper while Lisa climbed into the passenger seat.

Shayla read the note and was stunned stiff. Lisa watched her through the front windshield. She waved at Shayla to get her attention after a few seconds passed and she was still standing there.

Shayla finally looked up with an odd expression. She opened her door and took a seat, staring at the note again.

"What is it?" Lisa asked.

Shayla passed her the paper. She started the car but didn't immediately back out of her parking spot.

It only took a second for Lisa to read the message, because it only had three words. But she stared at it for as long as Shayla had, because the words were ominous and possibly threatening. The note was written with a black marker. The letters were big and all uppercase.

Lisa handed the paper back to Shayla and looked around curiously, as if the person who left it might be somewhere nearby. There were a lot of coworkers headed for their vehicles or driving slowly through the parking lot. Lisa didn't think any of them were watching, judging Shayla's reaction, but she couldn't say for sure.

Shayla read the note again. She felt angry and apprehensive and violated. Someone walked up to her car to leave this message. They lifted her windshield wiper. They wanted her to know that they had access to her private life. The message made it clear they had been looking for her for an unspecified amount of time. It simply read:

FOUND YOU BITCH

"Wh, what the hell is that about?" Lisa asked.

"I don't know."

Lisa took the note from her and read it again. Shayla put her car in reverse and backed out of her spot. She continued to look around but didn't see any suspicious people loitering in the area.

Her heart thudded. Sweat accumulated in her armpits. Her anger started to rise, and she welcomed that emotion.

"This is some fucking bullshit," she growled. She gripped the steering wheel tightly, gritting her teeth.

"Who do you think left it?" Lisa wondered.

"You *know* who left it. Who *found* me in the last couple of weeks? Who was on the elevator asking my fucking name?"

"You think Alaina did it?"

"Who else could've?" Shayla wondered. "We work in the same building. It would've been easy for her to find out what car I drive."

"What are you gonna do?"

"I wanna kick her ass," Shayla said. "Bright and early, first thing tomorrow morning. I wanna yank that ugly ass ponytail off her head."

"*Okay*," Lisa said. "I know you *want* to do that, but what are you really gonna do?"

"I don't know!" Shayla banged the steering wheel with her fist. "Dammit! *I hate this shit*! I told you we should've got rid of that bitch the moment I saw her."

"Got rid of her how?" Lisa queried. "She doesn't work for you, so you can't fire her. You don't know her manager well enough to ask her to fire Alaina for no reason."

"There's got to be another way," Shayla said. "I mean, no, fuck that. I'm not working in the same building with that ho. We can, she can get fired for leaving this shit on my car, right?"

"Yes. If she would've signed her name at the bottom, we could definitely use it to get her fired. But you don't know that note is from her."

Shayla frowned. "Of course it is. Who else would've done something like this? Didn't you read it? It says *I found you*. Who else found me? That bitch is the only one."

"I'm not saying it's not from her," Lisa reasoned. "It probably is. I'm just saying you can't prove she left it, so what do you plan to do with it? If you file a complaint with some random evidence, all you're gonna do is shine a light on your own shit. They're gonna ask why you think she left it. Have you and Alaina had problems before? Do you have history with her?"

Shayla shuddered at the thought. "Then I have to confront her myself."

"You need to be careful with that too," Lisa warned. "If you do it at work, it might backfire."

"How?"

"What if she makes a scene? What if she denies it and reports you for harassing her?"

Shayla shook her head.

"You don't know what her motive is," Lisa said. "It might be a trap. Maybe she's setting it up to make *you* look like the troublemaker."

Shayla nodded slightly. She looked over at her friend and smiled. "I love your twisted mind."

Lisa was surprised to see her smile. "What'd I say?"

"You always make me think. Whenever I wanna fly off the handle, you make me look at all the angles."

"I might be wrong," Lisa said quickly.

"Yeah, but even if you are, it doesn't hurt to calm down and think about things. I'm not gonna let that ho play me. She didn't do nothing but leave a funky ass note on my car. That shit don't hurt me."

"Why don't you set up your cameras to record her," Lisa suggested, "in case she does it again?"

"The cameras don't work unless I have the key in the ignition."

"You could buy one of those–"

"Nah. I'm not putting effort into this. I'm not even worried about it. If she wants me to act a fool, she's gonna have to come with something a lot better than *that*." Shayla looked down at the note in disgust.

"So what are you gonna do?"

"Nothing. Why do I have to do something? So she found me. And what? What she gonna do about it? I'ma wait for her to try some more shit. I got a lot of patience."

"While you're being patient, make sure you're also watching your back," Lisa suggested. "It's a short jump from leaving nasty letters to throwing punches."

"I wish that bitch would run up on me," Shayla said with a sneer. Her eyes narrowed to the point that the whole world became blurry. "Shit. I wish a bitch would."

With her mind settled on doing nothing, rather than give Alaina the reaction she wanted, Shayla tried to get her thoughts off the cryptic message. Noting her stress, Lisa thought she should hold off on her new exposé. But that would be like letting the devil win.

No, Shayla made plans to go to the singles' meeting, and she had no intention of backing out. She couldn't let Pastor Tate get away with having an affair that led to a suicide. Plus she wanted to see Marcus Campbell again. Lisa thought the guy was a jerk for his brazen flirting at Sunday service, but Shayla had respect for a man who came right out and said what was on his mind. When they got home, she changed clothes and left thirty minutes later.

She arrived at The Hill at seven-fifteen and was not surprised to find the valet stand deserted. There were less than a hundred cars in the parking lot. Shayla found a spot close to the main entrance. She snatched her favorite bible from the back seat and pulled her skirt down when she got out of the car. An usher appeared, virtually out of nowhere, as soon as she made it to the sidewalk.

"Are you here for singles fellowship?"

"Yes," she said. "Am I late?"

"Yes, Ma'am. But not too much. It's right this way."

He walked towards one of the smaller buildings, and she followed. Another usher opened the door for them once they got there. Inside, she saw two more ushers in the lobby. They were all black and good-looking. They made eye contact with her, but none were wolfish enough to grin or undress her with their eyes.

"Good evening, sister," one of them said.

"Hi," she replied.

The man she was following led her down a hallway with ten or more doors on each side. He stopped at the one door that was open and turned to face her.

"This is it."

Shayla peeked inside. She saw 70 to 80 people seated at rectangular tables that were pushed together with folding chairs arranged on one side. There were six rows of tables. All of the chairs faced the front of the room. Shayla looked in that direction and saw Pastor Jefferson Tate seated on a more comfortable swivel chair. There was no desk or podium in front of him, only a bible in his hands.

He wore khakis with a maroon colored sweater. He looked her way and smiled. He looked casual and approachable. She smiled back at him.

"Hello. Would you like to join our singles' class?" the pastor asked. His voice was soft. He had a twinkle in his eye.

"Yes," she said and stepped inside. "Are there assigned seats, or can I sit anywhere?"

The meeting lasted an hour. Pastor Tate spoke about appropriate dating practices for God-fearing Christians. He read a little from the bible, but mostly he told stories about his own experiences and invited the crowd to talk about some of the problems they'd encountered.

Shayla was impressed with his teaching prowess. If she was looking for a home church (and if Pastor Tate wasn't a false prophet), she thought The Hill was a great place to become a member. Anyone can throw a bunch of bible verses at you, but it takes a special teacher to make it relatable to your everyday life. Tate made you feel like you could come to him with any problem, big or small, and he'd take the time to listen and try to help you out.

When the class was over, Shayla waited in line with a dozen other people who wanted to say something to him on their way out. When her turn came, she was surprised by how nervous she was.

"Hi," she said. "I'm Carrie. I wanted to meet you before I left. Sunday was my first day here." She grinned and cradled her bible like a schoolgirl.

"It's nice to meet you, Carrie," Pastor Tate said. He reached to shake her hand. His grip was smooth and tender, definitely a stranger to manual labor.

"I really liked your class," she said. "Your message Sunday was good too."

"Thank you. I appreciate that." He gave her a brief once-over. "Where are you from?"

"Burleson."

"You've come a long way."

"Everybody says you're the best."

Pastor Tate blushed. Shayla couldn't believe it.

"It's, really it's all about what you take from it," he replied. "Some people only see how pretty this church is. I hope you'll take the time to see it's what's on the inside that counts."

Shayla smiled. She knew he would always have perfect responses. This man would never get a boner at church. She doubted if she could get him to talk dirty on the phone. She ran into his type before, cheaters who won't make a move until they develop a bond of trust, generally over a three to four month period. She would never spend that much time working on this set up. Four weeks was her limit.

She looked back and saw several people were waiting behind her, so she cut their talk short. "Thanks again. It was really nice meeting you."

"You too, Carrie. I hope you come back."

She gave him another bubbly grin and poked her chest out before she walked away. The pastor's gaze didn't linger. He looked over her shoulder and offered the same friendly smile to the woman standing behind her.

"Sister Murphy. Let me guess, you haven't given up on that dating app..."

When she got outside, Shayla felt a tinge of rejection and disappointment. She didn't expect the pastor to get bug-eyed when he saw her, but she would've appreciated *some* show of interest. She disabled her car alarm and turned when she heard quick footsteps approaching.

"Carrie, wait."

Marcus Campbell rushed to greet her. She saw him during the singles' class but avoided eye contact, even though she was aware of him staring at her.

"Dang, you walk fast," he said.

Shayla folded her arms over her stomach. "It's you again..."

His jaw dropped. "What? I know you didn't – did you just say, '*It's you again*?'"

"Yes. I remember you from the other day."

"But you ain't gottta say it like *that*. Dang. You sound like I'm a stalker or something."

He wore blue jeans with a white button-down that wasn't tucked in. Shayla thought he looked better than he did on Sunday. She liked his sense of humor.

"If I'm annoying you," he said, "just tell me. I'll leave you alone. I never harass women."

"Really?" Her look was skeptical.

"Really."

"I find that hard to believe. The way you ran up on me and my friend, I figured you had at least one active restraining order."

He smiled. "You're kidding, right?"

"I don't know. My friend thinks you're a creep."

His smile fell, a little. "Why she think that?"

"She thinks you should go to the club, if all you're looking for is a hook up."

"I don't want those women. Any girl who's at the club at one in the morning, grinding on men, letting them grab her, is not the one for me. I don't want a rump-shaking, buy me a drink, weed-smoking hoochie calling my house."

Shayla chuckled. "You don't want a rump-shaker?"

His smile brightened. "Well, maybe." He looked her up and down, his eyes lingering on her juicy thighs. "But not at the club."

"I guess you think church is the best place to find women."

"All the good ones are here," he confirmed. "You got to have some sort of values if you come here ever week."

"Let me guess, these Tuesday meetings give you an even *better* chance of finding your soulmate."

"That's right," he replied without a lick of shame. "All the women here on Tuesdays are single, and they're looking for a good man. It's like a candy store!"

"You're too much!" Shayla said laughing.

"So, can I have your number?" he asked. "Or must my quest continue."

She shook her head. "Your quest?"

"To get some," Marcus said, nodding. "I'm on a quest to get some."

Shayla's mouth fell open and she burst into laughter again.

"Nah, I'm just kidding," he said, but she didn't think he was.

His brute honesty was probably offensive to nine out of ten women. But for her, it was a turn on. She wanted to follow him home, to see if he had the dick game to back up his big talk.

She gave him her number and hopped in her car, but she didn't drive off. She waited to see what sort of vehicle Marcus headed to. He chirped his alarm, and the headlights flashed on a new F-150.

That was a mild letdown, but she didn't hold it against him. The cowboys in Texas didn't all ride horses, but they liked to have a big ass truck in the driveway. Even if they rarely had anything to haul, they were ready if an opportunity to *Git 'er done* should arise.

Shayla called her friend Janet as she exited the parking lot.

"What's up, Shay. How's it going?"

"Not bad. I'm leaving The Hill again, just left singles fellowship."

"Singles? Why'd you go to that?"

"Pastor Tate teaches the class himself," Shayla informed her. "I talked to him for the first time."

"What'd he say? Did he make a move on you?"

"Nothing like that. There were a lot of people around us. I'm still trying though. I can tell you now, this ain't gon' be easy."

"I know it's not. I appreciate what you're doing for me, Shay. You don't know how much it means to me."

"Let me ask you something," Shayla said. "Do you know a man named Marcus Campbell?"

"Uh uhn," Janet said. "Is he an usher?"

"No, he doesn't have any church duties. A light-skinned dude with a moustache... Real handsome, always cracking jokes."

"I think I know who you're talking about. But I never knew his name. Do he be hitting on women at the church?"

"Probably."

"He a joke," Janet said. "He already tried to holler at three girls – that I know of. Why? Did he try to hit on you or something?"

"Yeah, he did," Shayla said with a chuckle. "I gave him my number."

"What? Why you do that?"

"I don't see why everybody's hating on him. I think he's funny."

"Hmph. I don't know about all that," Janet said. "He's not gonna get in the way of what you're doing with the pastor, is he?"

"No. I'll call you when I have another update."

"Alright, Shay. Thanks again. This, you don't know how much this means to me."

CHAPTER TEN
BIRTHDAY SEX

When she got to work the next day, Shayla tried to stick to the plan. Lisa told her to ignore the note Alaina left on her car because acknowledging it would give the new hire power. Shayla knew her friend was probably right, but by 10 am it was hard to focus on her work.

The thought that Alaina would creep through the parking lot like a thief and leave a childish note was unnerving. If Alaina thought Shayla was a *bitch*, why didn't she say it to her face?

With no plan in mind, she left her desk at eleven-thirty and went down to the advertising department. Her heart began to race when she stepped off the elevator, but Shayla couldn't stop her legs from moving. She walked into a cluster of cubicles looking right and left. When she didn't see Alaina, she circled the outskirts of the department.

When she still couldn't find her, Shayla weighed her options and then walked into the manager's office. Patricia was on her feet, rifling through her file cabinet. She looked up with a smile.

"Hi! What brings you down here?"

"Just looking around," Shayla said. "I haven't checked you guys out in forever. You got a lot of new faces. I have a cousin who wanted to know if you were hiring."

The lie came effortlessly.

"Oh, no," Patricia said. "We just hired a new girl a couple of weeks ago. You met her, remember? I took her around, introducing her to everybody."

"Oh yeah," Shayla said. "You said her name was Alaina, right?"

"Mmm hmm." Patricia nodded. "She's the only team member I needed. But I'll let you know if something else comes up. I think they might be hiring in payroll."

"My cousin wants to work in graphic design," Shayla said and then asked, "How's the new girl coming along anyway?"

"Oh, she's great," Patricia said. "She's picking up everything really fast. And she gets along with everyone. I don't have any complaints."

"That's good. Um, where is she now? I didn't see her when I walked through..."

"She took a few days off. She'll be out for the rest of the week."

Shayla frowned. "She called-in already? She hasn't even been here a month."

"She didn't call-in," Patricia said. "When I interviewed her for the job, she told me if I hired her, she'd have to take a few days off this week so she could move."

"Where is she moving from?" Shayla asked, but she already knew. Alaina's husband was once the pastor of First United in Mesquite.

"Mesquite," Patricia confirmed.

Shayla nodded. The city was 45 miles away. It probably would take a few days to get settled into a new place, especially with young children involved.

"So she won't be back until Monday?"

Patricia nodded and looked curious for the first time. "Was there something you needed from her?"

"No," Shayla said and turned to leave. "Just wanted to say hi."

She called her friend when she got back to her office.

"I thought you weren't going to do anything," Lisa said.

"I didn't do anything. I just asked a few questions."

"You went down there looking for her."

"Yeah, but–"

"What would you have done if she was there?"

"I..." Shayla frowned. She hadn't thought that far ahead.

"You're about to lose your job," Lisa warned. "You can't make a rational decision one day and then turn around and do something irrational."

"What rational decision did I make?"

"You said you would wait until you had proof before you confronted her or tried to get her in trouble at work."

"Alright, fine," Shayla conceded. "But I found out something."

"What?"

"Alaina took the rest of the week off."

"So?"

"You don't think that's interesting? She told Patricia she needed time to move from Mesquite."

"You already knew she was from Mesquite."

"Yeah, but why would she take a job in Overbrook Meadows and move her family down here, if she didn't plan on this being a permanent gig? If you were in her shoes, would you do something at work that could get you fired?"

"Okay, I see what you're saying."

"Plus, the first time she saw me here was almost two weeks ago. She had that long to decide if she wanted to keep this job."

"Obviously she decided you weren't that big of a problem," Lisa deduced.

"If she thinks that," Shayla continued, "why would she start shit with me? Maybe I wasn't a problem before, but I'm definitely a problem now."

"You're right, that's not too smart," Lisa agreed. "But what you're doing isn't smart either, Shay. You went to her department to confront her over a note you can't prove she wrote."

"I wasn't going to confront her. I was just going to say hi, you know, to see how she reacts."

"You're playing with fire."

"Trust me, I'm too smart to get burned. There's no way that bitch is gonna get me fired."

"I hope not," Lisa said, "'cause I'm not leaving with you."

"I'm the one who got you your job," Shayla reminded her.

"Yeah, I know. And I thank you. And if you get fired, me and the rest of the team at Midwest Media will wish you the best."

"You ungrateful heifer. What you doing for lunch?"

"Vending machine."

"Let's go to Lotus," Shayla offered. "I'll pay."

"Alright. I'll be ready in thirty minutes."

"Okay. I'll come down there."

Shayla disconnected and worked diligently while she waited for their lunch hour. She got a call from Freeman when it was almost time to go.

"Hey, baby. You called earlier?" he asked.

"Yeah. I knew you were in class. I just wanted to tell you *happy birthday*."

"Awww. You remembered."

"Of course I did. I got special plans for tonight."

"Really?"

"You're not working late, are you?"

"No. I'll be home before you."

"Cool. I'll be there at seven."

"I can't wait..."

When she got home, Shayla had plenty of time to bathe and get dressed for her evening with Freeman. She stepped out of the shower at six and slipped into an outfit she'd been thinking about wearing for weeks.

Her dress was fiery red. It was sleeveless and strapless with a sweetheart neckline and beautiful, silk fabric that flowed down to her calves. The dress was form-fitting, highlighting her waistline and voluptuous hips.

She styled her hair in a messy bun, so she could show off her slender neck and draw attention to her luscious cleavage. She finished the outfit with three-inch heels, a light coat of lipstick and a few sprays of Gucci perfume.

When she was done, her bathroom mirror told her she was the fairest queen of all. Her little sister seconded that notion when Shayla stepped out of her room.

"Dang. You look like a movie star," Carla said. "Where y'all going?"

"A show at the Jubilee, dinner at the Ritz, and a suite on the 18th floor. When we get there, I have a surprise for Freeman under this dress."

"I don't think I want to know what that is," Carla said with a grin.

"I'll give you a hint: They're crotchless."

"I knew I didn't want to know," Carla said. She folded her arms over her chest and sighed. "I want some penis so bad."

"*Carla!*" Shayla laughed. "What would Daddy think?"

"*He's* the reason I'm going through this in the first place! That dumb *purity pledge...*"

"It's not dumb," Shayla said. "I'm gonna take a purity pledge myself, before I get married."

"Really?"

"Yeah, I'm serious. Four months before I jump the broom, I'm cutting off all sex. I want to be horny as hell on my wedding night."

"I know my wedding night's gonna be off the chain," Carla said. "I'm down to try anything."

"Don't tell Jimmy that. He'll ask to stick it in your booty."

"I said *anything*," Carla repeated with a straight face.

Shayla laughed, her eyes wide. "Hmph. *I'll say.*" She looked up and saw Lisa grinning in the doorway.

"I wish a nigga *would* try to put it in my butt," Lisa said.

"It's not a bad thing," Shayla said, "if you're both mature and comfortable with it."

"I wasn't being sarcastic," Lisa clarified. "I really do wish a nigga would put it in my butt."

Carla and Shayla laughed.

"I'll see y'all later," Shayla said. She continued to the front door, leaving the sexless wonders to finish their explicit conversation without her.

She arrived at Freeman's apartment twenty minutes later. He answered wearing a dapper black suit. The look in his eyes as he took in her beautiful gown was worth more than any compliment he could've paid her. He drew her inside with a strong hand on the small of her back. He kissed her softly before speaking.

"I love you. You know that right?"

She nodded. Their bodies were very close. She loved the scent of his cologne and aftershave.

"I love you too," she replied.

She thought he'd spoil the moment by bringing up commitment again, but he grinned and kissed the side of her neck before backing away.

"You ready?"

She nodded. "I am. How about you, birthday boy?"

"I'm actually excited about this. Where you taking me?"

"A few places."

"My car or yours?"

"You can drive," Shayla said. "I'll direct you." She turned and walked outside.

Freeman followed with his eyes glued to her ass.

"I wish you were mine."

Shayla didn't hear him. She looked back with a smile. "What, baby?"

He shook his head. "Nothing." He turned away from her so he could lock his door, and she didn't see the mist in his eyes.

She took him to the Jubilee Theater, which was the only black-owned playhouse in the city. They enjoyed a production of God's Trombones, a play written by the founder of the establishment, a creative genius named Rudy Eastman. Shayla remembered Mr. Eastman from when he came to speak to her class at Finley High. Freeman was one of few people she knew who would enjoy and appreciate the cultural significance of the Jubilee.

After the show, they went to the Ritz Carlton near the airport. Shayla had been there a couple of times, once for a wedding and again for a business conference. She always thought it would be nice to take a recreational trip to the hotel. Freeman was the perfect person to share the experience with.

They ate supper in a dining room that was first class all the way, from the musician tickling the ivory on a grand piano to their waiter, who wore a dashing tuxedo and pronounced the wine selections with a perfect French or Italian accent.

Shayla ordered seared Alaskan halibut. Freeman had pistachio dusted lamb chops. They drank a bottle of Bulgarian wine. Freeman wanted to show his woman off when the waiter took the last of their dishes away.

He led Shayla to the piano and dropped a twenty in the tip jar. He asked the pianist if he could play something with an R & B feel. Looking at the balding, blonde musician, Shayla thought that was a silly request. But the pianist surprised her by saying, "I've always loved Teena Marie. How about this..."

Shayla's heart grew warm when she heard the first chords of *Fire and Desire*. Freeman took her hand and led her to an empty space near the floor-to-ceiling windows. He pulled her to him, and Shayla laid her head on his chest. They rocked slowly, enjoying the music and the beautiful view of the city. Many merry eyes fell upon them, but Shayla felt like it was just her and Freeman in the room.

When their song ended, he told her, "This might be my best birthday *ever*."

"The best has yet to come," Shayla replied as she led him to the elevator.

On the 18th floor, their lighthearted romance gave way to unrestrained passion. Freeman's hands were all over her from the moment Shayla secured the deadbolt and placed her clutch on the coffee table.

He approached from behind and placed two large hands on her hips. He led her to the bedroom, his hands swimming from her waist, up her sides, and back down to her thighs. He kissed under her ear and grinded his manhood against her ass.

His hands left trails of fire as they slid across her frame. She turned to face him, her breaths quickening. Freeman's eyes were half closed. His lips were parted. She kissed him deeply. His hands moved from her waist to her ass. With a cheek in each hand, he fondled and squeezed and pulled her hips closer to his erection. He slipped his tongue inside her mouth and she licked it feverishly.

Unexpectedly, he hoisted her into the air with hardly any effort and lowered her gently onto the bed. He dropped to his knees and pushed her dress all the way up her thighs. When he saw her crotchless panties, he stared with an intense longing that sent a clap of thunder down Shayla's spine. He leaned in and licked her slowly, from top to bottom. His hot tongue set off a racket of spasms that made her legs tremble.

He stood abruptly and casually removed his sports coat and then his shirt. Shayla watched him undress, until he was down to his boxers. His dark skin was like a black sea of rippling muscles. She couldn't wait to dive in. She moved to sit up, and he helped her off the bed. She turned so he could unzip her dress. She peeled it down her frame seductively.

Without being asked for a show, she began to sway her hips to the music in her heart. She wasn't an exceptional dancer, but she was skilled when it came to strip teases. Freeman sat on the bed and leaned back on his elbows. He watched her with what could only be described as carnal lust in his eyes. Shayla loved being the center of attention. She loved the way he devoured her with his gaze. He gnawed his bottom lip subconsciously, and her nipples hardened.

She watched the bulge in his boxers grow. When he sat up and reached for her, she pushed him back to the bed and crawled on top of him. She gave him the lap dance of his dreams while he groped her ass and licked the exposed skin between her chin and breasts.

Knowing he could take no more, she dismounted and instructed him to take his boxers off. She retrieved a condom from her purse. When she turned back to him, Freeman was nude, lying on his back. The sight of his pulsing dick made her heart skip a beat. She put the condom in her mouth and dropped slowly to her knees. With the skill of a nympho, she rolled it down his manhood with just her lips.

When she got it on, she backed away and admired her handiwork. She grinned. Freeman did too. She took him into her mouth again. To her surprise, he told her, "Wait." He stood and moved to switch places. She sat on the soft mattress, and he positioned himself between her legs. He pulled her thighs apart and descended to his knees. Shayla's head swam as she lie back on the pillows.

With so much sexual tension accumulating throughout the night, she was on the verge of a climax the moment he spread her labia with his tongue. Freeman sensed this, and he was eager to hear her scream his name. He licked for a heavenly minute and then inserted two fingers. He sucked her clitoris while finger fucking her. She grabbed hold of his head with one hand and gripped the sheets with the other.

She wanted to prolong her eruption, but it was impossible. She gave in to the sensations he provided her, moaning loudly. Her orgasm was like a thundering waterfall flowing from her womb. Freeman lapped her juices ravenously. He didn't complain when she closed her thighs on his face. He pulled her legs apart again and continued to please her. When her tremors finally ceased, he stood. She looked up at him weakly and almost passed out at the sight of his third leg. She couldn't believe she ever took all of that inside her.

She held her breath when he mounted her, in anticipation of the initial discomfort. But tonight there was only pleasure. He slid in smoothly, like a sword in its sheath. She gasped as an unexpected second orgasm racked her body like a seizure.

Damn, she purred. *I feel like it's* my *birthday...*

Freeman didn't respond, but that was just as well because Shayla wasn't sure if she had spoken aloud.

Their magical evening came to a dramatic end at 11:45 pm. An unfamiliar ringtone awakened Shayla from a blissful sleep. On the second ring, she thought the tone sounded familiar. On the third ring, she recognized it as her new cellphone#3. Her body resisted the effort to climb out of bed, but she finally made it to her feet.

She staggered to the nightstand and found the cellphone in her purse. The incoming call was from Marcus. She declined the call and then shut the phone off.

She crawled back between the sheets, hoping Freeman was still sleeping. But after a moment he asked, "Who was that?"

She rolled over and saw he was staring at her. "Nobody," she murmured. She rolled away from him and closed her eyes.

"You won't tell me, 'cause I don't mean shit to you."

"Don't start."

"Are you gonna be my woman?"

Shayla's eyes popped open. She grimaced silently. She felt Freeman's eyes on the back of her head. She couldn't believe he wanted to argue after the night they just shared.

When she didn't respond, he slid off the mattress and walked to her side of the bed. He was still nude. He stopped with his dick no more than four feet away from her nose. She looked up at it and smiled. If he was down for another round, she was too, but Freeman didn't look like he liked her at all.

"I told you I would only ask you one more time," he said. "And that was it. You need to answer."

Shayla rolled her eyes, but that didn't make her problem go away. He stared down at her coldly.

"Why you doing this now?" she asked. "Is it because somebody called me?"

"It's because I don't want to have another good time with you unless I know you're mine. I don't wanna live like this no more, Shayla. I want you to be my woman. Now answer the question."

"Live like *what*?" She sat up and pleaded with her eyes. "We have fun together, Freeman. We love each other. Why can't you be happy with that?"

Rather than respond, he returned to his side of the bed and found his boxers. He pulled them on and reached for his pants.

"What are you doing?"

"I'm leaving."

She couldn't believe it. "Leaving this room or leaving me?"

"Both."

She snickered. "Freeman, you need to calm down. We can talk about it later. We both have to work tomorrow. It's too late to be trying to go somewhere."

He buckled his pants and sat on the bed so he could put his socks on. Shayla sighed and scooted towards him. She reached to touch his shoulder. He jerked away from her roughly and stood again. He stepped into his shoes and looked around for his shirt. When he couldn't find it, he turned the lights on and spotted it near the doorway. He stared at her as he put it on.

"Do you want a ride back to your car?"

Shayla couldn't accept this was happening. "You're breaking up with me? Is this for real?"

"How can I break up with you, if we're not together? I'm ending our... Shit, I don't even know what to call it, but it's over." He grabbed his sports coat and put it on angrily. "Do you want a ride back to your car or not?" His eyes were wet, but they were also ice cold.

"I'm not going anywhere," Shayla said, her anger starting to rise. "I paid for this room for the night. I paid for everything! How you gonna leave me on your birthday?"

He reached into his back pocket and removed his wallet. He pulled out two twenties and tossed them on the bed. "Alright. You can take a cab. And don't worry; I'm not gonna slash your tires when I get home, even though you'd probably do that shit to me."

Shayla looked from the money to her man. "If you walk out of that door, you'll never see me again," she warned.

Freeman thought about that and shrugged. He exited the bedroom and then the hotel room and stepped boldly into a new chapter of his life. Shayla was left alone and confused in a pricey suite that still bore the aroma of their lovemaking.

CHAPTER ELEVEN
SISTER TO SISTER

Thursday was Shayla's day to drive to work, but after the morning she had, Lisa volunteered to take her car. Shayla sat in the passenger seat applying more makeup than usual. She looked like she didn't get any sleep at all.

"Why didn't you let him take you back to your car?" Lisa asked. She looked from the road to her friend's sullen features, not sure how badly she was hurting. Shayla always downplayed her heartbreaks. It was hard to get a read on her.

"I didn't want to ride back with him. That would've been a forty-minute drive. I didn't want to be stuck in the car with him, looking stupid. Plus I paid for that room for the whole night. We had only been in there an hour before he started acting stupid."

"Who was it that called you?" Lisa wanted to know.

"That man we met at church last week."

"That light-skinned clown?"

"He's not a clown." Shayla frowned at her reflection in the visor mirror. She found a napkin in her purse and used it to wipe off all the foundation she just put on. She'd rather go to work looking exhausted than walk around looking like Lil Kim.

"How can you like him?" Lisa wondered. "The way he was hitting on you at church is worse than what those deacons and pastors are doing. That last guy, what was his name, Youngblood?"

"Yeah."

"He wasn't nearly as bad as your new friend."

Shayla frowned. "You're crazy. Joseph Youngblood was married with six kids. He had all those usher boys looking up to him. He was making a mockery of God."

"Marcus is going to church to meet women. That's not a mockery?"

"Not to me. Marcus isn't married, and he's not trying to be a church leader. Where in the bible does it say you can't find your soulmate at church?"

"I think his approach is wrong."

"I've seen worse," Shayla said. "Last week this dude ran up on me at the gas station, talking 'bout, '*Damn, bitch, you fine than a motherfucker. Where you stay at?*'"

Lisa laughed at that.

"And *that* fool probably has three kids already," Shayla said.

"So what time is he coming over?" Lisa asked.

"Who?"

"The man you met at the gas station. When are you seeing him?"

"Oh, you got jokes."

"No, but seriously, is that why you let Freeman go, because you like Marcus?"

"I don't even know Marcus. I think he's honest and funny, but I didn't leave Freeman for anybody. He left me."

"You drove him off," Lisa argued. "You might as well say you left him."

"I'm not claiming that. Me and Freeman broke it off because he wants to get serious, and I don't want to get serious with him."

"Because he cheated on his wife..."

"While performing leadership duties at church," Shayla added.

Rather than point out the fact that Shayla purposefully committed adultery with all the men she exposed, and if there was such a thing as hell, Shayla had reserved parking, Lisa chuckled and asked, "Did you get to show off your lingerie before he left?"

"You *know* that nigga got some before he left," Shayla said with a smirk. "He a *buster*, but I never said he was a fool."

Shayla's day went as badly as she expected. She felt as if the work gods piled on more tasks when they knew she didn't have the patience or brain function to deal with them. When she got home, she planned to bathe and take a nap before dinner, watch some TV, take a nap after dinner and then wake up and get ready for bed.

She kicked off her pumps and put bath salts in the tub for part one of her night of relaxation. She hadn't listened to the message Marcus left her last night, so she took cellphone#3 with her when she climbed into the hot, bubbly water.

Her new friend's message was short and sweet: "Hey, Carrie. This is Marcus. Give me a call."

Shayla backed out of her messages and returned his call. She sank down in the water as the phone rang. Marcus answered after four long rings.

"Hello?"

"What took you so long?" she asked. "I almost passed out waiting on you."

"Um, who is this?"

"This is Carrie. You didn't save my number? Don't tell me you don't remember me..."

"Hell yeah, I remember you!" He was suddenly animated. "You got to be the prettiest angel I've *ever* seen."

"I'm not an angel," she said with a smile. "Although some people think I'm an angel of death."

"No shit? Why they think that? Have you killed somebody?"

"Not physically. Mentally and spiritually maybe..."

Marcus chuckled. "Alright. That's cool. Do you want me to call you the Angel of Death too?"

She laughed. "No, boy."

"I get it; that's kinda long. I can shorten it. How about *Death Angel* or *AD*? Or we can mix 'em up: *D'angel*."

Shayla giggled. "Just call me Carrie."

"Alright. Do you, do you think one day I'll be one of the people who calls you the angel of death?"

"No. I don't know. Maybe."

"Wow."

"I'm just kidding."

"Now I'm scared,"

"That's what they all say."

There was a pause.

"*Okay...*" Marcus said with a snicker. "So, what are you doing? Did I call too late last night? Was you sleep?"

"I was asleep," Shayla said. "My boyfriend broke up with me because of you."

"Huh?"

"He sure did."

"Are you serious? I got you in trouble?"

"You did. But he was gonna break up with me anyway. He used you as an excuse."

"I'm sorry about that. Why didn't you tell me you had a boyfriend? Or at least you could've told me when it was a good time to call. Even better, you should've had your phone on *silent*. Dang, girl. Don't you know how to cheat?"

"No, I've never cheated before. But it sounds like you have."

"I used to," Marcus admitted. "I stopped when I started going to church. I figured if I was gonna find the good woman I'm looking for, the least I could do is treat her right."

"How's the search going?"

"Not great. The bad thing about going out with a church girl is some of them really wanna *follow the bible*. They won't come to my place after our date. And if they do, they don't wanna drink wine and stuff. I picked one girl up to go to the movies, and she had this other lady with her. At first I was like, *Hey, ménage a trios in this bitch!* But then she said the other girl was her *chaperone*! I left both of 'em on the curb."

Shayla laughed. "You didn't really burn off like that, did you?"

"Yeah, I did. I told her, 'I believe in Jesus too, but you're a little *too* conservative for me. I wish you the best, though.'"

"At least you were polite."

"How about you?" he asked. "Did your boyfriend let you down easy?"

"No. He left me in a hotel room all by myself. He gave me forty dollars for a cab."

"For real?"

"For real. I don't know why I'm being so honest with you."

"It's because I was honest with you first," Marcus said.

"Maybe."

"So, you're officially single now?"

"Yep," Shayla replied, although she considered herself single long before Freeman made his climatic exit.

"Good. That's perfect. So, um, what you got on?"

She chuckled. "Nothing. I'm butt nekkid."

"For real?"

"I'm in the tub. The water's hot. I got a soft, soapy sponge. I'm rubbing it on my neck, and my chest, and my stomach. My belly button. My..." She sighed loudly.

After three seconds of silence, Marcus said, "You, your what, Carrie? Where you rubbing it now?"

"Use your imagination."

"That's the problem. My imagination's running wild."

"Good," she said. "I'll talk to you later."

"Wait, what? You getting off the phone?"

"I'm trying to take a bath. I need two hands."

"Oh. Okay. Well, um..." He cleared his throat. "Am I gonna see you at church this Sunday?"

"No. I don't think The Hill is for me. But I'll be at the singles fellowship next Tuesday. I wanna talk to the pastor one more time."

"Can I see you before then?"

"I don't think so, but you can call if you want."

"Alright. I got one more question: If we do go out, are you gonna bring a cock-blocker – I mean a *chaperone* with you?"

Shayla giggled. "What the hell's a *chaperone*?"

"Shit, if you don't know, I don't know either! Talk to you later, Carrie. Enjoy your bath."

"*Mmmmm...* Boy, you know I will. *Hmmmm...*"

"Damn, Carrie. What you–"

She disconnected and dropped the phone on the floor mat.

Shayla tried to have another relaxing day at home on Sunday, but she made the mistake of telling her sister about her slothful plans.

"Why don't you come to Daddy's church with me?" Carla asked. She stood in Shayla's doorway with a blouse and skirt on but no shoes.

"I, uh..." Shayla hadn't left the bed that morning. Her blankets were warm like a kangaroo pouch. "Aren't you going with Jimmy? I don't like being the third leg."

"It's *church*, Shay, not Benihana's. And Jimmy's not going with me today. He's out of town."

"Out of town doing what?"

"His job sent him to Austin."

"Are you sure he's in Austin and not with his side piece?"

Carla frowned. "He don't... Wait, why are you changing the subject? Are you coming with me to Daddy's church or not?"

Shayla laughed. "I don't wanna."

"Get up," Carla urged. "You go to all them other churches. Why you can't support your own family?"

"Alright, alright." Shayla rolled her eyes and sat up. Carla stepped out of the room, and Lisa appeared in the doorway. "Hey, Lisa," Shayla said. "You wanna come with me and–"

"Hell no!" Lisa said and continued to her bedroom.

Shayla cracked up.

"Looks like it's just you and me," Carla called from the hallway.

"Like the good old days," Shayla said and reluctantly got out of bed.

Pastor Benny's church was located in one of the worst drug areas in the city. Around the corner from the church was his rehab, known as the "men's home." This was a huge two-story complex that currently housed 21 men. Shayla had seen the occupancy get up to 35.

The men in the home came fresh off the streets. To join Benny's program, they had to make a six-month commitment to live in the house and follow a long list of rules. To Shayla, some of the rules were worse than a minimum-security prison. The men were not allowed to watch *worldly* tv or read worldly literature. They couldn't leave the home outside of church or fundraising activities. They couldn't have prolonged communications with the opposite sex unless it was a family member. Sex was certainly out of the question.

If they decided to stay, the addicts were provided food, shelter and clothing. They read from the bible multiple times a day and prayed more than that. They learned how to surrender their lives to God, and in return God delivered them from their sinful addictions to drugs, alcohol and other vices.

Throughout her life, Shayla had been observing these men. The thing she found most interesting was how often the same ones returned. Some would finish their six months before they got high. Some would leave after two months or even two weeks and get high. Some would graduate the program, stay sober for over a year, and then they'd get really good news one day or a really nice paycheck, and they'd inevitably get high.

The success rate of Pastor Benny's rehab was between five and ten percent, but it didn't appear anyone was keeping up with the stats.

Carla pulled into the church's parking lot at 9:50, which made Shayla early for service for the first time in quite a while. She didn't wear anything sexy that day, but the ushers were from the men's home, and these had to be the horniest guys in town. They greeted the sisters with bright smiles and sweaty brows that exposed their lust.

They held the door open, and one of them turned to check out Shayla's ass when she walked by. Ever since she was a teenager, she was aware of the sex demons in her father's ministry. She knew the usher would take a mental image of her ass to the shower with him that night. She didn't mind. In fact, the thought of all of the masturbation sessions she had inspired over the years put a wicked smile on her face.

And this was how Shayla started her day at church.

Pastor Benny spoke about how you should stay still and be quiet when God is speaking to you. Shayla thought it was a good message, but she heard it so many times, she could almost give the sermon herself. Rather than listen, she found herself daydreaming. When that almost put her to sleep, she moved on to her next favorite church activity: Judging others.

Pastor Benny's church was big enough to seat 200, but only half the seats were filled. The men from the rehab occupied the first three rows on the left. Their family members sat behind them. The seats on the right were for folks who had no connection to the men's home. Those people weren't interesting. Shayla spent her time ridiculing the people on the left.

The first thing she noticed was two addicts who couldn't stay awake during the service. She elbowed her sister when one of them started to drool on his tie.

"Check him out," she whispered. "You think he got some dope last night? Don't it look like he nodding?"

Carla smiled and chuckled politely but didn't offer her own observation.

Shayla was also amused by a young mother of three who had been coming to support her husband for years. She hung on Pastor Benny's every word, with hopes that something he said would fix her no-good spouse, who was affectionately known in the home as *Can'tGetRight*. Her husband sat next to her, bouncing his knee anxiously.

Shayla nudged her sister. "Don't he look like he want some crack right now?"

"That's Brother Sam," Carla whispered. "Daddy says he's close to a breakthrough."

"He ain't doing nothing but breaking his wife's heart," Shayla said. "What would possess a woman to keep giving a crackhead so many chances? She can find somebody else to help raise those kids."

"She promised to stay with him *for better or worse.*"

"Yeah, but–"

"Shht!"

Shayla rolled her eyes and closed her mouth for a while.

The last straw came at the end of the service, during the altar call. Their father stepped from the podium with sweat on his face, his arms outstretched.

"Now I know it's *somebody* in here this morning that needs some healing, God! I know it's somebody in this church that stepped away from your light, and they need a word from you today! Let them come forward *right now*, God! Come to this altar and give up that burden you're holding on to! Give up your deceitful ways! Give up your *lying* and your *stealing*! God can take that monkey off your back right *now*, if you come down here and lay your burdens at his feet!"

Unlike the last altar call Shayla witnessed, most of the people at Pastor Benny's church were sick with sin, and they were past the point of feeling shameful about it. All but two of the men in the rehab home lurched down the aisle with tears in their eyes. They fell to their knees at the altar and cried and begged God to, *"Change me, Lord!"*

"I don't wanna be like I used to!"

"I want you to take my life in your hands, Jesus!"

"I can't do it on my own! I need you God!"

"Please, God, make me better!"

Shayla had seen this scene play out many times. It was impossible not to feel moved by the raw emotions on display as her father walked from one man to the next, and, with a hand on their head or shoulder, prayed God would deliver them and make them whole again.

She told Carla, "I guess if it works, they can all go home after church instead of back to the rehab."

To her surprise, Carla turned to her with fire in her eyes.

"What the heck is wrong with you?" she hissed, her eyebrows knitted together in anger.

Shayla flinched, the smile frozen on her face. "What?"

"You ain't done nothing but make fun of people the whole time you been here!"

She was whispering, and with the commotion from the altar call, no one but Shayla heard her. But Shayla thought her sister was way too loud. She looked around nervously, her smile gone now.

"Chill out. I was just kidding."

"It's not funny."

Shayla was shocked to see tears mixed with her anger.

"These people lost their whole life out there on the streets," Carla said. "They lost their jobs, their family, their kids. They come in here sick and hopeless. The only thing they want is to stop getting high. Maybe they don't all make it, but when somebody drops to their knees and pours out their heart to God, you should show some *reverence*. Why do you hate this church so much? What did Daddy ever do to you?"

Shayla looked around again, stunned that her sister (her *little* sister at that) would check her like this. But she knew she brought it upon herself. She'd grown too accustomed to going to church with Lisa. It was okay to behave this way with her best friend. She should've known her sister would respond differently.

She lowered her head in shame. "I'm sorry."

"It's okay," Carla whispered. "But I wanna know what Daddy did to you. I know something's wrong, Shay. He knows it too. Why won't you tell us, so we can help you?"

Shayla felt horrible. "I'm alright. I said I was sorry. I didn't mean no harm."

Carla gave her a skeptical look, and their father finished praying for the sinners. He raised his hands in victory and shouted, "Praise Jesus!" and everyone started clapping.

The praise and worship team marched onto the stage, and one of the best drummers in town began to rattle the cymbals. The choir sang a men's home version of "What a Mighty God we Serve," and got the whole church rocking.

Shayla was glad for the distraction. She clapped her hands and sang along, and after a while the sting from her sister's rebuke didn't hurt so much.

She and Carla had lunch afterwards. By the time they got home, Shayla didn't feel the sting at all.

CHAPTER TWELVE
STRANGER THAN FICTION

After her tumultuous week, Alaina McGhee was the last thing on Shayla's mind when she returned to work on Monday. The new hire should be back from her time off, but Shayla didn't think about her until she and Lisa headed for the parking lot after their shift. There was a red piece of paper pinned under Shayla's windshield wiper. The sight of it brought back all the shock and anger she experienced last week.

"What the? I can't believe this bitch!"

Lisa made it to the car first. She plucked the paper from the windshield and grinned when she turned it over. She looked around and Shayla did too. All of the cars in the lot had the same flyer affixed to them.

"A new Chinese restaurant," Lisa informed her. "They're up the street. Wanna check 'em out?"

Shayla rolled her eyes and unlocked her car.

"That ain't funny," she said when she and Lisa were seated in her Acura.

"Sorry. I take it you didn't say anything to her today?"

"No," Shayla replied. "To tell the truth, I forgot about her until I saw that stupid flyer."

"You're gonna leave her alone, right?"

"I'm gonna wait it out," Shayla promised. "I'm sure Patricia told her I came by looking for her, so Alaina knows I'm on to her. I don't think she'll try anything that stupid again."

"What if she does?"

"Then I'll confront her. If we gotta work together, then we have to have it out, one good time. I think if I talk to her, she'll understand why I did what I did to her husband."

Lisa chuckled. "Yeah, *I made out with your husband, but it wasn't to hurt you...*"

"I wasn't gonna say it like that."

"How would you say it?"

Shayla shook her head. "I have no idea, girl, but not like that."

On Tuesday Shayla could think of nothing but Alaina McGhee, but there was no incident that day. She didn't run into the new hire during her shift, and there were no incendiary messages left on her car when she got off.

Shayla couldn't believe her life had come to this, waiting for a disgruntled wife to harass her. Lisa couldn't believe something like this hadn't happened before, given the number of women who were upset with her. When she considered that, Shayla had to agree she was fortunate. She counted her blessings and didn't second guess herself when it was time to go to The Hill that night for singles fellowship.

Lisa, on the other hand, couldn't believe she wasn't taking a hiatus. She followed her to the living room when Shayla got ready to leave.

"Seriously, don't you have more important things on your mind, like your stalker?"

"This is the last time I'm going to The Hill," Shayla replied. "I'm gonna tell the pastor I decided not to become a member."

"You don't need to go there to tell him that. If you don't show up anymore, I'm sure he'll get the message." Lisa's comment oozed with sarcasm.

"I need to do it face-to-face," Shayla countered. "I want to give him a chance to make a move. I printed some business cards, just for him. If I can slip him a card, then that's it. If he wants to see me again, he'll call."

"What about that boy you like up there?" Lisa asked. "Is he the real reason you want to go tonight?"

"I did tell Marcus I would see him today," Shayla said with a grin.

"I'm warning you, Shay; he's a pervert."

Shayla took offense to that word. After struggling with her sexuality since adolescence, she had come to understand that she was what some people would consider a *pervert*.

"I'll be back in a few hours," she said as she exited the front door.

"Be careful," Lisa said and locked it behind her.

Shayla arrived at The Hill fifteen minutes late. She was ushered to the singles' class by a bearded brother who didn't speak much. He didn't respond to her flirting, even though Shayla knew she looked good in a pair of skintight jeans. The top three buttons on her blouse were open, revealing a glimpse of her black lace bra. If the ushers were so well behaved, she figured Pastor Tate was equally infallible.

That night the mild-mannered pastor wore Dockers with a short-sleeved golf shirt. His loafers were clean but well worn. He only wore two pieces of jewelry, his wedding band and a modest wristwatch.

Pastor Tate spoke about what Christians could do, in lieu of sex, when their hormones started to get the best of them. He was so informative, Shayla jotted down a few pointers that might help Carla and Jimmy make it through their last couple of months of abstinence. Once again the pastor's style was informal. The audience laughed at his jokes and were obedient enough to pipe down when he told them, "This is serious. I want y'all to pay attention…"

Shayla noticed Marcus trying to get her attention. She pretended not to notice him, and eventually he stopped looking her way. When the class ended, she stood in a short line of people who wanted to say something to the pastor on their way out. By the time it was her turn, she had her spiel memorized.

"Hi, Pastor Tate. I enjoyed your class again. I wanted to tell you how much I appreciate everything you guys do at this church."

He smiled. It was a warm, doting smile. "Thank you, Carrie. I'm glad to hear that."

Shayla was taken aback. "You remember my name?"

"Sure I do." He stared deeply into her eyes. "I try to remember everyone who has attended my services more than once. With over three thousand members, I'm not always successful. But I just met you last week, so you're fresh on my mind."

So far this was the closest he had come to flirting. But Shayla couldn't say for sure if that's what was happening. The comment and the look in his eyes were probably innocent. Most would think he gave off grandfatherly vibes.

"That's nice of you," she replied. "Now I feel even worse about what I was going to say."

Pastor Tate's head tilted slightly, but his smile remained. "What's that?"

"I decided not to become a member of your church. I've been looking for a church home. There are a lot of churches closer to me, but I wasn't feeling any of them. When I came here, I thought this place was perfect. It's far away, but with everything y'all offer, I thought it'd be worth the trip..."

"You changed your mind?"

"Not because of anything y'all did wrong," she said quickly. "It's the time it takes to get here. Gas prices are going up, and I ran into some traffic on my way here tonight. I got upset, and I don't like to get upset on my way to church."

Pastor Tate nodded. He looked her up and down briefly. The move was so quick, Shayla couldn't tell if he was checking her out.

"You shouldn't get upset when you encounter a traffic jam," the pastor advised her. "Delays are a part of life. If you leave home a few minutes earlier, you'll be prepared for a minor setback. If you don't encounter one, you'll be early, and there's nothing wrong with that."

He smiled. She smiled too.

"On the other hand," he continued, "you should feel comfortable with every aspect of your new church. There's nothing wrong with including driving distance in your decision. In the old days, before everyone had a car, people would walk to the church closest to them. If they didn't like it, oh well. They weren't gonna walk another five miles to find a better one."

He chuckled at his joke, and she did too.

"But in this day and age," he said, "you don't have to settle, especially when it comes to your faith. I'm sure you'll find a place of worship closer to you that suits your needs. We're sorry to lose you, but I understand, Carrie."

That was the response she expected. The pastor would look like a fool if he begged her to stay. The next step was to get her business card in his hand. For this, Shayla's speech was both factual and fictitious.

"I, um..." She giggled. "I know you probably have tons of people working on this, but I work in advertising for Media Marketing. I think you have the best church in the metroplex, and I would love to push more customers your way."

She dug in her purse for the business card she made him. Media Marketing was one of her company's competitors. Shayla used their logo on the card, which indicated she worked in the advertising department. For the office phone, she gave him the number for cellphone#3. She offered the number for cellphone#2 as her fax number.

The fair-skinned pastor looked at her card like it had vomit on it. His smile faltered. Shayla didn't expect his demeanor to change so drastically.

"Uh, actually we don't view this as a business, Carrie. I don't look at any of our congregation as *customers*. That's, that's not appropriate."

"Oh my God, I'm so sorry," she said. "That's the vocabulary I'm used to using at work. I know you don't see us as customers. I apologize."

His smile returned.

"But there's nothing wrong with a church advertising," she said.

Pastor Tate nodded. "Of course there's nothing wrong with it, Sister Carrie. But I don't handle those matters directly. You should call our secretary. She's here until five on weekdays."

Dammit. Shayla fought her frustration and maintained composure.

"I'll make note of it," she replied. "But if I forget, could you please give her my card?" Her arm was still outstretched.

Pastor Tate's smile faltered again. This time he looked around the room. There were two ushers standing near the entrance. Both were watching their interaction. There were several people standing behind Shayla who were probably listening to the conversation.

Stop looking at my card like that! Shayla wanted to scream. *Take it. It won't hurt you...*

Sweat accumulated on her forehead as she waited. She didn't wipe it off, because she didn't want to draw attention to it.

"I'll, um..." He took the card. He checked out the front and then flipped it over. "I'll give it to my secretary," he said and stuffed it randomly between the pages of his bible.

Shayla sighed inwardly. She felt like a thief slipping out of a department store with no buzzers going off.

"Thank you. I look forward to hearing from y'all."

"That's alright," Pastor Tate said, looking over her shoulder to see who was next. "You have a nice evening."

When she got outside, the night sky was warm and beautiful. Shayla knew she wouldn't make it far before her admirer chased her down. She stopped in the parking lot when she heard him approaching.

"Carrie! Hey, wait up!"

She turned and smiled at Marcus. Her smile was genuine. The warm sensation in her chest was real too.

"Why you try not to look at me while we're in class?" he asked when he was close enough to speak without yelling. "I know you saw me trying to get your attention."

She giggled. "Who said I saw you?"

"I *know* you saw me, just like I saw you. You had my full attention from the moment you walked in with them jeans on."

"That's the problem. The pastor was supposed to have your full attention."

"I can see he has *yours*," Marcus said. "This is two weeks in a row you stopped to talk to him."

She gave him a look. "And?"

"I'm just saying." He looked down at his shoes coyly.

Tonight he wore a black suit with an olive green shirt and no tie. Shayla couldn't get over how sexy he was. His curly hair was a welcome rarity. His hazel eyes were equally exotic.

"You jealous?" she asked him.

"A little," he admitted and met her eyes. "You got a crush on pastor?"

His childish demeanor made her laugh. But he was so close to the truth, her ears burned.

"You must really like me, if you're jealous of the pastor."

"He's a pastor," Marcus said, "but when it comes to beauty, he's still a man. He sees how fine you are, just like I do."

His remark made her heart flutter. Marcus said so many things that were right on the money. Shayla wondered if he might be her kindred spirit.

"Where you going now?" she asked. "Wanna get something to eat?"

His jaw dropped. "What? Girl, you *know* I wanna get something to eat! Come on, I'm parked over here..."

"I'll follow you to a restaurant, but I can't stay out too late. What's close?"

"There's a Dixie House down the street."

Shayla didn't care for the restaurant chain, mainly because *Dixie* sounded like a place that still had *Colored* and *White Only* fountains. But she didn't want to drive far, so she agreed to it.

Marcus hopped in his truck, and she pulled up behind him. As they exited the parking lot, it occurred to her that this was the first romantic interlude she ever had at church that didn't involve a takedown. There probably wasn't anything significant about that, but Shayla thought it was special.

At the restaurant, she dined on pot roast, while Marcus dug into chicken fried steak. For the first ten minutes, neither of them spoke much; they were so busy stuffing their faces.

Marcus finally put down his fork with a chuckle. "I guess you're not a vegetarian..."

"No, I like meat," Shayla said with a smirk. "Hot, thick, meat."

Marcus cleared his throat comically and took a sip of his tea. He watched her over the glass. She returned his gaze.

"There's something I've been wondering," she said.

"What's up?"

"Are you all talk?"

"What, what you mean?"

"You're so persistent. Loud, *boorish*, confident... Cocky."

"You think I'm boorish?"

"Does that offend you?"

"I'm not offended," Marcus said. "Hell, I don't even know what it means."

She laughed.

"Are you gonna tell me what it means?"

"Rude," Shayla said. "Obnoxious."

He shook his head. "Maybe I should be offended."

"I went on a date with you, so I must like it."

He sat back and his chest swelled. "Yeah, I knew you liked it."

Shayla rolled her eyes. "There you go again. You haven't said if you're the real deal or not."

"I don't know what you mean."

"I used to know this boy," she said, "when I was in high school. He was real good looking. Tall and popular. His name was Quincy. He loved to fight. Always wanted to prove how bad he was. Constantly hitting on girls. And all of us wanted him too. Until one day Trisha Turner went out with him..."

Marcus waited for the punch line.

"The next day she let it be known Quincy wasn't working with *nothing*," Shayla said. "He was so small, he couldn't even keep his condom on. He told Trisha to give him one of the little rubber bands from her hair. She did it too, but she started laughing when he tried to put it on the base of the condom. Quincy couldn't perform after that."

Marcus didn't know whether to laugh or feel sorry for little Quincy. He chuckled nervously. "That's... That's some story, Carrie."

"It's a true story." She stirred her tea with a straw, watching his eyes.

"Sounds like you want to know if I've got any shortcomings you should know about," Marcus deduced.

"Anytime I meet a man as headstrong as you, I think about Quincy."

He looked around and then shook his head. "I don't think I've ever been put on the spot like this, definitely not on a first date."

Shayla's eyes narrowed. She knew it!

His face reddened.

She sighed. Well, at least she got a nice meal out of it.

"You know what's unfair?" Marcus said. "A woman's pussy stretches to fit anything from a twelve-inch dick to a fat ass baby. But us men are working with the same dick we had since we passed our growth spurt. We always get judged on who y'all have been with before."

Excuses, excuses, Shayla thought.

"If your ex-boyfriend was a porn star," Marcus went on, "seven and a half inches might not be enough for you. But if you're a virgin, seven and a half is big as hell."

"It's okay," Shayla said. "I was just kidding."

"No you weren't. You wanna know how big I am."

She grinned. "Are you gonna tell me?"

"I already did." He wiped the sweat from his brow. "Dang. Why it's so hot in here?"

"Seven inches?" Shayla asked.

"*And a half*," Marcus said. "You, you ain't gon' gyp me outta my *half!* That half inch is the best part! Wh, where's our waiter? Can we get some fans turned on in this bitch?"

She laughed.

"Nobody ever does this," Marcus said.

"Does what?"

"Get the upper hand on me."

"I don't mean to emasculate you. And for the record, seven and a half is plenty big."

"Alright," Marcus said. "Can we, can we change the subject? I don't wanna hear nothing else about my dick unless I'm using it."

"Okay. I'm sorry to make you uncomfortable. Want me to make it better."

A sinful grin brightened his eyes. "Yes'm."

"Not like that. I mean I can tell you something personal about me."

"Oh, okay. That, that's cool too."

She shook her head with a giggle. "Okay. Now this is serious business. It can't leave this table."

"Alright." He nodded and leaned forward.

"I didn't go to The Hill because I'm looking for a new church. I went there to take Pastor Tate down."

Marcus eyes widened with shock and confusion.

"This isn't my real job or anything," she said. "I'm not a detective. It's just a hobby. People call me to their church when one of the leaders is acting a fool. I collect enough evidence against them to cause a divorce or get them kicked out of their position, or both."

Marcus' smile disappeared by degrees as he listened to her. He frowned.

"You serious?"

"Yep," she said with a nod. "I've been doing it for almost ten years. I'm pretty good at it."

"Wha, why would you want to take down Pastor Tate?"

"I'm told he's a whore." There were few people in her life who knew about her vendetta. Shayla *never* told anyone at the church she was currently working. She wasn't sure why she was telling Marcus, but it didn't feel like a bad thing. She felt she could trust him.

"Pastor Tate had an affair with one of my friends' sisters," she said. "When she found out he wasn't going to leave his wife for her, she committed suicide. Tate had more affairs after that, and my friend thinks he's still sleeping around."

Marcus was stunned silent. Shayla knew what was going through his mind. It's hard to accept that someone you look up to for spiritual guidance is not as holy as you thought they were.

"That's some crazy shit," he said at length.

"A lot crazier than your seven and a half inches."

"What, wait. I thought you said that was okay."

"It is," she said and smiled. "I'm just trying to break up some of this tension."

"You, you're serious?" Marcus asked. "About the pastor..."

"I wouldn't make up a story like that."

"And you were really sent here to take him down?"

"A friend that goes to your church asked me to give it a shot. She knows I've done this before."

"I don't, I don't understand," Marcus said.

"I know how you feel. It's not the easiest thing to come to terms with..."

They talked for another twenty minutes, during which Marcus accepted the fact that Shayla really was a spy (of sorts) and Pastor Tate might actually be a dirty old man. She knew telling him was a gamble, but she also knew Marcus wouldn't fly off the deep end. He already admitted he was at the church looking for a woman. He spent most of his time at the singles fellowship trying to get Shayla's attention, rather than listening to the pastor.

She guessed he hadn't developed a spiritual or emotional bond with Pastor Tate, and she was correct. Before they left the restaurant, she asked if he still wanted anything to do with her, and he responded in the affirmative.

"Yeah, Carrie. I never went out with a real-live private eye. And as fine as you are, I don't care if you said the *Pope* had a few mistresses. If you can prove it, I got your back."

She was glad he was in a joking mood. She had one more serious matter to clear up when they got outside. He walked her to her Acura and lingered there, no doubt waiting for a hug, or even better, a kiss.

"I got one more thing to tell you," she said. "My name isn't Carrie. It's Shayla. I use a different name whenever I go to a new church. I had to give you the same name I gave Pastor Tate. Sorry.”

Marcus shook his head in wonderment. “This is like a movie.”

“I don’t have any more secrets,” she promised. “I laid everything bare. You can take it or leave it.”

“What do I get if I take it?”

“I don’t know. You have to take it first.”

Rather than hit her with his own snappy comeback, he stepped to her unexpectedly. With a hand around her waist, he pulled her close and leaned in for a kiss.

Shayla closed her eyes. He pecked her softly, and then again, slower the second time. She didn’t think he had the gumption, but Marcus’ hand slid down her backside and lingered on her right cheek. She immediately began to feel aroused. He kissed her a third time, and she pulled back.

“Um, can I help you?” she asked.

“Naw. What’s up?”

“I think your hand is lost.”

His grip on her ass tightened rather than loosen.

“I just wanted to make sure everything else about you was real,” he said and removed his hand.

“Really? So, what do you think?”

“That’s Grade A ass right there. The real deal. No fillers.”

She grinned. “Well thank you, I guess...” She turned to get in her car.

“When can I see you again, Carr– I mean Shayla?”

“I’m not sure. I’ll call you.”

“Could, can I have one more kiss?”

She looked back at him and thought he was adorable. She nodded and he closed the distance between them with one big step.

She thought he’d try to slip her some tongue the second time around, but she realized there was another reason he wanted to be closer. As soon as their lips touched, both of his hands clamped on her ass like a magnet. She didn’t mind. She wrapped her arms around him and lightly sucked his lips. When he backed away, she knew he was feeling boneriffic.

“I think I love you, Shayla.”

"You don't have enough blood in your brain to think about anything," she replied. She gave him a flirty smile and turned back to her car. "See you later, Mister Marcus."

"Alright, Shayla. I can't wait."

CHAPTER THIRTEEN
NO CHAPERONE

On Wednesday Shayla was in a good mood at work. Things
got better when she checked her cellphones during her first break.
She had two messages on cellphone#3. The first was from
Marcus:

"Hello, Miss Lady. I was just calling, you know, to see if
you made it home alright. I had a good time at dinner. I *really*
enjoyed our kiss. I thought I'd be bugging about that stuff you told
me, but, on the real, I'm honored you trusted me enough to tell
me. Anyway, give me a call back – and don't make me wait too
long. I know how you women like to keep a brother stressing.
Does she like me? Is she gonna call?" He chuckled. "Damn, I
been talking for a minute. I should erase this. Naw, you know
what? I'ma send it. Just like this. I ain't scared."

The call ended abruptly. Shayla smiled.

I guess he wasn't scared.

Her next message was much shorter:

"Carrie, this is Pastor Tate, from The Hill..."

Her eyes widened. She sat up in her chair and grabbed a
pen.

"I've been thinking about your offer, to help the church
with advertising. I know I sounded doubtful yesterday, but I think
this is something we might be interested in. You can call me back
at 817-555-6331."

Shayla jotted the number, her mind racing. Yesterday
Pastor Tate said this would be something his secretary would
handle. But he called himself. She remained doubtful that he was
what Janet said he was, but his call was suspicious.

There was only one way to know for sure.

She activated her call recorder and took a deep breath before she returned his call. After four rings, a voicemail came on.

"Damn," she whispered.

"Hello," an automated voice said. "You've reached 817-555-6331. No one is available to take your call at this time. Please leave a message after the tone."

BEEP.

"Hi," Shayla said. "This is Carrie from Media Marketing. I'm sorry, I was away from the desk when you called earlier. I'll be in the office for the rest of the day, if you'd like to call back. Can't wait to hear from you."

She disconnected and rubbed her hands together. She had goose bumps on her arms. She loved this, the thrill of the hunt, the chase, the cat and mouse game she and the pastor were about to play. This is why people bungee jumped. Shayla felt the same adrenaline rush, and she didn't even have to mess up her hair.

She waited a few minutes for him to call back, but at eleven she had to meet with her team of marketing consultants. When cellphone#3 vibrated in her back pocket 30 minutes later, she apologized to her co-workers and excused herself from the conference table.

"Hello?"

"Hi, Carrie?" It was her prey.

"Yes, this is she. Who's calling?"

"This is Pastor Tate, from The Hill."

She grinned. "Good morning. It's nice to hear from you."

"I, um, is this a good time?" His voice was softer on the phone than it was in person.

"Yes," she said. "I'm sorry I missed your call earlier."

"Are you at work?" the pastor asked.

"Yes, I am."

"This, this isn't your work phone?"

She wasn't surprised by the question. The voicemail greeting on cellphone#3 was the same recorded message he had. He wanted to know why she hadn't personalized the recording to include her company's name.

"This is my cellphone," she said.

"Then, there's no office phone number on your card," Pastor Tate noticed. "Just this number and a fax number."

Suspicious, are we?

"I'm not in my office very often," she offered.

"Oh. You're, uh, you're located in Arlington, right?"

She knew he was still looking at her card. The address for Media Marketing was printed as clear as day.

"Yes. On Cooper. Would you like to stop by to discuss our services?"

That was a bluff. If the pastor agreed, she would find a way to steer their meeting to a different location.

"No," he said. "I don't have time to come all the way to your office, but I can spare a few minutes during my lunch hour."

She shook her head, her smile growing by degrees. Did this fool think he was slick?

"I'm free for lunch," she said, without missing a beat. "But I can't drive all the way to Denton. Are you going to come to Arlington?"

"Sure," the pastor said. "How about the El Chico on Collins?"

El Chico? Shayla frowned. She wondered if this was her month for cheap dates. The last time she went somewhere nice, it was with Freeman – and she had to foot the bill that evening. Thinking about Freeman made her heart sigh. She quickly pushed him from her mind.

"El Chico's fine."

"12:30?" the pastor asked.

"That's perfect," she said, although technically her lunch was from twelve to one. "I'll be there."

She left the office forty minutes later. She was glad it was her day to carpool because Lisa didn't have any surveillance equipment in her BMW.

When she arrived at the restaurant, briefcase in hand, there wasn't anyone waiting for her in the lobby. Before she could inquire about the wily pastor, a hostess approached and asked, "Are you looking for Mr. Tate?"

Mister?

Shayla raised an eyebrow. Why would a God-fearing pastor not want people to know he was a God-fearing pastor? The evidence was starting to mount. She nodded at the bubbly blonde. "Yes, I am."

"Right this way."

The hostess led her to a booth along the east wall. Pastor Tate was seated there, looking over the menu. He looked up at her and offered a nervous smile. He stood and reached to shake her hand.

"Hello, Carrie."

"Good afternoon," she replied.

Pastor Tate wore black Dockers with a green button-down tucked in neatly. Shayla wore a pink blouse with a white skirt that clung to her hips and thighs like shadows on the sidewalk.

The pastor pretended not to notice her curves, but the gig was up. Shayla was almost certain everything Janet said about this man was true. Not only did he contradict himself by driving 45 minutes to Arlington on a day when he was *supposedly* pressed for time, but he met her without a chaperone. There was no church secretary sitting next to him.

She took a seat across from him and placed her purse on the left side of the table. She had two hidden cameras in her bag. One of the lenses was concealed in the large buckle on the front.

Before speaking, she reached into her purse and removed a tube of Chapstick. She applied a thin coat while the pastor watched. When she returned the Chapstick, she casually flipped a switch on the inner lining of her purse to turn the camera on. There was no green indicator light on this device, so she had to assume everything was working properly.

She leaned back and crossed her legs. She looked the preacher in the eyes.

"Nice day, isn't it?"

"Yes," Pastor Tate said, and this was the first time his grin was even slightly perverted. "It is a beautiful day."

During their meal, he asked a lot of questions. Some of them were about Shayla's job, but most were meaningless, or so it seemed. It didn't take her long to realize he was sizing her up. He wanted to know where she was born, raised and what her parents did for a living. He asked where she went to high school and college.

She didn't expect questions of this nature and had to scramble to not only make up answers on the spot, but she had to remember her answers so they wouldn't coincide with things she'd already told him.

The conversation didn't shift to advertising until they were finished with their meal. She told him she wanted to start off with flyers. Her company had a street team that could put an advert on thousands of cars and doorknobs within twenty miles of the church. She wanted to put ads in the local papers and buy space on billboards in Denton. Depending on the pastor's budget, she also wanted to produce a few commercials for the local radio and television stations.

Pastor Tate listened politely and didn't ask how much all of this would cost until she finished her spiel.

"It depends on if you want the television and radio," she said. "Without TV ads, you'd probably be looking at forty. Our fees might go up to a hundred, maybe one-fifty if we do TV and radio."

"A hundred and fifty?..."

"Thousand."

Pastor Tate's eyebrows knitted. He sat back and shook his head. She knew it was all for show. She could've offered to do it for a dollar-fifty, and he still would've turned her down, because this meeting had nothing to do with business.

"That's a little steep."

"It's competitive," she replied.

"I don't think we can afford that."

She liked this chess match, but it was time to put this fool in check, or at least take out a pawn.

"Shouldn't you have a chaperone here with you?"

The pastor was caught off guard. His face flushed with crimson. "You, um, I mean..."

She waited.

"This, um, we're... This is a business lunch," he said at length. "We're not doing anything inappropriate." He looked around suspiciously.

"Yeah, but I thought you religious men were supposed to have a chaperone if you're meeting a single woman. Things could, *happen*, and you won't have anyone to back up your story."

Her eyes were serious, her lips parted. Sex oozed from every pore on her body.

Pastor Tate swallowed roughly. He reached for his glass. She was shocked to see his fingers trembling. He took a quick drink of water and carefully placed the glass back on the table.

"Thing, things like what?"

"Oh, I don't know..." She was as cool as a cucumber. "What if I told you I liked you? What if I said I think you're fine and we should, you know..."

The pastor's eyes grew large. She began to wonder if she was wrong about him.

"I'm, I'm married," he said.

She sensed she was pushing too hard, but she didn't care. Either he was a cheater or he wasn't. His personal opinion of her didn't matter in the least, so she kept her foot firmly pressed on the gas.

"I know you're married, but that doesn't mean I'm not attracted to you. If you're attracted to me too, things could happen. I won't tell, if you won't."

She leaned forward to sip her tea, her eyes locked on his. Rather than lift her glass, she lowered her head until her mouth encountered the straw. She licked the tip before she wrapped her lips around it. She maintained eye contact as she sucked. When she was done, she pushed the straw out of her mouth with her tongue, and then she licked the moisture from her lips.

Pastor Tate's mouth hung open. He licked his lips too. He tried to speak, but it took a moment to get the words out. "I, I gotta go." He looked around anxiously for the waiter. Sweat glistened on his forehead. "I, I'll get the check."

She was disappointed but it didn't show. The smile never left her face as she rose to her feet. "I didn't mean to offend you, Pastor. I was just telling you things *could* happen, if you meet a woman like me without a chaperone."

"No, it's, it's not that," Pastor Tate said. "I just, I guess I lost track of the time." He looked at his watch. "I have to get back to the church."

"It's cool." She folded her napkin and dropped it on the table. She was conflicted. It was obvious the pastor would cheat if she pushed hard enough, but that wouldn't be considered a success. Any man might lose track of his morals if a voluptuous woman threw herself at him. Shayla was only interested in exposing *predators*.

"I'll, I'll call you if I change my mind about working with your company," he said.

"That's fine."

She grabbed her purse and left him sitting there, thinking this would be the last time they saw each other. But when she looked back after a few steps, Pastor Tate's eyes were firmly glued to her ass. There was no mistaking it. She knew she was wrong for celebrating his failure, but the sight of his lust-filled stare filled her heart with glee – and disgust. She continued towards the exit with a renewed sense of hope.

On the way back to the office, she called her friend.

"I'm still not sure about this one," she reported.

"Why you say that?" Janet asked.

"I got him to meet me for lunch, but he freaked out when I started flirting with him."

"You probably have to take it slower," Janet suggested.

Shayla shook her head. "Girl, I don't know how much slower I can take it. You know I'm not getting paid for this. I should've been back at work thirty minutes ago. I'm just now leaving Arlington."

"I can pay you," Janet offered. "I got a little money left from Beverly's life insurance."

Shayla rolled her eyes, her mood suddenly downcast. She realized what was happening: Every time she sounded like she might back out, Janet brought up her dearly departed sister. Shayla thought it was a low blow.

"I don't want your money," she said. "I never charge for this. I'm doing it because I can't stand a lying-ass, cheating-ass pastor. All I'm saying is it's not feasible for me to play around with this dude for too much longer. I got a regular job and other stuff going on."

"I know," Janet said. "Just do what you can, Shay. If you have to quit, I understand. I'll find some other way to get him..."

Shayla considered what "other way" Janet had in mind. Her friend had a serious motive for revenge, but she doubted Janet had the means to take down a powerful pastor. She would probably key his car or slash the tires and call it a day. That type of retribution would never hurt a man like Pastor Tate.

"Give me a little more time," Shayla said. "I'll call you when I have another update."

She was still upbeat when she got off work, but the day took a turn for the worse when she and Lisa approached her car in the parking lot. There was another note under Shayla's windshield wiper. Before she jumped to conclusions, she looked around to see if she was the victim of another mass flyer distribution.

Not this time.

Every other car in the parking lot was bare. She was the only one who had been targeted.

She stomped to her Acura angrily, vaguely aware that Lisa said something like, "Oh, damn," in the background. Shayla snatched the letter off her car and unfolded it. She stared at the four words written in black marker. It was the same handwriting as last time. She guessed it was the same marker too. She wasn't aware that she was fuming until the paper started to shake in her hand, and a bright fire blazed in her peripheral vision.

She crumpled the note and kept her fist balled. She dropped her briefcase. She looked around but didn't see Alaina watching them. She looked back at their office and then headed in that direction. If Alaina had any sense, she'd be long gone by now. If she was stupid enough to still be on the property, Shayla planned to slap her lips clean off her face, consequences be damned.

"Wait!" Lisa grabbed her arm. She had to pull hard to halt Shayla's progress. "Stop it! Where you going?"

Shayla was too angry to speak. She shoved the note into Lisa's chest and then raised a trembling hand to her own face. She rubbed her temple and continued to look around the parking lot. The hairs stood on her arms. If she didn't release her tension, an explosion was imminent.

Lisa took the note and read it quickly. She stared into Shayla's eyes and then took the keys from her hand. "Get in the car," Lisa said as she disabled the alarm. She grabbed Shayla's briefcase and tossed it on the backseat. When she looked back, her friend hadn't moved.

"Come on, Shay, get in."

Shayla reluctantly got in on the passenger side. Lisa blew out a sigh of relief as she made her way to the driver's seat.

By the time Lisa got the Acura started, Shayla looked to be in a trance. She stared straight ahead. Her hands rested in her lap, both balled into fists. Shayla's eyes were wet, but the tears didn't spill. Lisa put the car in gear and got moving before her friend decided to jump out and hunt down her nemesis.

"Are you alr–"

Shayla screamed loudly and unexpectedly. Lisa was so surprised, she stomped her foot on the brakes. Neither woman had her seatbelt on. The sudden stop jarred them enough to snap Shayla out of her daze.

"Dammit, girl! What you doing?"

"What *you* doing?" Lisa snapped back. "Why you screaming?"

"I'm frustrated!" Shayla yelled. "I had to get it out!"

"Why are you still yelling *now*?!" Lisa shouted back.

Shayla sighed. Her nostrils flared. "Just drive."

Lisa eased off the brakes, and they got moving again. When Midwest Media began to fade in the rearview mirror, she asked, "Are you alright?"

"Hell no, I'm not alright." Shayla looked possessed, but she wasn't trembling anymore. She wasn't yelling either.

"What do you want to do?" Lisa asked.

"It's not a *want* anymore," Shayla said. "I'm gonna kick her ass. That's the bottom line."

"What about your job?"

"I don't care about my job. I'm not working with that lady anymore. If I get fired, so be it."

"You're not gonna attack her at work."

"Why not? She's attacking *me* at work."

Shayla snatched the new letter from her friend. She reread it, and her heart started to race again. The first note Alaina left read "**FOUND YOU BITCH**." The new one said "**COMING FOR YOU WHORE!**" Apparently Alaina wanted to take it up a notch. If she thought Shayla was going to run and hide, she had another thing coming.

"You don't even know if Alaina left that," Lisa reasoned.

"Who else could've left it?"

"I don't know, Shay. You know you have a lot of enemies."

"I don't have *a lot of enemies*."

"Every man you exposed is your enemy," Lisa countered. "Every one of their wives is your enemy. Every member of all those churches who blamed you and still supported their deacon or pastor is your enemy."

"Well, if you see any of them at Midwest Media, point 'em out, and I'll kick their ass too," Shayla growled. "But for now, I only know about *one* enemy that works with me, and *that* bitch is getting her ass kicked."

"Are you at least gonna ask her if she did it before you start swinging?"

"If it'll make you feel better, yes, I'll ask her."

"It would also make me feel better if you don't confront her at work."

"She's leaving these goddamned notes at work!"

"First of all, *maybe* she is," Lisa argued. "Second, even if you're right about her, that doesn't mean you have to throw away your career."

"Work is the only place I get to see her," Shayla whined.

"I work in Human Resources," Lisa reminded her. "I have access to her file. I can get you her home address, her phone number, whatever you need."

Shayla was so upset, she had forgotten about that.

"But you could still get fired for harassing her away from work," Lisa warned. "And if somebody finds out I gave you her personal information, I could get fired too."

Shayla was listening, but she didn't care what Midwest Media had to say about it. Jobs come and go. You have to live with your sanity forever. Her career wasn't worth risking a mental breakdown.

Then again, that was selfish thinking. Shayla had brought this upon herself. It wouldn't be right to do something that might cost Lisa her job. She remained quiet for a few minutes, and gradually her anger receded.

"If you can give me her phone number and her address," she said, "I'll take care of it away from work."

Lisa wished she hadn't brought that up, but it bought them a little time. They could go home and rest, and after a full night's sleep, Shayla was sure to come up with a better plan.

If she didn't, Lisa would have her back 100%. She loved her job at Midwest Media, but like Shayla, she recognized it was only a job. She could find gainful employment elsewhere. But a best friend, that's something you should treasure more than silver and gold.

In some cases, a best friend is even worth dying for.

CHAPTER FOURTEEN
HARLOT

When they got home, Shayla made Lisa promise she wouldn't spill the beans about the new note like she did with the last one. Lisa swore she'd keep her lips sealed, and she did, but it wasn't easy. Carla noticed the tension as soon as her roommates walked through the door.

"What's wrong with y'all?"

Carla sat on the sofa watching her favorite reality show. Shayla didn't envy her sister's twelve-hour shifts at the hospital, but she got a little jealous when Carla had four days off in a row.

"Nothing," she said. "Had a bad day at work."

"What happened?" Carla looked from Shayla's eyes to Lisa's. Lisa knew she couldn't mask her emotions, so she barely paused on her way to the kitchen.

"What we got to eat?"

"I ordered a pizza earlier," Carla said, and then looked back to her sister. "You got into it with somebody? Did it have something to do with that girl you wanted to get fired?"

"I really don't want to talk about it," Shayla said. "Not right now."

"How come–"

"At least let me get out of these clothes first," Shayla said and continued down the hallway.

As she undressed, she tried to come up with a lie that would get Carla off her back. When she got down to her bra and panties, she heard a familiar ringtone chirping in her purse. It was cellphone#3. She almost didn't answer it. The seduction of Pastor Tate was becoming less fun the longer it dragged on.

But she remembered Marcus still had the number for that cellular. She retrieved it, and her mood brightened when she saw it was her new friend rather than the skittish pastor.

"Hello."

"Hey, baby."

"*Baby*? You don't know me well enough to be calling me baby. You don't even have my real phone number."

"What number is this?" Marcus asked.

"This is a dummy phone," Shayla said, "for the *dummy* I'm trying to take down at your church."

"Dang. How many cellphones you got?"

"It depends on how many jobs I'm working on. Right now I have three, but I haven't used the second one in a while."

She sat on the bed, perplexed that she was so honest with him. She always said she wouldn't keep any secrets when she found the man she wanted to spend the rest of her life with. But she didn't think Marcus was that man.

She lie on her soft mattress and propped a pillow under her head, her legs hanging over the side. Her door was open, but she didn't feel like getting up to close it. It wasn't like her roommates hadn't seen her in her undies.

"I've been meaning to ask how it's going with Pastor Tate," Marcus said. "Are you still working on that?"

"As a matter of fact, I saw him today. We met for lunch. Supposedly he wanted to talk about some marketing I offered to do for the church. But he came alone, and he turned me down when I gave him some prices. I thought he was ready for a takedown, but when I started flirting with him, he got scared and said he had to go."

Marcus chuckled. "You flirted with him?"

"That's how I catch them in the act. I need him to proposition me. If I can get him to talk dirty or tell me about some of his past affairs, that's even better."

"Do you, you be touching on these pastors, the ones you expose?"

Shayla almost lied. But Marcus seemed to have a *What the hell* attitude, and he gave her one as well. She knew he'd either accept her for who she was, or he wouldn't.

"Sometimes I have to," she confided. "If I make out with a pastor and get it all on video, it's hard for him to talk his way out of it."

"Is that all you do, make out with them?"

"When I first started, I was into the sexual gratification as much as I was into exposing them," she admitted. "But I haven't slept with a pastor in a long time, at least five years."

"Wow," Marcus said. "I mean, I'm glad you changed, but, man... I don't think I would've wanted to be with you, when you were sleeping with them. Honestly, the idea of you kissing Pastor Tate makes me feel weird."

"I don't want you feeling weird. I won't tell you about it, if you don't want to know."

"Nah, it's cool. I guess I'm tripping 'cause I know Pastor, a little bit. I liked that dude."

"You don't have to worry. I'm not going to sleep with Pastor Tate. I promise."

"Cool," Marcus said, and thankfully he changed the subject. "So back to your cellphones... Why'd you give me a dummy number?"

"Because when I went to The Hill, my name was Carrie, and this is Carrie's phone number. You have to be *real* special to get my real number."

"So, hold up, let me save it in my contacts... Okay, what's your real number?"

She grinned. "Didn't you hear what I just said?"

"I must be special," Marcus deduced, "'cause you already gave me your real name."

"Yeah, but–"

"And you let me grab your real booty and kiss your real lips. You slipped me some real tongue too."

Her chest grew warm.

When she didn't respond, he said, "Sorry, did I embarrass you?"

"Not at all."

"Really?"

"Why would that embarrass me?"

"Damn," Marcus said. "See, that's what I like about you: Most girls think I talk too much, saying inappropriate shit. I be trying to make them laugh most of the time, but mostly it's me keeping it real. That's one thing about me, Shayla; I always keep it real."

"Like with your seven and a half inches?"

When he didn't say anything, she said, "Did I embarrass you?"

"Nope. I can tell you're interested in my seven and a half, or you wouldn't have remembered."

She giggled.

"It's thick too," he said. "Wanna see?"

She laughed. "Boy, stop. But I will give you my real phone number."

"Okay. What is it?"

Shayla gave him the number, and, not surprisingly, her real cellphone started to ring a moment later.

"You don't trust me?"

"Why you say that?" Marcus asked.

She got up and dug cellphone#1 from her purse. The smile slipped from her face when she saw who was calling.

"Oh, it's not you."

"What's that?" Marcus asked, hearing her other phone ring. "You getting another call?"

"Yeah. Can I call you back?"

"For sure. Talk to you later."

He disconnected without asking, *Who's that?* which was a big deal to Shayla. Even a man as fine as Michael B. Jordan could be a turnoff if he's insecure.

Shayla answered her main phone with a lot less cheer in her voice.

"What you want?"

"To let you know how much I can't stand you," Freeman growled.

She almost hung up then, but if he wanted to vent, she figured she owed him that much.

"You don't have to call to tell me that, Freeman. You already showed me how you feel when you left me at the hotel by myself."

"No, I want you to understand what you did to me." He sounded sober. His voice rattled, like he was near tears. But most of all Shayla heard white hot anger in each word he spoke. She knew it wouldn't take long before he ended each sentence with the word *bitch*.

"Tell me then, Freeman. And after this, I don't want you calling me no more."

"You ain't got to worry about me calling back, bitch, 'cause–"

"*There we go.*"

"What?" he snapped.

"Nothing!" she snapped back. She sat up with a scowl on her face. "Finish what you got to say, man."

"I left my wife for you," Freeman stated. "I left my whole family. I moved out of my house for you."

"I didn't tell you to do none of that."

"Yeah, you never told me to do nothing, Shayla. You just strung me along like a goddamned puppy 'cause I was stupid enough to follow your ass."

"Yeah, you followed like a dog in heat because that's all you ever cared about."

"*Bullshit*! Don't you dare say that! You know I loved you! I did everything I could to show you!"

"Alright, Freeman! Fine! I'm sorry, okay? If I hurt you, I apologize. What more do you want from me?"

"You know what I want from you?"

"No!"

"I'll tell you what I want from you!"

"Well, tell me, nigga! Damn! What you waiting on?"

"I want *you* to repent!" Freeman shouted. "You're so quick to judge everybody else, why don't you face up to what you did? I want you to admit that you're a harlot, and you–"

"A what?"

"A *harlot*!" Freeman repeated. "You lured me with your sex and pulled me away from God. You're doing the devil's work, and you're going to hell, Shayla! All you do is sin! You're *sick* with sin!"

"Are you done?"

"Yeah, I'm done!"

Rather than hang up, she now had a few things to get off her chest.

"Well, let me tell you something, you dumb motherfuc–"

"Shut up, whore!" Freeman spat and hung up in her face.

Shayla knew she shouldn't let him get to her, but for the second time that day, she was filled with rage. She wanted to throw her phone, but it was too expensive to break for a punk like Freeman. She looked around for something less valuable to destroy, and that's when she noticed her little sister standing in the doorway.

Carla looked more concerned than shocked about what she just heard. She waited a few seconds and then said, "I guess you don't wanna talk about this either..."

"I'll be in there in a minute," Shayla said with a sigh. "Close my door. Let me get some clothes on."

The next morning Shayla still felt grumpy. She decided that she needed immediate closure with Alaina McGhee. Waiting for Lisa to get her contact information no longer felt like the best approach. The quickest way to handle a problem was to attack it head on, so she called the manager of the advertising department at nine a.m.

This was the second time Shayla had inquired about her, so Patricia Moresby asked, "Is something wrong?"

"No," Shayla said. "It's not about work. Me and Alaina used to go to church together. I want to ask her something about our old pastor."

"Do you want me to have her call you?"

"Actually," Shayla said, "I was hoping you could send her to my office. It doesn't have to be now. Whenever she's not too busy."

"I can send her after the morning break," Patricia offered.

"That's perfect," Shayla said and hung up. She no longer thought Alaina would attack her, at least not at work. But she remained apprehensive about their meeting. There were too many unknown variables.

She wanted to get Lisa's take on this, but she knew her friend would be upset that she scheduled the encounter in the first place. Rather than seek counsel, Shayla watched the clock for the next hour and a half, until ten-thirty rolled around. Alaina knocked on her door a few minutes later.

Shayla told her to "Come in."

Alaina stepped cautiously into the office with a worried expression. She wore a white blouse with a long, black skirt. She had her hair down, which made her look more professional than the ponytail and purple scrunchie she had the last time Shayla saw her. Alaina wore too much lipstick, but she was attractive, even in her state of unease.

"You wanted to see me?" She stood in the doorway like a child summoned to the principal's office. Shayla didn't have one ounce of leverage over her career, but Alaina didn't know that.

"Yeah, I wanted to talk," Shayla said. "You can sit down."

Alaina approached the desk and reluctantly eased down in the chair. She looked around the office with quick eyes that never settled on anything.

Shayla was anxious too, but she drew confidence from Alaina's dread.

"Do you know who I am?" she asked.

Alaina nodded. "Your name is Shayla Humphries."

"Why'd you ask my name on the elevator?"

Alaina shrugged. She looked down at her hands.

"Do you remember me, from before you came to this company?" Shayla asked.

Alaina's throat caught. She looked around the office again, as if a mob of goons was waiting to jump her if she gave the wrong response.

Shayla liked to see her like this, but she felt she might be crossing the line. If Alaina reported the shakedown, Shayla would have a lot of explaining to do.

"Look," she said, "I'm not your manager. You don't have to talk to me, if you don't want to. You can walk out right now. But I think we have some issues we need to address. And I think you know what I'm talking about."

Alaina relaxed a little. She sighed and folded her arms over her chest in a defensive gesture.

"I know you from when you came to my church."

Shayla's knee started to bounce. Her fingers began to tremble as well. She placed both hands in her lap to hide her nervousness.

"That was a long time ago," Shayla said. "Why do you remember that?"

Alaina shrugged. "I don't know."

"You don't like me, do you?"

Alaina hesitated. She shook her head and started to get up. "I think I wanna go back to my department."

Shayla's heart stopped cold. Not only did she not have the answers she sought, but Alaina looked like she might file a complaint.

"Wait," she said, rising to her feet as well. "Please, talk to me. I just wanna clear the air. I'm not trying to start any trouble."

Alaina continued to shake her head, but she sat back down. Shayla did the same. When Alaina met her eyes again, Shayla was surprised to see she was close to tears.

"My husband said you was the one – in the video."

The blood drained from Shayla's face. Suddenly unsure of herself, she reverted to lying. "Wh, what video?"

Sensing a shift in power, Alaina narrowed her eyes.

"You the one who said you wanted to talk about it. Now you wanna play dumb?"

Shayla shook her head. She bit the bullet and cleared her throat. "Okay. I'm not going to deny it. I made a video about your husband."

"You was kissing on him," Alaina said, her boldness growing. "You and him was going to the motel."

"We didn't go to a motel," Shayla said quickly. "I never slept with your husband."

"I saw the video. Everybody at church saw it. You, you made a fool out of me." The tears rolled down her cheeks, even as her defiance grew.

Shayla pushed a box of Kleenex across her desk. Alaina plucked one and blew her nose.

"Alright," Shayla said. "I know what I did was wrong. But I never wanted to make a fool out of you. I only wanted to expose your husband. People had been talking about him having affairs with a lot of women. Someone from your church asked if I could help take him down. But as far as you—"

"Who the hell do you think you are?" Alaina asked. Her face was wet, and her eyes were growing puffy. But she'd been waiting four years to ask Shayla this, and she didn't sound meek at all.

"I, I'm nobody special," Shayla said. "This is just something I do, from time to time. It's a long story, about how I got started. But I never exposed anyone who was innocent. I know you probably don't want to hear this, but your husband wasn't being true to you. He was sleeping with women from your church. My friend said—"

"So?" Alaina cut her off.

Shayla was taken aback. "She, um... What?"

"So what if he was sleeping with other women?"

"I, I don't understand."

"That's 'cause you ain't got no business doing what you doing. Why didn't you ask me about it, if you were going to expose him?"

"I don't, I usually don't talk to the, um..."

Alaina didn't let her off the hook. She waited, impatiently.

"I just... I've never talked to one of the wives before," Shayla said.

"Why?"

"I don't know."

"Yes, you do," Alaina said, nodding. "You didn't talk to me, because you knew I wouldn't want you to do it. If it was supposed to be helping me, you would've told me about my husband and let *me* make a decision. But you didn't do that. I had to hear about it right along with everybody else. You embarrassed me. You made me look – like the biggest fool in the world!"

Alaina sobbed loudly. Shayla looked around nervously, her heart hammering. If someone walked into her office, she'd be hard pressed to tell them what was going on.

"Why you do it?" Alaina wanted to know. "Why you do that to me?"

"I, I didn't think about you," Shayla admitted. This was going as badly as she expected. "Everything I did was to hurt your husband. It didn't have anything to do with you."

Alaina's eyes widened, and Shayla regretted her choice of words.

"That don't even make sense!" Alaina spat. "You said you did it because he was cheating on me. Now you're saying you didn't care about me."

"I did," Shayla said, "but not like you're thinking. My goal was to hurt your husband. Yes, I got involved because he was married to you. But no, I didn't take your opinion into consideration, because I know most wives will stay with their husband, even if they know he's cheating."

Alaina wiped her eyes and snatched more tissue from Shayla's desk. "I knew about what my husband was doing for *years* before you came along. You didn't tell me nothing new. The only thing you did was get it on camera, so I was forced to look at it. You humiliated me in front of the whole church. That's the *only* thing you did for me."

"I also did it for other women in the church who felt like your husband took advantage of them," Shayla argued. "It was for the rest of the congregation who had no idea what kind of man they were depending on for spiritual guidance. I did it for the whole church, Alaina. For God, for everybody."

"Well, I guess you got what you wanted. They kicked him out, and our marriage couldn't hold on after that. I had to start over with my life. I moved down here by myself, just me and my kids."

Shayla thought Alaina should be happy with the changes. "Isn't that better?" she asked. "Why are you so upset with me?"

"You ain't never gon' get it," Alaina guessed. "Yeah, my husband was doing me wrong. But we have three kids. I never worked, the whole time I was with him. He took care of us. He paid the bills. He was a *pastor*. I know you probably don't think too much about pastors, but where I come from, pastors are important. They're *special*. Being a pastor's wife is special."

"I understand," Shayla said, but Alaina wasn't done speaking.

"It was an *honor* to be with that man. When I found out he was cheating, yeah, it hurt, but it's more to life than worrying about who your husband's sleeping with. He came home to me every night. His kids looked up to him, and they loved him.

"Sometimes that's enough to keep it going. Sometimes you have to take the good with the bad, and you'll figure out that if you got way more good, then you can get used to the bad. Like when he used to leave his drawers on the floor, it wasn't nothing to pick 'em and go on about my business. You get used to the bullshit, after a while."

By no stretch of the imagination could Shayla see a correlation between allowing your husband to cheat and him leaving his dirty underwear on the floor. But she met plenty of women like Alaina in her lifetime. There was no point in trying to convince her to see things differently. In any event, Shayla wasn't trying to make a friend. She only wanted the threats to stop.

"Why are you leaving notes on my car?" she finally asked.

Alaina frowned and registered genuine confusion. "Wha, what car?"

Shayla's heart sank. At that moment she knew Alaina didn't have anything to do with it. "Somebody left a note on my car, here at work. I thought it might be you."

Alaina shook her head. She sniffled. "I don't even know what kind of car you drive. I, I just moved down here from Mesquite. I ain't got nobody helping me. I wouldn't do nothing to get in trouble at work…"

Shayla watched her eyes. There was no doubt she was telling the truth. She looked away for a moment and tried to think of someone else who had the motive. She looked back to her co-worker. Alaina still looked confused.

"I, I guess that's all I wanted to talk to you about," Shayla said. "Again, I apologize, for everything. I did want you to leave your husband, but you're right, I should've considered how you felt about it. I was wrong for that.

"We won't see each other very much, here at the office. But I hope that if we *do* have to work together, we can do so professionally – without letting our personal feelings get in the way."

Alaina nodded. She swiped a few more tissues and tried to clean herself up before she returned to her department. She stood and deposited all the used Kleenex in a waste basket Shayla kept next to her desk.

"I know I look like hell," she said offhandedly.

"You look pretty good," Shayla said, "all things considered."

"Where's the restroom on this floor?"

"It's near the elevator."

Alaina nodded and headed for the door. She looked back before she exited.

"You, um, I don't wanna encourage you, but I do think my life is better now that I got a divorce. Even though I wasn't gonna leave my husband before you showed up, everything he was doing, it did hurt me. I used to think about it a lot, sometimes when I was home alone, and I knew he was with his women. I guess you are helping some people, but I think you're going about it the wrong way."

Shayla nodded vacantly. "Thanks."

Her brain raced as she watched Alaina leave. If the new hire didn't leave the notes on her car, then Shayla had another stalker out there, somewhere. Lisa said she left so many enemies in her wake, it was impossible to guess who her antagonist might be. Shayla figured that was probably right.

The first letter they found read, *FOUND YOU BITCH*. The second one said, *COMING FOR YOU WHORE!* Whoever left the messages wanted her to know they were getting closer. A confrontation was imminent.

Rather than drive herself crazy trying to solve the mystery, Shayla knew the easiest way to get her stalker to step out of the shadows was to make herself available to them. She wasn't keen on the idea of being human bait, but it couldn't be *that* big of a risk. What was the worst her adversary could do, kill her?

Hmph. Shayla balked at that idea.

CHAPTER FIFTEEN
SHOW AND PROVE

"Dammit, Shayla! What is wrong with you?"

"What? What are you talking about?"

"You keep going behind my back," Lisa said.

"I'm not going behind your back." Shayla pulled down the visor to block some of the sunlight peeking through the downtown skyline. The fire in the sky was starting to descend, but they had two hours of daylight left.

"We talked about this yesterday," Lisa reminded her. She sat in the passenger seat wearing a scowl. "You said you wanted me to get her phone number so you could call her."

"No, *you* said you wanted to do that."

"But you agreed! You said you would handle this away from work."

"Alright, well the next time someone threatens you, you try to wait till the end of the day to find out who it is. I held out for as long as I could."

"You couldn't even make it through lunch."

"No, I couldn't," Shayla conceded. "But I didn't get anyone in trouble. It's cool now. Me and Alaina are cool."

"What if it didn't turn out like that? What if she had got mad and reported you?"

"But she didn't. Instead of complaining about what could've happened, we need to figure out what to do from here."

"No." Lisa shook her head. "*You* need to figure out what to do from here."

"So you kicking me to the curb? You don't got my back no more?"

"What difference does it make?" Lisa folded her arms over her chest and stared out of the passenger window. "You not gonna listen to what I have to say anyway. Even worse, you'll pretend to listen and then do whatever the hell you want. You don't care about your job or nothing."

Shayla sighed. "Okay, I know we decided not to mess with her at work. I did it anyway, and I'm sorry. Your advice is always better than mine. If I would close my mouth and listen to you sometimes, I wouldn't be in this predicament in the first place.

"But that being said, I am in this predicament, and, and it's scary, Lisa. I don't know who's out to get me. I couldn't go through a whole day of work without finding out if Alaina was the one messing with me. I just, I couldn't do it. And even though it seems like I never listen to you, I need your help. I'm back at square one. I don't know where to go from here."

Lisa reluctantly returned her gaze to her best friend. She studied Shayla's eyes and saw sincerity. She shook her head and blew out a sigh.

"I should let you suffer in the hole you dug for yourself."

"What would Jesus do?" Shayla asked.

Lisa rolled her eyes at that, but she smiled.

"Alright, buttface. So, Alaina didn't do it?"

"No," Shayla said, already appreciating their brainstorming session.

"You sure?"

"I'm almost positive. Alaina and her husband got divorced. She's trying to start a new life here. She's not going to do anything stupid that would get her fired."

"Alright," Lisa said. "So if we rule her out, what other leads do we have?"

"You said it could be anybody. I make enemies at every church I go to, right?"

"You don't think so?"

"No. I mean yes," Shayla said. "You're right."

"Is there anyone in particular, anyone who was especially mad at you?"

Shayla thought for a few seconds and shook her head. "Sometimes the men curse me out. Sometimes they give their wife my phone number and let her call and curse me out."

"Did any of them tell you they would get you back?" Lisa asked. "Any of them say they were gonna find you?"

"Only about a third of them."

"How many is that?"

"Over what time frame?" Shayla asked. "I do about seven exposés a year."

Lisa frowned. "You don't even know if it's a man or a woman. It could be Freeman, for all you know."

"Freeman?"

"You said he called you a harlot. That's the same as calling you a whore, like in that letter."

"Yeah, but I got the first note *before* me and Freeman broke up."

"You said he was upset with you already," Lisa argued. "He'd been asking you to be exclusive, and you knew it wasn't gonna work out. If he was pissed off before the breakup, he could've left the first note, just to mess with your head."

Shayla frowned. Lisa's theory was plausible, but she couldn't imagine Freeman doing something so devious.

"I don't think it's Freeman. But you're right, it could be..."

"Or it could be someone who's even more pissed," Lisa warned. "If they know where you work, you have to assume they know where you live too. This could get dangerous, Shay. I think you should call the police."

Shayla shuddered. Once again, her friend's advice was the best course of action, but Shayla knew she couldn't do it. The police would want to know why she was being harassed, and she'd have to tell them about her hobby.

They might tell Shayla her videotaping and phone taps were illegal. They may ask her to give them a copy of all the videos she'd made over the years, so they could sort through them in search of a culprit. Shayla never purposefully broke the law, but she felt like a criminal just the same. A drug dealer couldn't call the police if someone robbed his dope house. She didn't want the police prying into her personal life either.

"I'll call the police only as a last resort."

Surprisingly, Lisa let her leave it at that.

When they got home, Shayla was desperate for a pastime that would get her mind off her troubles, at least for a while. She hopped on Hulu, thinking she'd bathe and then binge on *Living Single*. Marcus called while she was in the shower. She returned his call after she put on a tee shirt and sweat pants.

"Hello?"

"Mr. Marcus."

"You know that's a porn star's name, don't you?" he asked.

Shayla did know that. Anyone who knew anything about black porn had heard of Mr. Marcus and his iconic baseball caps.

"No," she said. "I never watch porn. Is he any good?"

"I don't know. I mean, when I watch those movies, I don't never be watching the *dude*, if you know what I mean..."

"What about his scene with Super Head?" Shayla asked. "You had to notice how happy he was, when she was doing her thing."

"So, you have heard of him."

"I read his biography on Wikipedia. But I've never seen his movies. I don't watch those kinds of videos."

"They talked about how happy he was on Wikipedia?" Marcus asked skeptically.

"They had screenshots," Shayla said. "Everything was blurred except his face."

"I'm at the computer. I can go to Wikipedia right now and prove you're lying. Or I can assume you're being honest, because you're always upfront with me..."

"Wikipedia changes every day," Shayla said. "They might have taken those screenshots off."

Marcus laughed. "You're full of it. But I still like you. What are you doing on this beautiful Friday evening?"

"Nothing. Watching TV."

"Have you had dinner yet? You wanna go out?"

"Sure, but I'm not driving all the way to Denton."

"I'll come to Overbrook Meadows. Can I pick you up?"

"No," Shayla said, not wanting him to know where she lived. "I'll meet you somewhere."

"What do you want to eat?"

"There's a PF Chang's on Hulen and 30. Do you know how to get there?"

"I'll look it up."

"I have to find something to put on. I can be there in an hour and... fifteen minutes."

"Alright," Marcus said. "I'll be there."

Dinner at PF Chang's was wonderful. Between the flirting and general getting-to-know-you talk, there was plenty to chat about. Marcus' focus kept returning to Pastor Tate's exposé. Shayla told him there was no new news. He was interested in how the exposé would play out, if it did run its course.

"You said you slept with some pastors before, right?"

Marcus' mocha skin looked delectable under the restaurant's dim lights. Shayla was itching to run her fingers through his short, curly hair.

"Why do you keep asking about that?" she asked. "No one wants to hear about who their girl slept with in the past."

That put a smile on his face. "So, you're my girl?"

"No. But if that's what you're hoping for, the same rules apply."

"I don't really care about your past. But it might give me insight on how things are gonna go in the future."

"With Pastor Tate?"

He nodded.

"You said you were okay with my detective work." Shayla never considered herself a *detective* until Marcus called her that.

"I am okay with it. But if you are gonna be my girl, I have a right to be, you know, curious."

"If it's too much for you to handle, let me know."

"No, it's not too much. But I don't know of any man who would be comfortable sharing his woman."

"Don't think of it as sharing. It's just acting. Do you think Jada gets mad every time Will Smith has to do a love scene?"

"Actually, I think she probably does. But with Will, she knows the sex isn't real. You said you actually had sex with some of the others."

Shayla sighed, starting to feel uncomfortable. "Look, man, what I did in the past is in my past. I told you I haven't slept with any of them in the past five years. If you wanna condemn me for something I did that long ago–"

"I don't want to condemn you."

"Then why you keep bringing it up?"

"I'm sorry. I'm trying to digest what you told me. But, you know, it's not that easy."

"I get it. That's why I don't tell anyone about it."

Marcus grinned. "Why'd you tell me?"

"I don't know."

"You must like me," he decided.

Shayla grinned too. "You must like me, if it bothers you so much."

"No doubt. I like you a lot."

"Then trust me," Shayla said. "I'm not gonna sleep with Pastor Tate."

"You could've said, '*I'm not gonna sleep with anyone but you*,'" Marcus suggested. "That would've made me feel a lot better."

Shayla fixed low, seductive eyes on him. "What makes you think I'm gonna sleep with you?"

He chuckled. "You said you were."

"When did I say that?" she asked with a frown.

"When you ordered that bottle of wine," Marcus said, nodding towards her sake. "Everyone knows there are certain items on the menu that have *sex* written next to them, in invisible ink."

She laughed. "I didn't see nothing like that on my menu!"

"You can't see invisible ink without a special light."

"That bottle only cost 26 dollars. I hope you don't think I'll put out for a $26 bottle of wine."

"No, I'm hoping you'll put out because I'm handsome and sweet and I have my own car and my own house. Plus I'm smart and funny, and you already said you was dying to see my seven and a half inches."

Shayla burst out laughing. "I never said that!"

"Why you fighting it? You should give in to your desires."

"Boy, you're the only one at this table with a bunch of *desires*."

"Alright," Marcus said. "You ain't gotta come back to Denton with me, to check out my crib..."

"I'm *not* going to Denton," Shayla agreed. "I already told you I don't feel like driving that far."

"I guess we don't have to go to your place either..."

"No, we don't," Shayla said. "If I wanted you to know where I live, I would've let you pick me up tonight."

"Hmmm." Marcus sat back and thought about it. "I guess the only thing left is for us to get a room. Would you prefer a motel or a hotel?"

"Definitely a *hotel*."

"This is your city," he said. "What's nearby?"

"I like the Embassy Suites downtown."

"Cool," Marcus said and summoned their waiter. "You ready to go?"

Shayla laughed. "Go where?"

"I thought we were going to the Embassy Suites."

Shayla started to burst his bubble, but Marcus was right about everything he said. She thought he was smart, handsome and a great catch. And they'd been talking about his seven and a half inches for so long, she was itching to see it and touch it and maybe ride it like a pogo stick.

"Alright," she said and dropped her napkin on the table. "Let's go."

Their night at the Embassy was nothing like Shayla expected. Given Marcus' wild style and cocky flirting, she thought he'd be loud and aggressive in the sack. She expected some hair-pulling, ass-smacking and a few demands for her to tell him

Whose pussy is this? or *You like it, don't you?* and *Tell me you like it.*

But Marcus' bedroom demeanor was quite the opposite. He was eager, but he didn't show it. He kissed her softly and caressed her body with soft hands that were curious and loving. He sucked her neck with intensity but not hard enough to leave a mark on her skin. He was smooth and mellow, like a shot of liqueur. His tongue was sweet, his breath pleasant.

Shayla considered taking the dominant role, but Marcus showed that his meekness should not be mistaken for weakness. Behind his cool demeanor lurked a mass of powerful muscles, a strong, steady heartbeat, hot blood coursing through his veins. He was a beautiful thoroughbred, waiting for his moment to burst through the gates and run free, to thrive and conquer.

He slipped Shayla's panties off, and she was treated to a mesmerizing display of cunnilingus that made her eyes water and all four of her limbs tremble. She thought she had an excellent head doctor with Freeman, but compared to Marcus, her old boyfriend was amateurish at best.

Marcus used his fingers and mouth to give her a fit of conniptions for a mesmerizing ten minutes. From the first lick, he had her in a state of shock. Most men wade in slowly with a few light kisses or a cursory suck of the labia. But Marcus dove right in with a huge slurp from top to bottom. Shayla felt like every one of his taste buds had a tiny tentacle, briefly sucking her hot flesh as it passed.

He sucked both labia and then parted them and flicked his tongue like a whip. He stiffened his tongue and explored her depths. He zeroed in on her clitoris right away. He sucked and kissed until it was hard and throbbing. He alternated his licking from slow, mind-numbingly teasing, to quick flicks of his tongue that made the muscles spasm in her left butt cheek.

She reached between her legs, and her fingers disappeared in his curly locks. Marcus placed his hands on her thighs and pushed them further apart. His hands slid up to her knees and back down to her hips. He caressed her ass and then lifted it from the mattress and pulled her closer to his face. Shayla yielded to his will, and when he had her kitty right where he wanted it, he rewarded her obedience with what Shayla quickly dubbed *The best head she ever had.*

He probed her love with two fingers that stimulated her G-spot. He didn't stop licking when she whipped her head from side to side. He didn't slow up when her breathing became labored, and her bare chest glistened with sweat. He continued to suck and finger fuck her, coaxing her orgasm like a patient hunter.

When she told him she was about to cum, he changed his style and position to delay her orgasm. He turned his head and licked her sideways, gnawing on her labia with his soft, pink lips. He buried his face in her wetness. Shayla would swear she felt his tongue three inches deep. He looked up at her when she reached her apex a second time. It drove her crazy to see his eyes while his tongue pleased her.

When her moans of pleasure became yelps of passion and longing, and the mere thought of cumming in his face made her heart palpitate, he denied her yet again. He backed away, his mouth and cheeks glistening with her essence.

Shayla wanted to protest, but she could barely speak. She was less than a second away from an orgasm. She couldn't believe he chose that moment to stop. And she knew he had done it on purpose!

Her frustration began to rise when he took his time putting on a condom, but when he became one with her, she couldn't remember what she was upset about.

He stared into her eyes as her walls contracted, squeezing his manhood rhythmically. He lowered his hips slowly, filling her with what felt like a hell of lot more than seven and a half inches. He didn't stop until their skin became one and his fat head pressed the back wall.

Shayla closed her eyes and exhaled a soft moan as she succumbed to a beautiful eruption that was well worth the wait.

"*Marcus*," she whispered.

"*You so wet*," he replied.

Those were the only words Shayla remembered him speaking that night.

CHAPTER SIXTEEN
PUSHING HARD

The couple slept late. They were awakened on Saturday morning by warm rays of sunshine peeking through the curtains of their hotel room. Shayla got up to shower. Marcus joined her in the tub a few minutes later. The shower wasn't very large, but they desired closeness, so it was just right.

Marcus used the hotel soap to lather up a hand towel. He used it to caress every inch of Shayla's body. She returned the favor. By the time she finished cleaning between his legs, he was rock hard and ready to get dirty again.

She eased down to her knees and pleasured him while the warm water drenched her hair and sprayed her back. She sucked him until she tasted his pre-cum, and she sucked harder when he tried to pull away.

When he came, she closed her eyes, loving the wetness in her mouth, on her body, her face. Marcus was so excited, they left the bathroom without drying off. They made love again, and there was something about the wet, slippery slickness of their naked bodies that made everything feel more erotic than last night. Or maybe it was the strengthening of their bond that heightened their sensuality.

The only thing Shayla could say for sure was she didn't envy the housekeeper who had to get the room back in its original condition.

"Let's get out of here," she told Marcus at a quarter after eleven. "I don't want her to see us leaving. It's embarrassing."

He was in the bathroom styling his hair. He looked back at their bed and laughed. The sheets were tangled and wet. At first glance, it was impossible to tell what the stains were.

"Damn, baby. You was *leaking*," he joked. "I ain't never seen nobody get *that* wet."

Shayla stepped into her heels and joined him in the bathroom so she could assess her frizzy mane.

"That wasn't me," she said. "That was you drooling all over my pussy."

"Bullshit. I wasn't drooling. When I eat pussy, I swallow every drop. You taste great, by the way."

Shayla was fully satisfied, but the thought of his superb mouth skills excited her.

She wrapped her arms around his waist and kissed him. "You're really good at that. Probably the best I ever had."

"I was gonna tell you the same thing," he replied. "That move you pulled in the shower... *Oh my God*. You got mad skills, ma. Skills to pay the bills. Matter of fact, I'll pay your bills, if you want – just one of them though. And it has to be something small, like the internet. But *yeah*... I'll pay that motherfucker!"

Shayla laughed. "What you got to do today?"

Marcus shook his head. "Nothing. Wanna get a room?"

"We already did that," she said with a chuckle.

"We can do it again. We can get some lunch and go to the movies and then go to the zoo or something. Then we can get dinner spend another night together."

"Are you serious?"

"For sure – unless you don't wanna be with me all day..."

"No, that sounds cool. But I have to get my hair done at some point."

"Alright, how about we get some lunch, and then we'll go back to our places and change. I'll get us a room at the Worthington, and you can meet me there whenever you're ready."

Shayla smiled. That sounded like a wonderful idea. "I like a man that takes charge."

"Cool," Marcus said. "In that case, why don't you–"

There was a knock on the door, followed by a female voice. "*Housekeeping!*"

Marcus and Shayla looked from the door to the nasty bed and then back at each other.

They laughed.

Shayla couldn't remember the last time she spent two days with one man. She combed her memory bank and realized Marcus was indeed the first. Contrary to their sultry start, sex wasn't the main focus while they were together. Marcus was genuinely fun to be around, no matter what they were doing. He cracked her up at lunch, and he was quiet and contemplative at the movies. He wowed her with his golfing skills when they went to the Colonial, rather than the city zoo.

And somehow, their second night together was more passionate than the first. They explored each other's bodies like students, finding ways to please every areola, earlobe and belly button. Marcus sucked everything from Shayla's collarbones to her toes, and by the end of the night, she had to crown him the king of stimulation.

There was no one better.

Period.

They woke up early on Sunday morning. She thought he should go to church, but Marcus said he'd have to drive all the way to Denton and stop by his house to change. Even if he didn't run into heavy traffic, he'd be an hour late. He vetoed the idea.

Shayla thought about what Freeman said, about her pulling him away from God. She didn't want to do the same with Marcus, but it felt good to cuddle against his warm body, without a care in the world.

When she finally returned home on Sunday afternoon, Lisa and Carla knew she was smitten. Shayla wouldn't confirm this, but she told them this was the happiest she'd been with a man in a long time. The fact that she had been honest with Marcus from the start made their burgeoning relationship that much more beautiful.

At four o'clock on Monday afternoon, Shayla was hard at work on a new promotional package when she got an unexpected call on cellphone#3. She almost didn't answer when she saw that it was Pastor Tate. His exposé was no longer worth the trouble, but she could imagine the disappointment in Janet's voice if she told her friend she gave up on it.

She activated her call recording app before answering. "Hello?"

"Hi. Um, Carrie? This is Pastor Tate, from the Hill."

Shayla sighed. She couldn't believe she was ever excited to hear from this man. She wished he'd crawl into a hole and stay there until he died.

"How are you?" she asked, her voice as upbeat as ever. "I'm fine."

She waited and then asked, "So, what can I do for you?"

"Um, well, I spoke with our secretary and the treasurer," he said, "and I'm thinking I might have been too quick to turn down your proposal the other day. I think, maybe I should've heard you out."

Shayla rolled her eyes. She was sick of these pretenses.

"Would you like to see the numbers again?" she asked. "I can draw something up and email it to your secretary."

"Uh, no. Actually, I'd like to see you in person," Pastor Tate said. "Whenever possible, I think it's better to communicate face-to-face."

His game was tired and lame. And Shayla's patience was running thin. She needed evidence of adultery, and she needed it now.

"It's already after lunch," she said. "Would you like to come by my office? I can schedule an appointment for tomorrow morning..."

"No, I would, I would like to meet for dinner tonight, if that's alright."

Okay, that's good, Shayla thought. *Now we're getting somewhere.* But still, she wouldn't agree to meet with this man unless he incriminated himself during this phone call. Playtime was over.

"I can meet you for dinner. Are you going to bring your secretary with you this time, so we don't have another misunderstanding?"

Pause.

"Uh, no," the pastor said. "I spoke with my treasurer, at length. I have a clear understanding of our budget now."

"Are you bringing your treasurer?"

Pause.

"No. I, I'm not bringing her either."

Shayla's excitement started to grow. This was how she was used to things going. The next step was to get him to acknowledge that this wasn't their first date. She also wanted him to admit that he knew it was wrong.

"When we had lunch last week," she said, "I told you it was not appropriate for us to meet without a chaperone. I told you that maybe I think you're fine, and, with me being a single woman, things could happen. You got all scared and said you had to go..."

"I, I remember..."

"Now I'm telling you straight up," Shayla continued, "I do think you're fine, and I'm still a single woman. If you meet me for dinner by yourself, *things – will – happen*." She spoke slowly and clearly, both for his benefit and for the exposé video she planned to make later.

"Where would you like to meet?" he asked.

Shayla smiled. She was in her zone now, and it felt good. She couldn't believe she ever considered backing out of this job. This is what she was made to do. It was her calling.

She gave him the name of the classiest French restaurant in the city, because Pastor Tate was a millionaire, and it was about time he started acting like it. They made plans to meet at seven o'clock. Shayla hoped to have him in her car no later than 8:30 and completely out of her life fifteen minutes after that.

She called her friend Janet when she got off the phone with the slimy pastor.

"Hey, Shay."

"Hey, girl. Just wanted to give you an update. I just got off the phone with Tate. I got the conversation recorded. It's good stuff. We're gonna meet tonight for dinner. I told him something was gonna go down if he came without a chaperone, and he basically said that was cool."

"That's good, Shay. You got him."

"Not yet. I don't have enough evidence. I'm really starting to hate this man. I want to bury him."

"What more evidence do you need?"

"You'll see," Shayla said, thinking about how Joseph Youngblood pulled his dick out in her car. If she could get Pastor Tate to do that, there was no way anyone in his church could stand by him.

"I'll call you tonight when I get through," she told her friend. "Get those email addresses ready..."

She arrived at Mille Fleurs at seven-fifteen wearing a gown that was both classy and sexy. It was black and sleeveless, flowing down to her ankles while exposing a nice amount of flesh about her chest and back. She wore her hair down and layered. A thin coat of lipstick shimmered on her lips.

If Pastor Tate was thinking with his brain rather than his balls, he would've noticed the large Coach bag she toted didn't match her outfit. A black clutch would've been more appropriate. But Tate was as foolish as the others. He rose to his feet when the hostess led Shayla to his table. He pulled her chair out and continued to smile dopily when she took a seat and reached into her purse in search of a napkin to discard her gum.

She turned the camera on with the stealth of a magician and then moved the purse slightly to the side, so the buckle fully faced the target. Pastor Tate watched her every move, and his goofy smile remained.

That's right, Shayla thought. *Smile for the camera, baby.*

"You sure look nice tonight," he said. The pastor wore a black suit with a white shirt and tie.

"I forgot my briefcase," Shayla said right away. "I won't be able to go over those numbers I promised you."

"That's alright. Don't even worry about that, Carrie."

Shayla enjoyed her meal and the ambiance of the fancy restaurant, but this wasn't a date, Pastor Tate wasn't her man, and she wanted to get down to business. She didn't get any good evidence with her purse camera when they met at El Chico's. She was determined not to let that happen again.

"So, is this an official date?" she asked when the pastor leaned back in his chair with a full belly.

He thought about the question and smiled. "If you would like to see it that way."

"I want to see it as it really is," Shayla said. "I don't want to get the wrong idea about you and end up with hurt feelings."

Her comment struck a chord. Tate might have thought about how badly things had ended with Janet's sister Beverly. More likely, there was a multitude of jilted lovers in his past.

"I'm married," he said, and Shayla had to fight off a smile. It was always good to get them to acknowledge their spouse.

"I'm not leaving my wife," he continued. "Not leaving my family."

"I didn't ask you to leave anyone. I asked you what *I'm* doing here, what we're doing here, together..."

The pastor looked into her eyes and sighed. He leaned forward with his elbows on the table, his hands clasped together. "No man is without sin," he told her. "It's not easy for me, to do the right thing, every time – especially when a beautiful woman like yourself professes her attraction to me."

Shayla didn't like the slow, deliberate way he was being careful with his words. Even worse, she didn't like how he pointed out the fact that she was the one pursuing him.

"I didn't tell you I was attracted to you until you asked me out," she said, hoping to get things back on track.

"I didn't ask you out that day, Carrie. That was a business lunch."

You sonofabitch. She wanted to throw her water in his face.

"This is what I'm talking about," she said. "I don't want to be responsible for anything that might happen between us. I definitely don't want to think you feel a certain way about me if you don't."

"It's not like that. I do have feelings for you, Carrie."

"What about your wife?"

"She, she's... My feelings for her are different. We share a bond, a *spiritual* bond, that can never be severed."

"She doesn't turn you on?"

The pastor rubbed his chin. He stared at her cleavage unabashedly. "Not like you."

Good. Good. She kept reeling him in.

"Aren't you worried about her finding out?"

The mark grinned. "You don't have to worry about that, Carrie. My wife and I have, an understanding."

Shayla's eyes brightened. That was a great scoop. She pressed for more. "She doesn't care if you cheat on her?"

Pastor Tate frowned. "I didn't say that."

"You said y'all have an understanding."

"There's no such thing as a faithful wife who doesn't care what her husband is doing. I said we have an understanding. She is aware. She doesn't ask, but she is aware."

"Does she know where you are right now?"

"She, she is aware..."

Wow. Shayla didn't expect this conversation to reveal so much. Pastor Tate's revelation wasn't mean-spirited like Joseph Youngblood talking about how much he couldn't stand his Millie, but it was just as damning. The next thing Shayla wanted was for him to confirm that she was about to be the next notch on his bedpost.

"So, what are you plans for me?"

He frowned. "You, I don't like to talk about these things. Why don't we let our relationship take its natural course, and we'll see where it goes?"

Shayla liked how he used the word *relationship*, but that wasn't enough. "I like how rational you are," she said. "You want to take things slow, and that's cool with me. But I keep telling you; I don't want to get the wrong idea. If you're not talking about fucking, then tell me straight out."

Her vulgarity turned his face tomato red, as she knew it would. "We can, we can do whatever you want, Carrie."

Grrrr! She felt like pulling her hair out. It was as if he knew she was recording him.

"You're the man," she said. "And you're the one who's married. I'm single, so it's not about what I want. Why can't you speak your mind? Are you nervous?"

"I, I am. And, yes, I would like to do that, what you said."

She sighed inwardly. She knew that was the best she'd get out of him. Hopefully it was enough. "You ready to go?"

"Yes," the pastor said, looking around for their waitress. "Do you have to go home?"

"I'm not leaving you until I get what I came for."

Pastor Tate's smile was both mischievous and oblivious.

When they got outside, he finally asked if Shayla wanted to accompany him to a hotel room. She was pissed that he didn't ask in the restaurant.

"Yes," she said. "But not yet. I think we need to talk more."

"Okay, I'm parked right over here..." He headed for a new Navigator, but she didn't budge.

"Let's go to my car. You're parked all out in the open. I'm parked on the side over there."

Pastor Tate checked out his parking spot and then followed Shayla's gaze to her Acura. He considered his options for a lot longer than she expected.

Finally he said, "Okay," and followed her.

Once inside the quiet confines of her bait car, she put her key in the ignition and quickly went through the process of turning the cameras on. Pastor Tate looked around anxiously, possibly sensing his impending doom. Shayla took a deep breath, drawing his attention to her heaving bosoms.

"Okay," she said. "What's the deal?"

He leaned in and kissed her. Shayla was startled and unexpectedly turned-off by the move. Her eyes remained wide open, her pupils darting wildly. The pastor reached and touched her breast, causing her to gasp. Never before had her car felt so small. Never had she felt so violated. Even the sweetness of his breath was revolting.

Without thinking, she pushed his hand away. "Stop."

He pulled back, and she could tell by the look in his eyes that she messed up badly.

"Oh my God. What am I doing?" The pastor's face became paper white. His jaw trembled. He stared into her eyes and covered his mouth with a trembling hand. "I am so sorry, Carrie. I thought... Oh my God. What have I done?" He reached for the door handle. "I'm sorry. I didn't mean..."

She grabbed his arm. "Wait."

He turned back to her, shaking his head. "I would never, I have never violated a woman in this manner." He stared down at his knees, refusing to meet her eyes.

"I'm, I don't feel violated," she said, though there was no word that better described her feelings.

"You, you didn't just see the look in your eyes," Pastor Tate said. "I..." He looked up at her and then averted his gaze just as quickly. "No one's ever made me feel like that, like I'm, hurting them."

She placed a hand on his lap and tried to salvage the exposé.

"I'm sorry. I didn't mean it like that. I do like you. You just, you caught me off guard."

He looked up at her, reluctant to accept the explanation.

She moved her hand higher up his thigh until she encountered his manhood. His mouth might have been saying no, but his dick was saying, *Hell yes!*

She coughed as a wave of nausea rolled through her. Pastor Tate's erection wasn't very large, but touching it (Shayla thought she might roll over and *die* if she saw it) filled her with revulsion. The worst part was she had no idea what was going on. Was it this particular pastor, or had she simply lost the taste for her hobby? Her heart told her it was probably the latter.

At that moment she knew she should probably put him out of her car. But she was so close. She could edit out his hesitation if she could get him to become aggressive again. She swallowed the acid in the back of her throat and struggled to get her racing heartbeats under control. She prayed her eyes wouldn't reveal her inner turmoil.

She tightened her grip on his dick and started to massage and then stroke him through his slacks.

"Come on. Don't be like that. Loosen up. Don't you want me?"

The terrified pastor met her gaze. He nodded stiffly.

"Then show me," she said. "Touch me."

He reached slowly for her breasts again. His mouth hung open. His breathing was almost labored. He watched her eyes closely. She forced an encouraging smile.

His touch was fiery. He rubbed and then squeezed her breasts when she didn't protest. A few of the larger beads of sweat on his forehead rolled slowly down his face. Shayla's stomach tightened, and she had to fight off another wave of nausea as his hand disappeared inside her dress. He pulled her bra down and cupped her bare breast in his warm palm. He pulled her dress aside with his free hand and inhaled sharply when her nipple was in plain view. He leaned forward and kissed it.

"Sweet Jesus," he moaned, and then he started to suck.

Shayla closed her eyes and squeezed him harder, asking herself, *How much more do I need? This is enough. It's got to be enough.*

"Oh my God, I want you so bad," he whispered as he attempted to please her. "You got me so hot, Carrie. I wanna eat you out. Can I lick your pussy? Do you want me to eat you?"

She didn't respond, partly because she knew it was a rhetorical question, but also because she wasn't sure what would come out if she opened her mouth. She was pretty sure it would be a scream.

This is enough. It's got to be.

Pastor Tate's mouth was hot, but to Shayla, his saliva was ice cold. She could endure it on her chest, but when he licked his way up her neck and slipped his tongue in her mouth, she could maintain the façade no longer. Though he was attractive, Shayla felt like someone was force-feeding her raw oysters.

"Okay," she said, pushing him away again. Her heartbeats were thunderous, but she tried to convince him it was passion he was looking at. "We need to get to a motel right now," she said, her voice quavering. "I can't, I can't take it no more. I want you so bad." She tucked her breast back in her bra and straightened her dress as she spoke.

Pastor Tate was drunk with horniness, and he was completely deceived this time. "Okay, Carrie. I want, I can't..." He swallowed hard. "Yeah, we need to get us a room. Do you mind paying for it? I don't want to show anyone my ID. I'll pay you back when we get, inside."

She nodded quickly. "Yeah, daddy. That'll work. Hurry up and get in your car. You can follow me. There's a Great Western right up the street."

Pastor Tate nodded too. "Okay. Alright. That's, that's fine." He took a deep breath and blew it out loudly. "Whoo!" He wiped the sweat from his forehead and grinned at her. "I don't think you know how fine you are. I can make you real happy, Carrie. Anything you want, all you have to do is ask."

It was good to get confirmation that he lavished his mistresses with gifts (most likely purchased with money he received from the church), but Shayla didn't care about the exposé anymore. She just wanted him out of her car and her life.

"Alright, baby, that's good. You got me so wet. Come on, daddy, let's go. I'm *ready*."

Pastor Tate's heart stuttered at the thought of her slickness. "Damn, Carrie. Let me, I wanna feel..."

He reached between her legs and tried to pull up her dress, but she blocked him again. Before he reacted, she said, "Baby I don't want no more touching 'til we in the room. My panties already soaked. I can't get no more excited."

Pastor Tate's mouth fell open. He blinked quickly, and then he adjusted his boner so he wouldn't look conspicuous when he got out of the car. He nodded.

"Alright, Carrie. Let's go. Which way are you headed?"

"I'm making a right on Brentwood Stair. The hotel's right up the street, about two miles on the left."

"Oh, okay." Pastor Tate wiped his sweat again and then sat up straight. "Do I look okay?"

Like Satan himself.

"You look fine, baby. Hurry up. Why you stalling?"

"I'm not."

He opened the door and took a jerky step out of her car. He stuck his head back inside to say something else, but Shayla had backed into her parking spot, and there was no parking block to impede her forward progress. She started the car and threw it in drive. She kept her eyes forward, too afraid to look at him again. Pastor Tate tried to hold on to the vehicle when she started to move, but he was no match for the 300 horses under her hood. He pleaded for her to, "Wait, Carrie!" but she couldn't have sped away faster if there was someone shooting at her.

She jetted out of the parking lot and thankfully didn't collide with a van full of senior citizens who were moving very slowly in the middle lane. She made the right turn she told him about, but then she made another right two blocks down the street and booked it for the freeway.

Even when she got on the interstate, she couldn't stop shivering. Every part of her body the pastor had touched seemed to be blazing and itching, as if his hands were made of poison ivy. She didn't realize she was crying until the world disappeared in a blur, and an 18-wheeler blared its horn when she veered out of her lane.

She wiped the tears from her eyes and grabbed the wheel with both hands. She took a deep breath and tried to shake off the tension and dread. It was over, and there was no use crying about it now.

The bible says the wages of sin is death. Shayla always believed that anything that didn't kill her would make her stronger. She hoped that was true, because the thought of going through all of this for nothing seemed like an unnecessarily cruel punishment, even for a wretched sinner like herself.

CHAPTER SEVENTEEN
THE BIG PICTURE

Shayla's tears had dried by the time she made it home. She heard Lisa in the kitchen, but thankfully Carla was out on a date with her boyfriend. Shayla went straight to her room and began to download the files from her purse camera and the one from her Acura. Lisa appeared in her doorway a few moments later.

"Welcome back. How'd it go?"

Shayla tried to offer her friend a smile, but it cracked and crumbled. Lisa rushed into the room.

"Are you alright? What happened?" She wrapped an arm around her shoulder. Shayla leaned into her embrace.

"It didn't go well," she said, fighting the urge to start crying again.

"What'd he do? Did he hurt you?" Lisa asked, fearing the worst.

Shayla shook her head. "No. It wasn't even that bad. That's what I don't understand. I've done worse with other people. But tonight, it felt different. I don't know why."

"Did you get it on video?" Lisa asked. "Can I see it?"

"Yeah. I'm working on it now."

She returned her attention to her laptop. Lisa sat on the bed next to her.

"Shay, tell me what he did to you."

Shayla shook her head. "Tate didn't do anything but touch me and kiss me, and... I don't know. I freaked out. He started tripping on the way I was acting, and he freaked out too. I caught myself and tried to pull it back. I told him I was okay, but I felt like screaming, when he was in my car."

Lisa could hear the turmoil in her voice. "Look at me."

Shayla turned towards her. Her eyes were wet, not bloodshot, but definitely pinkish.

"I don't understand what you're saying," Lisa told her. She was so concerned, it looked like she might start crying too. "What was different? What happened?"

Shayla wiped her face and sniffled. "I'm trying to tell you; he didn't do anything to me – nothing I haven't done many times before. It was different, but it wasn't him. It was *me*. And I don't know why. He made me feel, violated. I was scared. It's, I don't know..." She shook her head and returned her attention to her laptop.

Lisa held her tongue until she had the video ready.

There were four files in all. The first was from her purse camera at El Chico's. The video quality was good, but she didn't get Pastor Tate's full face in the frame. That video was useless anyway, because the pastor didn't say anything incriminating. In fact, he became nervous and said he had to leave when Shayla tried to flirt with him.

The second file was the phone call Shayla recorded at work. This one did have useful information. The highlight was when Shayla told the pastor that if he met her without a chaperone present "*things – will – happen.*" There was a pause, and then Pastor Tate asked, "Where would you like to meet?"

The third file was another recording from Shayla's camera purse, this time at the French restaurant. The camera angle on this video was perfect. The evidence was even better. Shayla got the pastor to acknowledge that his wife was aware of his affairs. He tried to push responsibility for their tryst back on Shayla, but she could edit that part out.

The last file was from the surveillance equipment in her Acura. This scene was the hardest for Shayla to relive. She and Lisa were completely silent while they watched. When it ended, Shayla turned to face her friend. They watched each other for a few seconds.

"What the hell was that?" Lisa finally asked.

Shayla sighed. "I have no idea."

"What, why'd you do that?" Lisa wondered. "You had him right where you wanted him. I mean, I personally wouldn't have liked his disgusting hands all over me, but you do that stuff all the time. Do you think he's ugly? Did his breath stink?"

"If it was that easy, I wouldn't even be tripping right now," Shayla replied. "I wouldn't let nothing like that throw me off track."

"You looked scared to death," Lisa said. "And you scared him."

"I know. That's when I knew I messed it up, when I saw the look in his eyes. He was so embarrassed. I tried to pull it back, but I ended up, you know, basically *begging* him to, to touch me..." She lowered her head and rubbed her hands together. She hadn't felt shame like this in a long time.

"So, you can't use it?" Lisa asked.

"No, I don't think so. He's an adulterer. I can prove that. But if I showed this video to his church, they would take his side and turn on me. Even if I edit out the part when he wanted to leave, you can still see that I was urging him on. If I had strung him along for a month, I could've gotten better evidence. But the way I rushed it, it makes me look like a ho."

Lisa nodded. "And you still don't know why you freaked out?"

Shayla shook her head and shrugged.

"Do you think it was just this one time, or do you think you changed for good? Are you feeling like you don't wanna do anymore exposés?"

It was too soon to call it, but if she had to decide now, Shayla was ready to give up her hobby.

"I don't know," she told her friend. "Let me, I have to think about it. I need to call my friend and tell her what happened."

"Alright." Lisa got up and gave her a brief hug on her way out of the room. "I love you, Shay. It'll be okay."

Shayla knew her best friend had her back, through thick and thin, but it still felt good to hear it. "I love you too, Lisa."

She took a long shower before she called her friend from college. Janet always sounded depressed as of late. She became more downcast when Shayla gave her the bad news.

"But why can't you still make a video?" she wondered. "You said you had four files. I know it's something you can use off one of them."

"The first three aren't that good," Shayla explained. "He was being careful the first time we went out. I could probably use the phone call, because I told him something would go down if he saw me again, and he said that was cool."

"That sounds good," Janet said quickly. "Why can't we use that?"

"Because without all the videos together, it's not enough proof," Shayla reasoned, "especially since it's just a phone call. He can say I spliced some different conversations together to make it sound like he was talking about cheating."

"But, but you got *four* files," Janet pressed. "I just need *one*. Please, Shayla. I don't want my sister to die for nothing. We got to take him down!"

Shayla sighed as she opened her lap top. "The last video is definitely out. I got him to come to my car, and we started making out–"

"That's perfect, Shay. I want that one."

"No, Janet. You didn't let me finish. I messed up in that video. I came on to him, instead of the other way around."

"It can still work," her friend argued. "Even if you threw yourself at him, he didn't have to respond."

"I've been doing this for a long time," Shayla said, growing frustrated. "You haven't done it *once*, so don't tell me what good evidence is."

"Okay. Alright, Shay. I'm sorry. I didn't mean to – I know you know what you're doing."

Shayla's eyes were knitted in annoyance, but she wasn't the type to hold a grudge.

"It's okay."

"What about that phone call you talked about? You said his wife knows about his affairs..."

"She does. That's probably the best file I have, but it wasn't a phone call. I used a hidden camera at a restaurant. I got his face in view the whole time. If I was going to make a video, that would be a good one. But even that video isn't perfect. He was still talking like I'm the one who came on to him."

"Can't you find *some* way to use it?" Janet persisted.

Shayla considered it, but again she rejected the idea. "It won't work. It doesn't prove he's actively having affairs. He could lie and say that happened a long time ago, and he and his wife went to counseling for it already. I'm telling you, unless I present all the videos together, including the one with me and him in the car, this exposé won't work. The church won't turn on him because of one conversation."

"Can, can I see it anyway?" Janet asked.

Shayla frowned. "Why?"

"You, you don't understand what it's like – to lose your sister." Janet sniffled. "She told me what was happening, with her and the pastor, and now she's gone, and it ain't no way to prove it.

"I know she was telling me the truth, but I never had no way to back it up. I couldn't talk to nobody about it, 'cause wouldn't nobody believe me. But you got that bastard on tape saying he do be cheating on his wife. That's the closest I ever came to having real proof, Shay. You got to... Please, Shay. You gotta let me see that video. Even if it's just that one, I need to see it. Please..."

Janet's persistence was annoying, but Shayla had empathy for her friend. If Carla or Lisa died prematurely, and there was someone to blame for it, she'd do whatever she could to make sure the rest of their life was as horrible as possible. The video Janet wanted to see didn't have Shayla's face in it, so there was no way it could come back to hurt her.

"Alright, I'll send it to you," she told her. "If you think it's worth using, I'll go ahead and make a final video. I can use some scenes from the other files, but I have to cut a lot out of them. It's gonna look so jacked up when I get through, everybody will know they're not seeing *everything* that happened. But some people will think it's enough. I don't know if he'll lose his position, but he will lose a lot of respect."

"That's great," Janet said, suddenly bright and cheery again. "Are you sending me the video now, the one where he says he cheats on his wife?"

"Yeah," Shayla said. "I'm–"

Her phone beeped.

"Hold on a second." She checked the display and saw that she had an incoming call from Marcus. "I gotta call you back," she told Janet.

"Are you sending the–"

"I'm sending it *right now*," Shayla said with undisguised irritation. "I'll talk to you later. Bye."

She hung up on her. She emailed the file to Janet while she accepted the new call.

"Hello, Marcus?"

"Hey, baby. What's going on?"

"Things are not that great," Shayla said with a sigh. "I finished up with your pastor tonight, but it didn't go like I expected."

"What happened? You couldn't get any evidence?"

"No, I got some. It's probably not enough to use. I got him to admit that his wife lets him have affairs."

"What? He told you that?"

"Yeah. I got it recorded. He told me at a restaurant."

"What'd you have, a microphone in your shirt?"

"No," Shayla said. "I had a camera in my purse."

"No shit?"

"Yeah, but he messed that video up. He kept saying I was the one who was coming on to him. I don't like to use videos like that."

"That's... I don't get it," Marcus said. "Ain't that what you're doing, coming on to him?"

"Basically, but usually when I do an exposé, I'll express interest the first time we meet and then let them make the rest of the moves. That way, everything I record will show them being the aggressor. But with Pastor Tate, I had to drag him along the whole time."

"Did, did you have to kiss him?"

Shayla hesitated. He already told her he wouldn't like it if she and the pastor made out. She only promised that she wouldn't *sleep* with Tate. Even though she kept that promise, she was reluctant to tell him what happened.

Her eyes widened. It suddenly occurred to her that Marcus might have had something to do with the way things played out tonight. It was possible that her promise to him manifested as guilt when she was in the car with the pastor. She didn't remember thinking about Marcus at the time, but she was falling in love. Maybe on a subconscious level, she wanted to be true to him.

"I thought you was gonna be honest with me," he said when she didn't answer his question.

"I, I'm sorry," Shayla said, trying to come to terms with her revelation. "It's not that. I was thinking about something."

"Are you thinking about how much you wanna tell me and how much you're gonna leave out?"

"I don't know what to tell you, because I'm not sure what happened," she replied. "I got him to come to my car, but I freaked out when he kissed me. It's, I don't know why that happened. I felt scared and disgusted. And then he got scared and wanted to leave. I know I messed up the video."

Her heart pounded. That was mostly the truth. The only thing she left out was how she tried to salvage the video before he got out of the car. It wasn't really a lie if she didn't mention that part, was it? Her heart told her it was, but her brain said it wasn't.

"He got scared?" Marcus chuckled. "What does that mean? He's not really a cheater?"

"No, he is," Shayla assured him. "But I don't have time to wait for him to shed his sheep's clothing. I got a life, you know? I got other stuff going on. Plus, ever since I started going out with you, this hasn't been as fun for me. I never felt guilty before, but you make me feel like, I don't know, like I'm doing you wrong or something."

There was a pause and then another chuckle.

Marcus said, "You for real?"

"Yes."

"You said you been doing this for ten years. I'm the first person that's ever made you feel guilty about it?"

Shayla gave it some thought and said, "Yeah, you are. Maybe it has something to do with you going to that church and knowing the pastor. When I send an exposé video, usually I never look back. I know I'll never see those people again.

"But the idea of sending a video to your church, knowing you'll see it..." She shook her head. "That, it gets to me. It makes me think. It makes me feel like, like I'm the one who's sinning. Like I'm the ho, and the pastor just got caught up in the mix."

"Man," Marcus said. "That's some deep shit right there."

"Yeah," Shayla said, her face growing warm.

"Do you feel like that because you love me?"

She snickered. "Just because I'm changing doesn't mean I'm whipped."

"I didn't say that. I was–"

"I'm kidding," she said with a grin. "I think you're special, and I'm glad I met you. I think my feelings for you have changed me. I'm feeling you. A lot."

"You got a nigga smiling big over here."

She could hear the cheer in his voice.

"You got a girl smiling big over here too," she said.

"I love you," Marcus said.

Shayla hesitated. She had only been dating him for a few weeks. She didn't know if he really loved her, or if she was ready to take the leap herself, but it felt good to open the gates and let her heart run free. "I love you too."

"For real?" he said. "You mean it?"

"Yeah, I think so..." Her eyes became misty again – but this time it was a good cry. "I do love you. I can't wait to see you again."

CHAPTER EIGHTEEN
THE PROPHET HOSEA

By the next morning, Shayla felt a little better about the incident with Pastor Tate. She talked to the two people who were most concerned about the exposé. Both Janet and Marcus were okay with the way things had turned out.

Shayla called her man when she got off work that day to ask if he planned to attend singles fellowship. Marcus had gone to The Hill every Tuesday since she met him. He surprised her by saying no.

He told her, "What I need to go to McDonalds for when I already got me some filet mignon."

Shayla never wanted to be the cause of him skipping any church services, but she was flattered by his remark.

At work on Wednesday, she ran into Alaina McGhee in the lobby during their lunch break. Alaina looked her in the eyes and smiled and said, "Hey, Shayla." Shayla was so taken aback, it took her a couple of seconds to respond.

"Oh, hey, Alaina."

Alaina continued on her way, laughing with another coworker, and Shayla got moving too. She didn't think Alaina would curse her out if they ran into each other at work, but she didn't expect her to be so cordial. She called her friend downstairs to get her take on it. Lisa was equally surprised.

"I would still be cutting my eyes at you."

"I know, right?" Shayla agreed. "Do you think, maybe she forgives me?"

"If she was married to a pastor, she must be religious. I think if you're a real Christian, you have to forgive those who trespass against you, right?"

Shayla laughed at her friend's wordplay. "For an atheist, you sure know a lot about the bible."

"I know a lot about *everything*," Lisa said. "One day you have to accept the fact that I'm the smartest person you know."

"Don't hold your breath."

It didn't seem possible to leave the ugly incident with Pastor Tate completely behind her, but Shayla hoped that was the case. And she *almost* made it. She almost forced her mind to forget about the lunch and the dinner and the way his tongue felt like raw oysters in her mouth. But sometimes her awesome God was also vengeful.

The bottom fell out from under her on Wednesday night, at ten p.m. sharp. She would never forget the exact time, because she had been waiting to call Marcus for a couple of hours. She knew he went to Wednesday night services at The Hill, and she was determined not to disturb him.

She knew the service ended at nine o'clock, but The Hill was a southern, Baptist church, so it wouldn't officially end until the Holy Ghost allowed it to. At nine-thirty Shayla checked her phone, wondering if Marcus was going to maintain his routine of calling to tell her goodnight. At nine-forty-five she began to feel the first tinges of concern.

She occupied her mind with an old re-run of Night Court, hoping to take her thoughts off whatever Marcus might be doing. When the show went off at 9:59, she checked her cellphone again. She hadn't missed any calls. She stretched out on her bed wondering if this was really happening: Was she already sweating this man?

Before she had time to give it serious thought, her phone rang at 10:00. It was Marcus. She answered with a smile on her face, but the happy times didn't last ten seconds.

"Hey. What are you up to?"

"Hey," Marcus said, his voice subdued.

"How was church?" Shayla asked. "You okay?"

"Nah," Marcus said with a sigh. "I'm not okay. Shit's all fucked up."

Shayla felt a sudden chill roll through her body. She sat up in bed, her stomach tightening. "What's wrong? What happened?"

"Pastor Tate wasn't at church tonight," Marcus reported. "The assistant pastor gave the sermon."

Shayla brought a hand to her mouth, her eyes wide. "Wha, what happened?"

"Well, at the time, I had no idea," Marcus said. "But I noticed everybody was acting funny, kinda sad, you know, like somebody died. And then when the assistant pastor got behind the podium, you could hear this hum around the whole church. People usually don't talk like that during service, but today everybody was talking. It took Pastor Miles a while to get them quieted down..."

Shayla's heartbeats slowed, but her face flushed with heat. She knew this scenario well. She heard similar accounts after every one of her exposés. But that didn't make sense, because she never did a video for Pastor Tate. Marcus didn't ask for any input, so she kept her mouth closed tight.

"Pastor Miles said the church is under attack," Marcus went on, "and we all have to stand together if we want to get through this. He said people was trying to slander Pastor Tate, and we should pray for the pastor and his family. He said there was demons trying to destroy our faith. But we got to be stronger than the devil."

Shayla listened intently. She understood every word he said, but she couldn't believe it. This was a carbon-copy of her exposés – but she never completed her work at The Hill. She wondered if an unknown third party was trying to take Pastor Tate down at the same time she was. She shook her head. That wasn't just wishful thinking, it was ludicrous. Plus Marcus' tone made it clear that he was speaking to the guilty party.

"And then Pastor Miles started talking about *harlots*," Marcus said. "Do you know what a harlot is?"

Shayla couldn't have been more stunned if God reached down from heaven and slapped her across the face Himself. *Harlot?* Was this some kind of joke? Shayla was positive Marcus and Freeman never crossed paths. The fact that such an obscure term would come from both of them was amazing – or it would've been if Shayla wasn't the harlot in question. For her, it was one of the sickest coincidences ever.

"That's alright," Marcus said. "I didn't know either. The way Pastor Miles explained it, a harlot could be anything – something worldly that pulls you away from the things of God. But I looked it up, and I found out a harlot is a *whore*. But I'ma get to that in a second."

In a second? Shayla was already struggling to breathe. No way could she make it to the end of this awful story, but she dared not interrupt.

"After church everybody was talking again," Marcus said. "I couldn't get any good information from nobody, 'cause I'm new to the church, and a lot of people be acting like they don't like me. But from what I did pick up, you know, just from eavesdropping, Pastor Tate was sleeping with some woman, and somebody had it on video."

"Wha, what?" Shayla wasn't asking him to repeat the comment. But she felt like she had to say *something*, because without her input, this conversation was becoming more warped by the second. Her heart hammered. Her forehead glistened with sweat. "I didn't send no video. I didn't sleep with him. I told you that."

"I know what you told me," Marcus said. "That's why I was like, *What the fuck?* You know? I love you so much, I was telling myself, *It's got to be somebody else. Shayla told me she wasn't doing the exposé.*"

"I didn't," she cried.

"Yeah, you did," Marcus said coldly. "When I got home, I wanted to look up what the bible had to say about harlots. After I did that, I went to check my email."

Shayla's mouth fell open. Her heart sank into the pit of her stomach.

"Imagine my surprise," Marcus said, "when I found an email from a weird address: pastortateisawhore at yahoo dot com."

"What are you talking about?" Shayla breathed. Her lips quivered. "I didn't send no emails. That, that's not my account."

"You don't wanna cop to it?"

"Cop to *what*?" Shayla said, more boldly this time. "I didn't do nothing. I didn't send no videos!"

"I guess that wasn't you in the video, either…"

"What–" Shayla caught herself, and the word *JANET* flashed in her mind. *That bitch!* She gave her friend one of the videos, and the idiot distributed it without her permission. Janet didn't have the expertise or equipment to edit the video, so she would've sent the raw file with no music and no headings. Janet would've left-in all of the parts that made Shayla appear to be the aggressor, too.

Shayla wanted to wring her friend's neck for jumping the gun like that, but it wasn't the end of the world. The video Shayla sent her had good information on it. Pastor Tate admitted that his wife knew about his affairs. Plus, Shayla's face wasn't in that video, just her voice.

She started to relax, but then her mind processed the information Marcus just gave her. He said, "*I guess that wasn't you in the video, either.*" Shayla inhaled sharply. Her mouth was bone dry.

"What are you talking about?" she managed.

"I, I'm trying to figure out if you lied to me, or if I only heard what I wanted to hear," Marcus said.

"I didn't lie to you," Shayla moaned, but she knew that she had.

"Yea, yeah you did," Marcus stated flatly. "You told me you freaked out when he kissed you, and that messed up your video."

Shayla shook her head in wonderment. This wasn't possible.

"What are you talking about? What video?"

Marcus grunted in frustrated. "Really? You don't know what I'm talking about? How many videos did you make, Shayla? I saw the one with you in the car. Was, is there another one? Is there a video of you and pastor at your house? At the motel? For, for real Shayla," he whined. "How many videos you make?"

Shayla began to cry. She wasn't aware of it until she felt the tears dripping off her chin. She retraced her steps and realized she made a fateful mistake two days ago. When Janet begged her to send the video of her and Tate at the restaurant, she mistakenly sent her the footage from her bait car.

It was a simple mistake. She hadn't changed the names of any of the files at that point. Plus she was in a rush at the time, because Marcus was calling, and Janet's pleas were starting to get on her nerves. She couldn't believe Janet would watch the video and then pass it around her church, knowing it wasn't the file Shayla meant to send.

But now wasn't the time to fret about that. At the moment, Shayla's boyfriend sounded like he was breaking up with her, and she couldn't very well blame him. She lied to him about what happened in her car that night. Her brain raced. She tried to remember exactly what she did when she tried to salvage her exposé. What did Marcus see in the video?

It was hard to think clearly with her head filled with the sound of her heart ripping in two, but Shayla remembered enough to know it was very bad.

She knew that she begged Tate to touch her when his moral compass tried to lead him the other way. She knew she caressed his manhood and urged him to give into sin.

Come on. Don't be like that.

Loosen up. Don't you want me?

Shayla shuddered, her tears now a steady stream.

Then show me. Touch me.

"Oh my God." She brought a fist to her mouth and sent a throat full of vomit back down her esophagus.

Alright, baby, that's good. You got me so wet right now. Come on, daddy, let's go. I'm ready.

"I'm so sorry," she said, sobbing uncontrollably.

"Yeah," Marcus said. "Me too. I wish I hadn't seen that. I don't know why I watched it. As soon as I saw that email account, I knew it was you."

"*I didn't do it.*"

"Shayla, you need to quit saying that. I saw the video with my own eyes. Everybody at-"

"I didn't send the video," she clarified. "I told you I wasn't gon' send it."

"Well, it got sent. I don't know how the rest of your missions go, but this one definitely made you look like a ho. And it's hard for me to say that, because I had feelings for you. I trusted you. I believed what you told me was going on…"

Shayla caught how he said *had feelings* and *trusted*, but she didn't want to accept that it was over. "I'm sorry, Marcus. *Please*. Please forgive me."

"Like I said, I looked up what a harlot is," he went on, not saying whether he would forgive her or not. "And this is what I found out: Did you know the prophet Hosea was married to a harlot?"

Shayla's mind was spinning. She couldn't believe he asked her that. Her father was a pastor. She practically grew up in the church. Of course she knew Hosea married a harlot. Why would he ask her such a crazy question at a time like this? Before she could wrap her mind around all the tangents of this God-awful conversation, Marcus continued speaking.

"See, Hosea wasn't a special man," he said. "I don't know if he knew his wife was a harlot before they got married, but he found out real quick after they jumped the broom. She was sleeping with *everybody*. And Hosea, I guess you could say he was a punk, you know, by today's standards, 'cause he didn't do shit about it. His wife would come home at all hours of the night. And when they started having kids, he knew at least one of them wasn't his."

Shayla listened and cried. Her head started to throb along with the knocking of her heart. She didn't know where Marcus was going with this or why she didn't simply hang up. For whatever reason, she was compelled to hear him out.

"One day God called on Hosea to go and speak to the people of Israel," Marcus said. "I know, it seems like Israel wasn't never getting it right. He always had to send somebody to tell them what to do. And of course Hosea didn't wanna go. He asked God, 'Why me?' And God told him, I mean, I don't know the exact words, but basically God said Hosea knew what it was like to be married to a whore. And God felt like the people of Israel were being whores by worshipping other Gods, or whatever they was doing."

"Please," Shayla breathed. "Please, Marcus. I'm sorry. I'm so sorry…"

"Anyway," he went on, "Hosea went to the people of Israel and told them, 'Y'all niggas is tripping. When you turn away from your God, who loves you, you're behaving like harlots; whoring yourself to other gods. But if you turn back to the only real God *right now*, He will still love you and forgive you.'

"And the people was like, 'Yeah, you right, Hosea,' and they stopped doing all of that evil shit they was doing. They went back to God and begged for forgiveness, and He forgave them. You know, 'cause that's what He does."

Shayla didn't think she could take anymore. She couldn't remember the last time her heart and soul felt pain like this. "*Please, Marcus.*"

"So then," he said, "Hosea went back home after he did his thing for God, and guess what happened..."

Shayla didn't bother speaking, and he didn't wait for her to respond.

"He ran into his harlot wife," he said. "But she wasn't pretty like she used to be. She was living on the streets, all old and used up. None of the men she used to whore herself to wanted anything to do with her now. She was ugly and filthy, basically like one of them old crackhead bitches you see near the homeless shelter.

"But here's the thing that makes this story so awesome," Marcus said. "Instead of turning his back on her like she deserved, Hosea told Gomer – that was his wife's name – he told her he would forgive her for what she did to him, just like God forgave the people of Israel. Hosea took his wife back, and they went home, and he loved her the same as he did when he first met her. They lived happily ever after."

Shayla's heart fluttered. She couldn't believe it, but Marcus was giving her another chance. She held her breath and waited, like a condemned inmate, for her reprieve.

"But, I ain't no prophet," Marcus said. "I wish I could forgive you like Hosea did, but I can't, Shayla. I thought I loved you, but you really are a harlot, and I can't be with no harlot."

He disconnected a second before the phone slipped out of her hand, and she rolled over and buried her face in the pillows.

Ten minutes passed before she got herself under control. She knew it wouldn't do any good, but when she could speak without slurring her words, she fumbled for her phone and called her not-so-good friend from college.

Janet answered the phone with an apology. "I'm sorry, Shay."

Shayla took a deep breath, and her tears flowed anew. She was angry and heartbroken, but most of all she felt betrayed. Everything she did at The Hill was to help Janet. Even when she wanted to back out, she stayed the course because of her friend. She never turned her back on a friend.

"You, you knew I sent you the wrong video." Shayla spoke in a harsh voice that was bass-filled and downright spooky. Janet didn't bother lying about what happened.

"I know you sent me the wrong video. But, but when I saw it, I thought we should use it anyway. You said it wasn't good because you came on to him too much, but it didn't look like that to me. He was all over you as soon as the video started. The way he was touching you, and the way he was *talking*, I thought that would be enough to get him kicked out. He was, he was talking like a regular dude off the streets."

"I didn't even block out my face," Shayla said. "You sent that video with my face still on it."

"I'm sorry," Janet said again. "I know if I had asked you to send it, you woulda told me no. You sounded like you wanted to give up, and, and I couldn't let you do that. I thought that if nothing else happened to him, at least the church would see this video and see him for what he is."

"You don't have the right to send my videos to anybody," Shayla said, her anger rising. "You don't have the right to send my video *with my face still on* it to anybody! I told you that video wasn't edited, Janet! Nobody thinks that was a good exposé. Everybody turned on me!"

"I know. And I'm sorry, Shay. If I wouda known it was gonna turn out like that, I wouldn't have sent it. But I had to do *something*. My sister's dead. She gone forever. My life ain't never gon' be the same without her. I'm sorry, Shay. I didn't mean to hurt you."

"You fucking–" Shayla shook her head fiercely. "You fucked up my *whole life*! You don't even know how bad... You don't know what you did to me!"

"My sister's *dead*, Shay. At least you still got a life."

"*I don't give a damn about your sister!*" Shayla spat, glad to finally get it out. "I tried to help you! I bent over backwards–"

"I said I was sorry, now I'm finna go," Janet said and hung up abruptly.

Shayla's fury was at an all-time high. Her eyes were red and devilish. She began to hyperventilate as she pressed redial. Carla rushed into the room and took the phone from her hand. Shayla looked up and saw Lisa was there as well.

The sight of her family and her dearest friend reminded Shayla that there was someone in this cruel, ugly world who loved her still. She released a floodgate of emotions as they held and comforted her.

An hour later all three ladies sat on Shayla's bed watching the notorious video of her and Pastor Tate. Shayla continued to cry, barely able to relive what had to be the worst moment of her life. Carla and Lisa fought to keep their eyes on the screen. When the video ended, an awkward silence ensued. Carla was the first to speak.

"Is, is this what you be doing, when you expose somebody?"

Shayla shook her head. She was beyond embarrassed. Her little sister thought she was some kind of sicko.

"I never got scared like that," she said.

"But this is what you do?" Carla asked. "You get them in your car and let them, touch on you and stuff?"

Carla made it sound so bad, Shayla almost fed her another lie. But everything was out in the open now. She nodded.

Her sister shook her head, her eyes filling with tears. "Shay, that's, this is *terrible*. Why would you let somebody do that to you, like you're a prostitute or something?"

Shayla always had plenty of reasons for why she did what she did, but at that moment, she couldn't think of one.

"This is *sick*," Carla said.

"Yeah, that'll help," Lisa said, jumping to her friend's defense. "It's not like her whole life isn't ruined right now. Go ahead and pile more shit on top of her."

"It's alright," Shayla said, resigned to her lowly fate. "It is sick. Everybody who saw it thinks it's sick. Even Marcus called me a harlot."

"If you know it's bad, why do you do it?" Carla asked. "Shay, you *know* you got problems. You need counseling. Why don't you find somebody you can talk to, so you can get some help?"

Shayla sniffled and chuckled. Her face was completely raw. "I should sit down and talk to somebody, huh? You think it's that easy, don't you?"

"It can't be that hard," Carla said. "And even if it is hard, don't you..."

Carla trailed off, and her eyes locked on an unusual occurrence over her sister's right shoulder. "What's that?" she asked as she rose to her feet.

Lisa turned too, and she jumped off the bed. "What the hell?"

By the time Shayla spun around, Carla had run to the window and pulled the curtain back. The sight she revealed was so abstract Shayla's brain refused to accept it as reality. It was after eleven p.m., but outside it was bright and sunny. As a matter of fact, it appeared the sun had come all the way down to earth and settled in their driveway. On its way down, the sun shrunk to the exact size of Shayla's car.

"*Fire!*" Carla screamed, and all three women were thrust into fight or flight mode.

Shayla didn't think she could withstand another adrenaline rush, but Lisa and Carla darted to the front room, and she was quick on their heels.

CHAPTER NINETEEN
THE FIRES OF HELL

When she got outside, Shayla was horrified to see her Acura fully ablaze. Bright orange and yellow flames licked the air a full five feet higher than the roof of her car. The heat was so searing, Shayla felt the warmth on her face as soon as she opened the front door. A strong smell of gasoline left no doubt this was arson.

All three roommates were educated and rational women most of the time, but the sight of such a huge fire flipped a PANIC switch in their brains. They stared. They screamed. They ran around like children. Carla thought they should take cover, in case the Acura exploded, like in the movies. Lisa wanted to grab the water hose and try to prevent the fire from spreading to her BMW or the shrubbery to the right of Shayla's car.

Shayla had the most to lose in this situation, but she had the least input. She staggered out onto the lawn like a zombie and stared in shock as she shuffled to the right, towards the rear of her vehicle. Thick plumes of smoke rose high in the nighttime sky. One of her tires farted and sank quickly as the fire melted the rubber like lard in a frying pan.

The trouble with The Hill and Marcus got moved to the back burner, and her exhausted brain was forced into action again. She considered the many items she'd never recover from the vehicle, but that wasn't as important as the fact that her stalker wasn't leaving notes anymore. Whoever it was meant business. Shayla now understood that her life might be in danger. Her assailant could've set the house on fire, making sure to start with the doors and windows to block off the escape routes.

As her shock and anger gave way to terror, she heard a sound that jolted her like an electric shock. She spun towards it, and a high-pitched squeal forced its way up her throat.

Lisa and Carla followed her gaze, and they saw the same thing: A burgundy Astro Van, an older model, sped away so quickly the tires spun in place for a moment, filling the night air with a loud screech that rattled every bone in Shayla's body. The van roared through the next stop sign and then made a speedy right and disappeared from sight.

The driver never turned his headlights on while the van was within view, and Shayla didn't have time to see the license plate. She never even saw if the driver was black or white, male or female.

At that point all three girls were *completely* freaked out, but someone had sense enough to yell, "Call the police!"

It was Shayla who got her legs moving the fastest. She sprinted to the porch and crashed through the front door, her eyes wide, her mouth stretched in a ghastly scowl. Her heart thumped like a twenty-inch woofer. The hallway seemed to tilt a full ninety degrees as she ran, and she had to lean on the walls for support.

When she got to her room, her main cellphone was ringing. She snatched it off the bed. She meant to hit the END CALL button, but in her haste, she answered it. She brought the phone to her face and made a few panting sounds that were meant to be *Hello*.

"Gotcha, bitch," a male voice on the other end of the line said.

Shayla stopped cold. Even her oxygen-deprived heart stopped beating as she realized she was speaking to the person who left the notes on her car. This was the person who set her car on fire moments ago. As Shayla strained her ears for clues, she heard street traffic behind the threatening voice, so this might also be the person who sped away in the Astro Van.

"But it ain't over, ho," he said. "Naw. It ain't over by a long shot."

The caller hung up, and Shayla stood in stunned silence. Gradually her eyes widened. She knew that voice. It was a southern black man, a country boy. It was definitely one of her exposés from the past.

She was mentally fatigued, on the verge of a full shut down, but she racked her memory bank and forced it to fill in the rest of the pieces.

Think. Think. Think!

Her iPhone slipped from her hand and bounced on the soft carpet as the name of her stalker was revealed, and mental images of the perpetrator flashed before her eyes.

The exposé of Pastor Chauncey Miller started like any other. During spring break of 2015, Shayla and Lisa traveled south for fun in the sun in Galveston. They made a pit stop in Houston to visit Shayla's seldom-seen cousin Denise.

Denise owned a beauty shop in Galena Park. She was pleased to learn Shayla was a new marketing consultant at Midwest Media. She was even more delighted to hear that Shayla had been dabbling in the exposé business, focusing her efforts on freaky pastors and deacons who swung their dicks wherever they chose and made a mockery of God each Sunday.

Over three rounds of Long Island iced teas, Denise told Shayla a story about a lying-ass pastor she had the displeasure of meeting a few months ago. Pastor Chauncey Miller presided over a 300-plus congregation at First Church of Christ on Morningside Drive.

According to Denise, Pastor Miller was the worst of the worst. He was tall, dark and handsome, and as smooth as his midnight blue Escalade. He was the father of *fourteen* children, currently on his third marriage. Supposedly he slept with a dozen members of his congregation, some of whom still went to the church and had fathered a child with one of them.

Things were so out of hand, two of his mistresses had a fight at the church picnic last Easter. When the hair stopped flying, Pastor Miller took the winner of the fight to his office for "special prayer." A few people thought she looked a little *too* happy when she rejoined the picnic thirty minutes later.

If that wasn't bad enough, Chauncey's brother Cassius was the church's only deacon, and he was as crooked as a thirty-dollar bill. Deacon Miller had been locked up for everything from extortion to possession of a controlled substance. When he got out of jail the last time, Pastor Miller baptized him in front of the church and declared him clean and whole again.

Between Pastor Miller sleeping with anything that moved and his brother dipping in the collection plate, it didn't appear the church would survive. But according to Denise, the congregation was filled with some of the most ignorant country bumpkins in the city. And Chauncey had a silver tongue like no other.

When he preached about Jesus dying on the cross, he dropped to his knees and cried real tears. When he told his flock that God would return every dime they put in the collection plate *ten times over*, women emptied their purses with total faith that their personal hardships were about to become a thing of the past.

By the time Denise was done talking, there was no way Shayla could leave Houston without seeing the First Church of Christ for herself. Rather than head for Galveston the next morning, she and Lisa set off for what would be Shayla's sixth exposé. They arrived at the church at 10:30 on a cloudy Sunday morning. Neither of them was prepared for the sheer *ratchetness* on display.

Not only did Pastor Miller have six gold teeth gleaming in his mouth, but he didn't look smart enough to read, let alone decipher the bible. He spent most of the service strutting around like a damned fool, while his brother stood stoically against the back wall, fixing a mean and suspicious glare on anyone who stared at him for too long.

Pastor Miller had his microphone turned up extra loud that day. And like any good southern preacher, he punctuated most of his sentences with an emphatic "*Ha!*" that made Shayla's skin crawl:

"I don't think y'all hear me up in here today – *ha*! I said I don't think y'all hear me up in this church this morning – *ha*! I'm asking you, church, who gon' be there to save you when the day of the rapture comes? – *Ha*! I say who gon' be there to save you on the day of the rapture? – *Ha*? Is it gon' be *yo mama*?"

"No!" the church cried.

"I say, is it gon' be yo daddy? – *Ha*!"

"Naw, he can't save me," a woman yelled.

"What about yo, I say what about yo *baby-daddy*?" Pastor Miller asked. He was marching back and forth, his elbows pumping, sweat dripping from his coal black face. "I say what about yo baby-daddy? Is he gon' save you from the rapture? – Ha!"

"No!" the multitude cried.

"Well who gon' save you? – Ha!"

"*Jesus*!" the church answered.

"I say who gon' save you!"

"*Jesus*!" they repeated.

"Jesus is the *only* one who can save you – ha!" Pastor Miller confirmed. "I say Jesus is the *only* one who got yo back on the day of the rapture – ha! Now let's get some music up in here! Where the choir at? Is y'all ready to praise Jesus?"

"Yeah!"

"I say is y'all ready to praise Jesus?!"

"*Yeah!!*"

"Well let's praise him then!" Pastor Miller yelled, and he surprised everyone (well, Shayla and Lisa at least) by throwing his microphone to the floor and breaking into a funky-chicken dance that Shayla hadn't seen since the days of James Brown.

She looked at Lisa, and her mouth fell open too, but everyone else jumped to their feet and had what Shayla could only describe as a *ho-down*, while the praise and worship team burst into a lively rendition of Amazing Grace, the likes of which Shayla had never heard before.

The scene was so surreal, Lisa wanted to get the hell out of there as soon as possible and never look back. But Shayla couldn't have been more intrigued. Pastor Miller was like Kirk Franklin on crack. And his shadowy deacon was one of the scariest goons she had ever seen. Together, the brothers were getting paid and getting laid, and if ever there was a reason for an exposé, this had to be it.

After church, Shayla proceeded with what would become her typical M.O: She filled out a New Visitor card and gave it to the deacon. She went back to Denise's house and waited patiently. Pastor Miller called approximately two hours later. Shayla told him she was from Abilene, and unfortunately she would probably never make it back to his church. Pastor Miller asked if he could see her before she left, to give her "travelling blessings." To this date, that was the lamest hook-up line Shayla had ever heard.

They met at Wendy's, and before her fries were cold, they made plans to hook up at a nearby hotel. She probably gathered enough for her exposé at the fast food restaurant, but when he wasn't jumping around like a fool, Chauncey was handsome, sexy and brimming with confidence. It wasn't hard to see how he charmed the panties off so many women. Plus, he got hard while they were at the restaurant, and Shayla thought he had a cucumber taped to his thigh.

Pastor Miller noticed her interest and told her, "Yeah, that's all me, baby," his gold teeth twinkling. "The good Lord blessed me, yes He did."

The final exposé video for Pastor Miller was probably Shayla's raunchiest, because back then, she was down for whatever her victims were down for – especially if they had dark skin, a flat stomach and a dick so big she couldn't close her hand around it. Pastor Miller worked her out for an hour. Later, Shayla was hard-pressed to cut his video down to just five minutes.

She edited the exposé with her laptop and gave the file to Denise the same day, and she and Lisa continued their trip to Galveston. Two weeks later, Shayla learned that she single-handed took down both Miller brothers.

"How so?" she asked.

"Well, Pastor Miller prolly could've talked hisself out of it," Denise reported, "except one of his mistresses got *real* mad, 'cause he told her he wasn't gon' sleep with nobody but her and his wife. So that heifer threw a fit at church, and then a couple more of them took her side, and the whole thing just snowballed. One of the elders said they wasn't gon' stand for that crap no more, and they brought in a new pastor from the east side.

"The new pastor came in wrecking shop. He wanted everything that was wrong with that church fixed, from the floor up. And you already know what he found when he looked at them books."

"What'd he find?" Shayla asked.

"That crooked ass deacon was embezzling his ass off," Denise reported. "They called the police on Cassius, and when they picked him up, guess what he had in his trunk..."

Shayla had no idea. "What?"

"A bunch of *crack*," Denise announced. "The pastor's brother was using church money to score *dope!*"

"Wow." Shayla was genuinely amazed.

"You did a good job," Denise said. "Everything is way better at that church now."

"Glad to be of service," Shayla said, but deep down she felt a tinge of regret for what happened to the deacon. She wanted to embarrass men. She even wanted to bring about their financial ruin. But it was never her intention to send anyone to prison. Even if Cassius deserved to be there, she didn't want to be the one to get the wheels of justice rolling.

The only other thing Shayla regretted about her trip to Houston was not obscuring her face in Chauncey's exposé video. She didn't start doing that until a year after his takedown. She often wondered if one of her early videos would come back and bite her in the ass one day.

Shayla sat in an interview room at the downtown police station and told the whole story. Lisa sat next to her, cradling her hand. Carla didn't make the trip, because someone had to stay with the firefighters.

The red-headed detective who had the pleasure of listening to Shayla's account had a lot of notes scribbled on his pad. He rose from his chair, shaking his head in disbelief. He left the room to verify as much as he could and to spread the story to some of the officers on his floor. This was one for the books.

"I'll be right back."

Shayla looked at Lisa. Her friend offered her an encouraging smile. Both girls were exhausted, but Shayla was a lot worse for wear. Not only did she lose a good man she dared to profess her love to, but she lost her SUV and all of the surveillance equipment hidden inside.

The women didn't talk much while they waited for the detective to return to the small room. They called Carla, and she told them the firefighters had the blaze extinguished. A tow truck was there now to remove the remains of Shayla's Acura. Lisa's BMW was parked in front of Shayla's car. The flames got hot enough to melt some of the paint off the rear of her vehicle, but Carla said it wasn't that bad. Shayla promised to get Lisa's whole car painted. Her friend didn't want to talk about that at the moment.

When the detective returned to the interview room, he had more folders and paperwork than he left with. He sat down and slid two mug shots across the table.

"Do you know these men?"

It had been five years since Shayla last saw the Miller brothers, but her recognition was immediate. She reached to hold Lisa's hand again, as a tremor rolled down her spine.

"Yeah. That's them. That's Chauncey, and that's Cassius," she said and pointed.

Both men were dark like coffee. Chauncey was the better looking of the two. He had a strong jaw line and small eyes with thick eyebrows. His hair was short, and his lips were full. He wasn't smiling in his mug shot, but Shayla knew he had a perfect set of choppers.

Cassius was physically similar to his big brother. He had a big, broad nose and the same beady eyes. But there was something in Cassius' stare that was cold and downright dangerous. The first time Shayla saw him, she thought he looked more like a nightclub bouncer than a deacon.

"Well, I don't think you could have picked two worse enemies," Detective Jeffries said as he flipped through the papers he brought with him.

Shayla nibbled her thumbnail as he proceeded to scare the living daylight out of her with a tale of two young boys from the ghetto who, try as they might, never managed to stay on the right side of the law.

Born to a crack addict dad and a heroin-addicted mother, the Millers never had a fair shake at life. They lost their father to the prison system before they were five, and they lost him again three years later in a riot at the Sugarland Unit. Four inmates lost their lives during three days of chaos and bloodshed. Chauncey's father was found with more than twenty stab wounds to the chest and neck.

When the brothers were ten and eleven years old, their mother died from an overdose, and they were sent to live with their ailing grandmother. When their grandmother died on Chauncey's 14th birthday, the boys were relocated again, this time to their uncle's house. By then they had been arrested half a dozen times each. Their uncle didn't care if they went to school or not, so they dropped out and continued a life of crime that would span the next three decades. Their only code of survival was to always have each other's back. They never needed a gang. It was just the two of them, like it had always been.

The Millers' crimes ran the gamut from drug dealing to pimping and robbery. The only time they were ever apart is when they were serving separate prison sentences, which rarely totaled more than three years at a time. It was during one such bid at Sugarland penitentiary that big brother Chauncey discovered Jesus.

Locked behind the same walls that slaughtered his father, Chauncey claimed he shed tears one night while reading his bible, and the Holy Ghost entered his cell. When he was released to his old neighborhood a few months later, he didn't want to rob and steal anymore. He told his brother that from that moment on, he only wanted to do God's work. Cassius quickly became a born-again Christian as well.

There was speculation as to whether the Miller brothers had truly changed their stripes, but it didn't take long for Chauncey to prove himself. He joined the United Missionary Church on Pleasantdale and quickly rose the ranks as a fiery preacher who could relate to sinners like no one else. Within a year of his release from prison, Chauncey rented a disheveled building that would later be known as First United. With the help of his brother and a small, but dedicated congregation, they built the church from the ground up.

By the time Shayla hit the scene, Chauncey's congregation was 300 strong, and his church had been renovated four times. First United was now a respected landmark, and Chauncey had become a community leader. There were some who believed Cassius was only in it for the loot and others who thought Chauncey was a little too friendly with the pretty women in his pews. But no one took a stand against them until a sexy, young thing named Shayla Humphries came to town.

With her exposé, she set off a string of events that would spell doom for the brothers. The parishioners could tolerate their pastor no longer when she released what was essentially a hard-core sex tape. They asked Chauncey to step down and forced him out of power when he refused. He didn't think they could take the building from him, after all the improvements he'd made there. But he was mistaken. Chauncey never bothered to purchase the church outright from the property owner. When his lease expired, the new leaders went behind his back and secured the building for themselves. That was the beginning of the end for both brothers.

Within six months of Shayla's exposé, the Millers were indicted for a variety of crimes, from possession of narcotics and embezzling, to attempted arson of their old church. They were sent back to prison. According to Detective Jeffries, Chauncey got out four months ago.

"It looks like they have plenty of motive to come after you," the detective told Shayla.

By then, she and Lisa were stunned silent.

"The bad thing is, this kind of stuff is hard to prove," he went on. "If someone saw them leave a note on your car, that's harassment. But even a jailhouse lawyer can get them off with community service and a restraining order. No one saw them set the fire. With the previous conviction for arson, we could bring them in for questioning, but this is all too circumstantial to press charges.

"The best I can do is contact Chauncey's parole officer and see if he can verify his whereabouts for tonight. I can ask the Houston office to question them, but the Millers know the system very well. If they refuse to speak without an attorney, that's it. We have to turn 'em loose.

"Let me work on this for a while," he said, "and see what I come up with. These men are street-smart, but it's impossible to travel four and a half hours without *someone* seeing you. They had to stop for gas, or maybe they got pulled over for speeding. I'll give you a call after I get in touch with Chauncey's parole officer."

CHAPTER TWENTY
WHAT HAPPENS IN THE DARK...

Shayla didn't remember going to sleep on Wednesday. She, Carla and Lisa stayed up most of the night talking and comforting one another. No one wanted to be alone in their bed. They gathered in the living room like children at a slumber party. The warmth of their bond was as nurturing as a campfire. Gradually their tension gave way to exhaustion, and one by one the roommates succumbed to sleep.

When Shayla awakened, it was seven a.m., and the front room was filled with bright rays of sunshine. For a moment, her heart swelled with the hope of a new day. But when she opened the front door, reality welcomed her with a cold, clammy embrace that felt like death. She sighed as she looked upon the drama she brought to their home.

How did they find me?

The driveway didn't look that bad last night, but now it appeared to be permanently scarred from the fire. Two thirds of the shrubbery that separated Shayla's yard from their neighbors was black and charred. The fire had even spread to portions of the front lawn.

Shayla stepped off the porch gingerly, watching out for broken glass and other remnants of her car still scattered across the grass. The scent of gasoline and burnt rubber invaded her nostrils and made her cringe. The aroma was so strong, her eyes began to water. Or maybe it was the sight of such wanton destruction that made her want to cry again.

How did they find me?

She stepped into the middle of the yard and shuddered as she assessed the damage to Lisa's BMW. Last night it looked like her friend's whip was virtually unscathed. She now saw that Lisa's car was almost totaled. They didn't make vehicles with as much steel as they used to. The BMW's plastic and carbon fibers easily succumbed to the intense heat. The rear license plate was blackened. It was now forever molded to the bumper, like a penny stuck in hot tar.

How the hell did they find me?

She heard a sound behind her.

She turned and saw that Lisa was awake as well. Her friend stepped out onto the porch and stared at her car with the same forlorn expression Shayla wore. Lisa didn't speak when they locked eyes.

"I'm sorry," Shayla said, but she'd uttered that phrase so many times in the last ten hours, her words were virtually useless. People are *sorry* when they're late to work. They're *sorry* when they forget a birthday. Apologizing for something this big was like putting a Band-Aid on a slit throat. Shayla knew it, and Lisa knew it too.

Shayla lowered her head in shame, and Lisa moved quickly to embrace her. Lisa wanted to tell her it would be alright, but she couldn't say that with complete honesty. It was no secret Lisa loved her BMW more than anything else she owned. She didn't think she could comfort Shayla without letting on how heartbroken she was.

Rather than speak, she simply held her hard-headed friend until Shayla's tears subsided. There were a few neighbors watching them, some from their windows and others from their front yards. They too decided to hold their tongue for now. They would have to rely on the rumor mill for a little while longer until someone built up enough courage to approach one of the roommates and ask them what the hell happened last night.

By ten a.m. everyone was awake and somewhat organized as they moved on to the recovery phase of their ordeal. Shayla and Lisa had to file claims with their car insurance companies. Lisa's BMW was operational, but she made arrangements to have it towed to a nearby dealership.

Shayla fought valiantly to take financial responsibility for the Beamer, but Lisa insisted on letting State Farm handle it. Shayla only had three thousand in her savings account. Her friend didn't want her to have to take out a loan.

"It's alright," she assured her when she got off the phone with her insurance rep. "They said I'm fully covered. I can get a rental today or tomorrow, whenever I want."

"Me too," Shayla said. She had gotten off the phone with her insurance company a few minutes prior. So far everything seemed to be working out, but Shayla's eyes were red and baggy. Her nose was pink from blowing it so much. "But your rates are gonna go up," she told Lisa. "You don't know how bad I feel about this. I'd do anything to make it up to you."

"You don't have to make it up to me. You didn't do anything wrong, Shay."

"Yes, I did. You know it's my fault."

"Look, girl, me and you been going back and forth about the rights and wrongs of your exposés for years. I accepted that you were doing the right thing – the right thing for you, at least. None of what happened changes that. I don't like getting caught up in this shit; I can't lie about that. But I'm not mad at you. I'm mad at the people who started the fire."

Shayla watched her eyes, wondering how her friend could be so forgiving. "No, I wasn't right," she said, shaking her head. "I was wrong, the whole time. Everything I did was stupid."

"If that's how you feel, I accept that. If you change your mind later, I'm not gonna hate on you. You're my best friend, Shay. I'm with you, no matter what."

Shayla's face burned. She didn't deserve a friend like Lisa. Most people run away from a burning building. Only a few run into the flames, searching for survivors.

"Has Marcus called back?" Lisa asked.

The question struck Shayla like a slap in the face. She thought she was done crying, but her eyes watered again. She shook her head. Marcus was one of the ones who ran away from Shayla's self-destructive tendencies. She couldn't blame him.

"It's alright," Lisa said. "I think it'll be okay, once he cools down..."

Shayla didn't respond. She would've agreed if Marcus broke up with her in a fit of anger. But it was nothing like that. He called and calmly explained why he didn't want anything to do with her. He said she was a harlot, and he didn't have the compassion of prophet Hosea.

Even if he did take her back, Shayla didn't think she could look him in the eyes again. Marcus would forever remind her of her dirty deeds with Pastor Tate. She couldn't talk to him without reliving the panic and disgust she felt in her car when the perverted pastor tried to reach between her legs. No, the only way for Shayla to truly move on was to leave every bit of her past behind her – Marcus included.

In a way, it might have been good that her Acura was set on fire. Fire was the only way to completely erase her sins. Like a phoenix, Shayla hoped to rise from the ashes with a chance to start anew.

The police called at one o'clock. The day-shift detective assigned to Shayla's case said he was able to make contact with Chauncey's parole officer in Houston. Unfortunately, the call didn't generate any leads. Chauncey was currently in good standings with his parole requirements, and he didn't have any outstanding warrants.

The parole officer offered to make a surprise visit to see if Chauncey was in town, but he didn't have enough leverage to track the Miller brothers down if they were in fact missing. The circumstantial evidence Shayla provided might have been enough for an arrest, if either Chauncey or his brother drove an Astro Van, but neither had a van registered in their name. The detective said even attempting to question them could be iffy.

"These guys are career criminals," he stated. "When you're dealing with career criminals, you can't just pull 'em in off the streets and throw them in an interrogation room. The Miller brothers have rights, and they're well aware of them.

"If we detain them and start inquiring about their whereabouts last night, they're gonna lawyer-up. I guarantee it. Plus they'll know we're on their ass, which will make it that much harder to find evidence we can use against them.

"These guys just got out of prison, Miss Humphries. Anyone else could probably get off with probation for arson, but that charge will get them five years, easy. When you throw in the harassment and threats, you can add another two years. Trust me, these boys will do whatever they can to avoid that kind of time."

Shayla held the phone tightly. She looked around nervously. The idea of two dangerous men knowing where she lived was unnerving. The detective probably didn't mean to frighten her with his "*whatever they can*" comment, but Shayla considered a variety of heinous acts that fell into the *whatever* category. According to the police, the Millers never killed anyone, but that didn't mean they weren't capable. Every killer has to start with his first murder.

"What if I drop the charges?" she asked. "Will they leave me alone then?"

She realized how silly her question was the moment it left her lips. The stress and fear was clouding her thought process.

"You, um, you wanna drop the charges?" the detective asked.

"I just want them to leave me alone." Shayla spoke with desperation. She wiped her nose with the back of her hand and sniffled loudly. "I don't want nobody to get hurt because of me."

"We, um, we haven't compiled enough evidence to press charges on anyone," the detective explained. "I can't say if they would leave you alone. But if you and your roommates don't feel safe at the residence, I suggest you make arrangements to sleep somewhere else for the next couple of days. Usually when people are harassed in this manner, it's because the assailant doesn't want to harm them physically. But you never know. You should definitely take whatever steps are necessary to assure your safety..."

Shayla thanked the policeman for his help and got off the phone, wondering if they really should vacate the premises. Her father had a huge, four-bedroom home, with only him and his wife living there. He would take Shayla, Carla and Lisa in without hesitation.

But if she ran to Pastor Benny, she would have to come clean; she would have to tell him about all the wicked things she had done, starting with how she couldn't look away from the sight of his adultery. She sensed the time for their long talk was finally upon them, but she was reluctant. Even this late in the game, the thought of such a conversation made her sick to her stomach.

If only Chauncey hadn't delivered that ominous message yesterday. Shayla thought she could accept everything that happened if he had told her, "*Bitch, we even now!*" Instead he said, "*It ain't over, ho. Naw. It ain't over by a long shot.*"

Did he mean to drag out his game of revenge for a few days or a few tension-filled weeks? Shayla thought she'd go insane if she had to wait that long.

As luck would have it, she only had to wait a few short hours to find out what more Chauncey had in store.

The first call came at 5:02 pm. It was a woman named Theresa, from Human Resources. When Lisa saw her number on the Caller ID, she assumed Theresa called to complain about the extra duties she had to take on because of Lisa's call-in that day. But she found that Theresa wasn't mad at all. In fact, she was upbeat.

"Girl, you not gon' believe what happened at work today."

Lisa was too naive to expect the worst. "What?"

"We working with a *freak*!" Theresa reported. "Somebody got put on blast!"

Lisa was frustrated and tired. She wasn't interested in more drama. "I'm not feeling good," she told her. "Let me call you back."

"Alright, you can call me back," Theresa said. "But make sure you do. You not gon' believe this, girl. You should'a been at work today. You woulda got one too."

Lisa was half a second from disconnecting, but Theresa's comment piqued her interest. "What, what are you talking about?"

"A *DVD*," Theresa said. "Everybody got one. It's on our cars, in the parking lot. I got one. I'ma check it out as soon as I get home."

Lisa rubbed a spot of tension between her eyebrows. She still wanted to hang up, but she sensed this conversation was crucial. Acid started to bubble in her stomach.

"What are you talking about?" she asked again. She rose from the couch and headed for Shayla's room.

"Everybody got a DVD, put under our windshield wiper," Theresa reported. "The CD case says, '*You work with a freak!*'" Theresa laughed. "Ain't that some shit? I don't know what's on this movie, but everybody thinks it's something *nasty*. Sarah said it might be a sex tape with Tom Randall. Wouldn't that be some shit?" she shrieked.

Sarah was another girl who worked with them in Human Resources. Tom was the CEO of the company. He was rumored to have had an affair a few years ago, but Lisa was certain it wasn't him on the mystery DVD.

Her heart was pounding by the time she made it to her friend's door. She pushed it open without knocking. Shayla was at her computer checking her emails. Her eyes grew wide with dread when she saw the expression on her friend's face. She rose from her chair slowly, a moan of despair growing in her chest.

"What's wrong?"

"I think he went back to the job today," Lisa said numbly. "Everybody got a video on their car..."

Lisa's sentence didn't make sense, but at the same time, it made perfect sense. Shayla stopped in her tracks. Her jaw became unhinged, but she couldn't speak right away.

"What?"

That was Theresa speaking on Lisa's phone. She was giddy about the prospect of seeing their CEO naked.

A multitude of questions ran through Lisa's head, but she couldn't get them organized. "When, when did y'all find them?"

"Just now," Theresa said, "when we got off. They wasn't there at lunchtime, so somebody must have left them pretty recently. They in a cheap, paper cover. They woulda got messed up if was hot or if it woulda rained, but it feels good outside. Who do you think it is? Didn't nobody see who left them."

Shayla was talking by then, asking questions Lisa didn't want to give the answer to. If she could completely distance herself from this situation, Lisa would do it in a heartbeat. She knew it was Shayla on the DVD, and she knew Chauncey was responsible for the distribution. The only thing she didn't know was what was on the disc and how Shayla would respond once she told her.

"Call me back after you watch it," Lisa told her friend from work. She disconnected and walked slowly to Shayla's bed. She took a seat and implored her friend to sit down with her.

Shayla shook her head, the tears already twinkling in her eyes again.

"I don't wanna sit down. Tell, tell me what's going on, Lisa."

Lisa looked away and sniffled. Her eyes glossed over as well. She opened her mouth to report what she knew, but Shayla's main cellphone started ringing at that moment, and Lisa didn't have to say a word.

From 5:05 to a little after ten pm, the phones rang nonstop. Some called with the same information about the mysterious DVD. Some called to say they got a call from someone else who said they saw Shayla in a sex tape. Some called after they got home and watched the video themselves. It was from these people that Shayla got the most information.

They told her the video was five minutes long. They said the quality was good, but they could tell the scene was dated. They said the camera angle never changed during the video, but it was better than most of the celebrity sex tapes that got leaked. They said Shayla's hair was short in the scene, and she was thinner than she is now, but her body was awesome.

Some of the people Shayla was close to told her they were appalled to see her behaving in such a manner, even if it was with her boyfriend. They said her language was coarse and vulgar. They didn't like how Shayla mentioned her partner's wife more than once and how she encouraged her partner to comment on how much he despised his spouse. They said Shayla said other things in the video that made it clear this was her first sexual encounter with the gentleman, which made her words and actions that much more deplorable.

Some of the calls Shayla received were from people she considered *friends*. These folks were a lot less brutal in their assessment, but it was hard for them to find anything positive about the exposé. They said Shayla was aggressive, definitely hamming it up for the camera. They said she was *skillful at sex*, rather than call her a *whore*. They asked if she was still dating the married man in the video. They apologized for the embarrassment she surely felt.

"I know how hard this must be for you, but it's not the end of the world. I don't think you can get fired for something like this..."

Shayla thought she worked with professionals with integrity and compassion, but she received a few prank calls from her coworkers at Midwest Media.

One man with a poor vocabulary (Shayla guessed he worked in the mailroom) told her, "Damn, bitch, I didn't know you got down like that! You was actin' all saddity when I tried to holler at you, but you wasn't saddity when you was sucking that nigga's dick! I knew you was a ho. All you bitches is ho's!"

Shayla's brain was drowning in a sea of depression by then, and she couldn't formulate a snappy comeback before he hung up.

Another male caller spoke in a whisper: *"I'm jacking off right now, Miss Humphries. I dreamed about your big ass for a long time, and now I'm looking at your whole ass crack. You are the best dick-sucker in the world! I can tell you like it from the back. Oh my God, I'm cumming right now, Miss Humphries! I swear to God, I'm cumming right now!"*

Shayla didn't hang up on that guy either. She started to, but a part of her wanted to hear it. She wanted to know what people really thought of her, when they had the option of being anonymous.

By then she wasn't crying anymore. She was completely numb, but her fingers kept answering the phone. Her ears kept listening. Lisa stopped coming to Shayla's room when coworkers phoned her, but that was okay. Shayla had so many people ringing her line, she couldn't get to them before some were sent to voicemail.

One anonymous call was from a woman whose voice sounded familiar. Shayla didn't understand why she was taking the exposé so personally: "You are one *nasty bitch*. How dare you disrespect our company like this? Don't you know there are Christians at Midwest Media? No one wants to see your *filth*! You and your boyfriend are disgusting animals. I don't know why you thought it would be cool to show this to everyone, but I think it shows what a lowlife you really are. I hope they fire you for this. I really do. I don't, I don't think I can ever look at you the same."

That message made Shayla so angry, she almost called the lady back and vented her frustration: *What the hell do you mean I showed the video to everyone? Why the hell would I do an exposé on myself, you dumb cow?*

The only thing that stopped her from making the call was another incoming call. She wiped her face with a shaky hand and cleared her throat before she answered it. She tried to sound natural, but the turmoil resonated strongly in her hoarse voice.

"Hello?"

"Sounds like you already heard..." It was Stephanie, one of her closest friends at the office.

"Yeah," Shayla said. "You got one too?"

"I didn't watch it," Stephanie lied, "but people have been telling me about it. Did you, do you know who's spreading it around? Everybody I talked to says they got one, Shay. They all, they say you was, it was real hardcore. Is, is it old? Are you still with that guy?"

"Keewhin." Shayla cleared her throat. Her windpipe seemed to be getting tighter and tighter. She wondered if it would close up entirely and choke off this wretched existence she called life. At this point, that didn't sound like such a bad way to go.

She cleared her throat again just as Stephanie said, "Huh?"

"Can you bring me the video?" Shayla asked. "I wanna see it."

Stephanie hesitated, not willing to part with her free porn. She could hear the sorrow in her friend's voice, but it's not every day you get to see someone you work with in such a compromising position. Stephanie wondered if she could make a copy of the video before she gave it to Shayla. If not, there was sure to be more copies at work tomorrow. There were plenty of guys at Midwest Media who lusted after Shayla. They were probably busy making duplicates right now.

"Oh, okay," Stephanie said. "Do you want me to bring it to your house?"

"Please." Shayla spoke very softly. It was the most demure Stephanie had ever heard her. "I'd really appreciate that..."

Stephanie arrived at the house at 9:15. The scent of gasoline was still noticeable when she got out of her car. She planned to ask what happened when she got inside, but she was never given the opportunity.

A woman she didn't know answered the door and asked, "Do you got the video?"

"Yeah," Stephanie said. She pulled it from her purse, and the stranger took it.

"Thank you," she said, and then she closed the door.

Stephanie stood there for a second, a little perturbed that they weren't going to let her watch it with them or at least offer her a little something for her troubles. Gas was nearly three dollars a gallon nowadays. And her personal time was very valuable.

"Bitch," she muttered as she stepped off the porch.

Inside the house, Carla removed the video from the cover and popped it into the DVD player. She called Lisa and Shayla to the front room, and they took a seat on the sofa.

Shayla briefly examined the handwriting on the CD cover and confirmed it was written by the same individual who had left the threatening letters on her Acura. It was hard to believe ex-

Pastor Miller had kept his exposé video for so long. But a few seconds after the DVD started, she knew this was the case. Shayla watched quietly as her past-self walked away from the dresser where she had positioned her purse. She made her way to the dark-skinned pastor, who was grinning broadly in the background, taking off his belt.

Shayla wore a skin-tight skirt that hugged her assets mercilessly. Her blouse was loose, and it was mostly unbuttoned, revealing a red, lace bra. She remembered wearing the blouse like that for their date. She thought Pastor Miller was a breast man, but she later learned it was her thick thighs that turned him on.

She began the exposé with her typical dirty talk. She wanted the pastor to acknowledge his wife. She wanted him to talk dirty, to show how un-Christian he was. When she got that out of the way, she revealed her true self: The exposé was only part of the reason she was in the motel room. From the moment Chauncey exposed his manhood, she only wanted sexual gratification.

If she was working on this exposé today, she would've stopped the show when Pastor Miller, dick in hand, told her, "You gots to be the finest bitch I done *ever* seen! Why don't you stay for awhile? I'll get you a house, baby. I makes plenty money. I'll pay all yo bills."

But her old self didn't stop or even slow down. Without being prompted, she took a seat on the bed and pulled him between her legs. She grabbed his manhood like a microphone and deep-throated him without a care in the world. Chauncey stared over her shoulder (directly at the hidden camera) with a shocked expression that gradually took on a look of eternal bliss.

"Damn, baby, you ain't even playing. Oh my God, you's a nasty bitch..."

That was all Carla could watch. She walked out of the room without a word. She knew her sister was going through an awful experience. Shayla needed her support, but she couldn't do it anymore. Despite their Christian upbringing, Shayla had clearly given her life to Satan. Carla loved her, but she no longer wanted anything to do with her.

Shayla knew what her sister was thinking when she walked out, and she didn't make any moves to stop her. With her sister gone, she was able to give Pastor Miller's exposé (which, ironically, was now her exposé) her full attention. To her surprise, Shayla found herself becoming aroused, rather than upset with what she was seeing.

At that point, she knew that Carla was right; she was sick. She wondered if she might have gone mad sometime in the last 48 hours. The incident with Pastor Tate, the break-up with Marcus, the horror of seeing her car on fire, and now this – that was enough to push anyone over the edge, wasn't it? It had to be. There was no other way to explain why her panties were becoming moist.

When the video ended, Lisa asked the same question she'd been asking since they first got word of the DVD: "You want to call the police?"

Shayla shook her head the first three times Lisa asked, and she shook it again now. What good were the police in a situation like this? If they couldn't arrest Chauncey for *possibly* setting her car on fire, what were the chances they could arrest him for *possibly* distributing a sex tape? In fact, Shayla distributed the video herself five years ago, so if anyone was guilty of revenge porn, it was her.

Lisa waited on the couch, open for a brainstorming session, but Shayla took the DVD from the player and walked slowly back to her room. Her phone was ringing when she got there. She climbed into bed and curled up in a fetal position before she answered it.

"Hello?"

"Yeah, I gotcha bitch!" Chauncey said. He laughed. "What it feel like, ho? How you like it?"

Shayla's heart rate increased, but her expression didn't change. She didn't even bother activating her call recording app.

"How you find me?" she muttered.

"What, you recording this?" Chauncey asked. "You trying to get me hemmed up, bitch?"

He knew her so well.

"No," she said. "I'm not recording."

"It don't matter if you do, bitch. I ain't gon' say nothing incriminating. You think it's hard to find a ho like you?" He chuckled. "Shit ain't hard, baby. You gave me a video with your whole face on it. Yo shit was so professional, I knew I wasn't the first, and I probably wasn't the last nigga you fucked with.

"*If I wanted to find you*, all I'd have to do is take a few screen shots from that video and print them. Take them pictures up north and ask around. If you been to some more churches, motherfuckers would remember you. If I keep following the trail, I'm bound to run into somebody who lost everything because of you.

"Maybe I'd run into three niggas you fucked over. Maybe one of them niggas remembered what kind of car you was driving. Maybe one of them remembered your license plate number. Maybe I know some people who can turn a license plate into a name and an address. It wouldn't be hard to find you, if I wanted to."

He was speaking in hypotheticals, but she knew he was detailing the actual steps he took.

"What I want to know is if we through, or you wanna take this to another level," Chauncey said. "Far as I'm concerned, I got you back, bitch. I'm done. Your life is ruined just like mine was. But if you wanna get them laws on my ass, we can keep it going. That's what you want, bitch? It's on you..."

"Fuck you," Shayla said. She wanted it to be over, but she didn't want to concede defeat.

"Naw, you already fucked me. That's why you getting fucked right now. And I know you can't take it. Is it over or what, bitch? I ain't got time to play."

She wanted to tell him *Go to hell! I'll kill you if I ever see you again.* Instead she said, "Just leave me alone." It was a hard pill to swallow, but she had to do what was right for her family and friends. They didn't deserve this.

"Ha ha! Yeah, that's what I thought, ho," ex-Pastor Miller said and hung up abruptly.

Shayla tried to hold it in, but the relief that he was done with her, coupled with the sorrow of how they got to this point, broke her down once again. She bawled like an infant while listening to the voicemails she had accumulated throughout the day. She hoped one of the messages would be from Marcus, but fate was not nearly that kind.

CHAPTER TWENTY-ONE
THE FINAL CHAPTER
DADDY DEAREST

Shayla's mind was so frayed, slumber was a welcomed respite. She knew sleep was akin to death, and she welcomed that too. She wasn't suicidal, but she wouldn't mind if God pinched the wick on her candle of life. Subconsciously, she embraced the thought. No more pain. She felt herself drifting, towards the heavens, perhaps. But God was too cruel to allow this.

She felt a hand on her shoulder, pulling her back towards the earth. She fought to shake it off, but it was no use. As her soul returned to the fleshy shell she'd left behind, she heard her father. He was trying to wake her for church, but she didn't want to go. She never wanted to see another church again.

But he persisted.

"Come on, baby girl. Wake up."

She rolled to him and opened her eyes. Her room was dark. Her home was quiet. Pastor Benny left her side and walked out of her line of sight. A moment later she heard a slight click as he turned on the bedside lamp. She closed her eyes. She listened as her father returned to her side of the bed. She smelled his cologne. She opened her eyes again and saw his face.

Her stomach twisted suddenly. She winced from the pain. She felt like she might throw up, but she didn't remember eating today. She felt the first jagged tendrils of a headache as it worked its way from the back to the front of her head. Her eyes were sore from crying.

She told her father, "I don't wanna go to church," and he smiled. It was a terrible smile, like a mother looking down on her stillborn infant, seeing death and beauty at the same time.

"We're not going to church, baby girl." Her father stood again. He went to the computer desk and placed a large hand on Shayla's swivel chair. He rolled it to the bed and took a seat. He wore a white button down with blue jeans. He looked tired, or worried. Shayla figured it was a combination of the two. She pulled her sheets up to her shoulders and looked up at him, as if he was there to tell her a bedtime story.

"What time is it?" she asked.

"Almost midnight."

"What are you doing out this late?"

"Carla called me." He leaned forward with his elbows on his thighs. He rubbed his hands together. "I don't know why she didn't call me sooner. I don't know why *you* didn't call me. You know I'm always here for you."

She chuckled. She didn't mean to, but it slipped out. And then she couldn't wipe the smile off her face.

Her father frowned. "I'm not always here for you?"

"I don't need you to be here for me."

He nodded. "Yeah. I noticed."

"So why bother coming now?"

Her father was stunned by her words. His daughter disappointed him quite a few times throughout her life, but she was never outright disrespectful.

"This is how you talk to your father?"

"I don't want to play these games anymore," she said. "You and me never talk. You always say what you want, and I say what you want to hear, and we both walk away knowing we didn't talk about nothing."

Pastor Benny watched her eyes. He didn't respond right away. "That's, uh…" He sighed. "Is that what's been going on with us? Is that why you don't talk to me, about things?"

"Why are you here?" she asked again. "Where's your wife?"

"She's in the living room."

"With Carla?"

He nodded.

"Carla told you to come talk some sense into me?"

"She told me there were some problems," Pastor Benny confirmed. "She said you didn't want to tell me about it, but things seemed to be getting out of hand. She told me some things that, I just can't believe, Shay. I don't know what's going on with you. I, I don't even know the person Carla described."

Shayla took a deep breath. When she let it out, her nostrils flared. She hated her sister for running her big mouth. And she hated her father for thinking he could pick up the pieces after all these years.

"Nobody's who they appear to be," she muttered.

"What does that mean?"

"Nothing," she said with a roll of her eyes.

Pastor Benny shook his head. He took his glasses off and rubbed his eye sockets.

"Is this what it's come to?" he asked. "You gonna disrespect me like that?"

"I'm tired. I don't wanna talk."

"Baby girl, you've been running from this talk for twenty years. And it don't look like running is helping. I wanna help you, Shay. Why can't you let me do that?"

She looked him in the eyes. It was clear he wasn't going to leave until they had their stupid *talk*, so she sat up on one elbow. "You think you can help me, Pa?"

Her tone was condescending, but he nodded quickly. "Yes. If you tell me what's wrong."

She shook her head, but she sat up all the way. "What did Carla tell you was wrong?"

Pastor Benny put his glasses back on. "She said you're having problems with some men from your past. She said they set your car on fire..."

Shayla nodded. "That's right, Dad."

She was still being ugly, but this was progress, so he pressed on. "She said..." He could barely bring himself to repeat it. "She said you've been making videos, with men. Sex videos." He looked away in embarrassment. They hadn't had a conversation this awkward since Shayla started her period.

"That's right, Pa."

"You, you've been doing that?"

"It's not as sordid as she made it sound."

"What–"

"I mean, yeah, it's sordid, but I wasn't doing it for sex. Just to take them down."

"Take them down?"

"Yeah, take them down. You know, like when somebody's in a position they don't need to be in. Somebody's gotta take them down."

Benny shook his head. "Shayla, I'm not going to sit here and tell you I understand this. What... Who gives you the right to take anyone down? What, what are you trying to accomplish?"

"I just want to make the world a better place," she said with a grin.

Her father's frown intensified. "Are you serious?"

"Sure. Why not?"

"Because Carla says you had sex with men, and you filmed it."

"That was a long time ago. I haven't had sex with one of them in five years." She thought this conversation would be hard, but now that it was underway, it actually felt good to get it off her chest.

"I, I don't understand."

"That's 'cause you don't want to understand. You're looking at it from the victim's perspective, because you're one of them."

"One, one of who?"

"A lying pastor."

Pastor Benny's eyes widened. "What?"

"What's wrong? You said you wanted to talk about it."

"I do."

"Then you can't be getting offended when I tell you the truth."

He shook his head in wonderment. "Shayla, have you gone crazy? Why are you talking like this?"

She smacked her lips and rolled her eyes. "I guess you're still in denial."

Her father tried to keep cool, but his anger started to rise. He rose from his seat. "Don't you talk to me like that! I know things are bad right now, but that doesn't give you an excuse to be disrespectful."

"Why weren't you respectful to Mama?" Shayla asked, not backing down at all.

The question caught him off guard. He hesitated. "What are you talking about?"

She looked over his shoulder and noticed her door was open. "You wanna close that?"

Her father looked back, and then he took slow steps in that direction. He closed the door and returned to his seat. He looked like he'd seen a ghost.

She smiled. "I guess we're really gonna talk about it..."

Her father nodded. "Yes. I, I think we should."

She nodded too. "You made me like this."

He shook his head.

"Yes, you did," she said. "You're the first person who showed me that just because you open a church and call yourself a pastor, doesn't mean you're not full of sin."

"That, that's true," Benny said. "No man is without sin."

"I'm not talking about little sins. I'm talking about the big boys. I'm talking about the seventh commandment. You know which one that is, don't you?"

The color drained from his face. "Wha, what are you talking about?"

"You know what I'm talking about."

"Shayla, you, you been talking in riddles all night. I thought you said you didn't want to play games anymore."

"I'm not playing games. You are. Why don't you admit what you did?"

"Wha, what are you..."

She snorted in frustration. "Okay, let me paint the picture for you: A Wednesday night, after church. I'm thirteen. Carla is nine. Mama's in the hospital, dying from cancer in the brain. You bring your secretary home. You take her to the living room to talk. Me and Carla go to sleep. Is this ringing any bells?"

Her father brought a hand to his mouth, but he didn't speak.

"Okay," Shayla said and continued speaking. "I wake up in the middle of the night, and I hear these sounds. You know what sounds I'm talking about. They were Mommy and Daddy sounds. But then I remembered that Mama wasn't home. She was at the hospital dying. *Well, who's making the sounds*, I wondered. I got out of bed to see. You know what I saw, don't you?"

Shayla had never seen her father so unsure of himself.

"That, that was a mistake," he said.

She laughed callously. "A mistake? No, Dad. When you give a cashier a five when you meant to give her a ten, that's a mistake. When you put your penis inside a woman who is not your wife, that's not a mistake."

He flinched. "That's, you—"

"I watched the *whole thing*," Shayla said. "I saw you smacking that ass, hitting it from the back. When she turned around and said, 'I wanna taste it—'"

"Stop."

"I saw the whole thing."

"*Stop*," he said more forcefully. His eyes watered and he looked away in embarrassment. Shayla saw that his whole body was trembling. "I, I made a mistake," he said. "I can't tell you how many nights I cried about that, begging the Lord for forgiveness."

As he spoke, thick tears spilled from his eyes. The only other time Shayla had seen him cry was when her mother died. She felt a little guilty, knowing she was the cause of his sorrow. But he was the cause of her sorrow many times over. He was responsible for a whole lifetime of pain.

"I saw it all," she said. "And the worst part was I couldn't even tell anybody because as I stood there watching, I couldn't look away. I couldn't go back to my room and mind my business, because I was fascinated by what I was watching."

Her father gasped. He looked like he'd rather be trapped in the bowels of hell than listen to what his daughter was saying.

Shayla, on the other hand, felt pretty good about the way their talk was going. It sucked that she had to ruin her life before she found the courage to confront him.

"Imagine what my childhood was like," she said. "I had to suffer with the pain of what I saw and the guilt of how I reacted. I hated you, Daddy, but I also loved you." She sniffled. She reached to scratch her face and realized she was crying again.

"I am so sorry," he said. He wrung his hands with nervousness. "I'm sorry for what I did to your mother, and I'm sorry for what I did to you. I did have an affair with my secretary. More than one time. And I did it while your mother was in the hospital; when she needed me the most. I was selfish, and I was wrong. If I had known you saw that, Shayla..."

He buried his face in his hands and sobbed openly. "Oh my God, can you please forgive me?"

She had been waiting for this moment, nearly all her life. She had the power to prolong his agony, but there was no point in it. "I forgive you, Dad. It's not your fault. Just a man being a man."

He looked up at her, his face wet and twisted with shame.

"No." He shook his head. "It's not that easy. I want you to know how hard I fought and prayed to overcome the demons that were attacking me. It wasn't easy. I almost killed myself, when your mother died. I was so ashamed of what I had done to her. But I overcame my issues, with the help of the Lord. I prayed, and I repented. I turned away from my sins, Shay. And He forgave me. I became a new person. And you can too. You don't have to go out, trying to hurt people because of what I did to you and your mother. God doesn't respect what you're doing, baby girl. You're not accomplishing anything."

She rolled her eyes at that. She was still crying, but her face was stone cold. "I know you don't believe that."

"Be, believe what?"

She looked him in the eyes. "Daddy, I know there's no God, and you know it too. Why do you lie so much? Your whole life is built on a lie."

Pastor Benny thought he'd heard the worst of it, but this new revelation was almost too much to bear. He grew lightheaded. His heart fluttered. He placed a hand on his chest, hoping he wouldn't pass out, or worse. "Baby girl, you don't believe in God?" He asked the question with the same shock he'd have if she told him she didn't believe in bathing.

She hesitated. This was the first time she admitted it to anyone, Lisa included. "Daddy, you know there's no God. Quit playing."

"Stop it, Shayla. That's blasphemy!"

Goosebumps sprouted on her arms, but she knew she wouldn't get struck down by lightening.

"Is that why you're living this way?" her father asked, his temper rising. "You're sleeping with those men because you don't believe in God?"

As he spoke, the pastor realized the clues were always there. The way Shayla responded when he asked her to come to church, the way she acted when she got there, her atheist best friend, her general irreverence towards the words of the bible. Pastor Benny fooled himself into thinking she was just rebelling against him, but deep down, he sensed it was something worse.

"Yeah," she said. "That's why I do it, 'cause I can't stand y'all *preachers*." She spoke the word with disdain. "You know there's no God, but you keep on anyway. You build those big churches and take those people's money. You tell them to pray for somebody to help them with their bills or their diabetes, and you know it won't work. *You know it*! All those dopefiends praying for deliverance, and ten years later they got the same monkey on their back. You know you're not helping those people!"

"Shayla please..."

She was just getting warmed up. "And then..." Tears continued to stream down her face, but her voice was strong and harsh. "And then y'all got the nerve to sleep with the women too! You take their money. You take their hope. You take their free will. And then you take the women too! I can't stand y'all pastors. You *know* you wrong!"

Her father's jaw moved, but he couldn't come up with the words to respond to the evil his daughter was spewing. The fact that he was responsible for this monster broke his heart like nothing before. All he ever wanted was to bring people to the light. He had no doubt that he saved countless souls in his lifetime. But if he couldn't save his own daughter, what good was he?

All of his words had failed him thus far, so he stood and drew her into his arms. She resisted at first, but Pastor Benny was strong, and Shayla was weak. He sat on the bed and cradled her like he did when she was a child. She began to sob loudly. She buried her face in his chest and gradually reached to hug him back.

Pastor Benny cried too. He cried for the sins he committed. He cried for not being more attentive to the signs when his first-born began to slip away and finally turn her back on Christ.

But even as he cried, a spark of hope warmed his heart. Shayla was disillusioned because of all the pain and suffering she saw in the world. She gave up on God because He didn't fix it, but God never gave up on her. Even in the midst of her sickest sins, He loved her still.

Thankfully, Shayla was young, and her support system was strong. Pastor Benny took responsibility for her lack of faith, and as he comforted her, he made a promise to right this wrong. Even if it took the rest of his life, he vowed to bring her back to the arms of the one and only God who loved her; the God of Isaac and Abraham, the God of Jacob and David and Moses.

The devil was truly a liar, if he thought he could have this pastor's daughter.

EPILOGUE
AUSTIN, TEXAS
10 MONTHS LATER

On Saturday, April 19th, Shayla got her first tattoo. It was a phoenix. It was mostly black, with bright reds and yellows and tattered feathers that looked like they were on fire. She chose the phoenix because she always loved the story of the mythical bird that lived for 500 to 1000 years. At the end of its lifespan, the phoenix would build a nest of twigs. And then there was a fire. Both nest and bird were burned to ashes, but that wasn't the end of life. A bright, new phoenix rose from the ashes, destined to live as long as the last one.

Shayla got the tattoo on her back, between her shoulder blades. She thought the tattoo was fitting – not just because of the car fire that was the start of her own demise, but because she felt like she had a new lease on life, like the mythical creature.

The road to redemption wasn't easy. Up to this point, she never had to do any serious work on herself, but Chauncey shined a bright light on all her faults. It was impossible to move on without acknowledging them.

The first thing she realized was Chauncey was right. He said she couldn't take it if she was the victim of an exposé, and that proved to be accurate. The day he saturated Midwest Media's parking lot with their steamy sex tape was officially Shayla's last day as an employee for the firm.

Lisa told her it would be alright; no one would remember the video after a month or two. Even Carla thought it was foolish for Shayla to throw away her career over the scandal.

"If they're not firing you, you'd be crazy to quit," Carla told her. "You're making seventy thousand a year. And you're a manager. If you suck it up, eventually people will forget."

Shayla thanked her little sister for the advice, but she rejected the idea. How could anyone forget about seeing their coworker in such a compromising position? Two weeks after the DVD was distributed, she had to change her phone number because perverts were still calling; breathing heavily on the phone, whispering their dirty thoughts while her sex scene played in the background.

No, she could never go back to work there. She couldn't look her boss in the eyes or the people who worked under her. Plus, there were at least three perverts in the building who called and said they were masturbating to her sex tape. Shayla feared they might stalk her if she returned.

She typed up a letter of resignation and gave it to Lisa to file for her. Only one person from the office called to try to talk her out of it, which was a good indication she made the right decision.

With no work for a while, she had time for something she'd been avoiding since she was thirteen. She found a counselor not far from home and embarked on a cleansing and maturation process that lasted three months.

Her counselor, a middle-aged woman named Mrs. Webb, had been married to the same man for thirty years. She had five children and two grandchildren and what Shayla considered a "perfect life." She almost rejected Mrs. Webb after meeting her, thinking there was no way a puritan like her could relate to the perverted, sex-driven story she had to tell.

But she gave the counselor a try, and by the end of their time together, she absolutely adored her. Mrs. Webb was a good teacher and a good listener. She helped Shayla understand that there was nothing wrong with the way she reacted to her father's affair. While it was true that most children would've turned away in shame, it wasn't uncommon for some to become captivated by what they were witnessing. Shayla learned that by self-shaming her curiosity, she laid the groundwork for the guilt and sexual frustration she experienced later in life.

Shayla came to understand that it wasn't her lack of faith in God that led her to believe she must right the wrongs in the world.

Instead it was her anger towards her father that caused her to embark on her illicit vendetta. She realized that she saw her father in every crooked pastor she met. The exposés were her way of punishing Pastor Benny without having to confront him directly.

With Mrs. Webb's help, Shayla accepted that there were no winners in any of her exposés. The men she exposed were hurt, their wives were hurt and everyone in the church who believed in their pastor was hurt. Most of all, Shayla was hurting herself. She was blurring the line between sexual gratification and "acting."

Mrs. Webb told her that if she had continued on the path she was on, she would one day find herself old, desperate and lonely, like a prostitute who traded her most valuable possession for money or drugs – never for love and companionship.

Towards the end of their time together, Mrs. Webb wanted to explore the possibility that her client might be a sex addict, but Shayla didn't want to change that aspect of her life. She promised to only make love to men she cared about, and her counselor was somewhat satisfied with that.

With the lessons she learned from Mrs. Webb, Shayla embarked on phase two of her maturation process: Making things right with Daddy. She thought she'd have to endure a ton of embarrassment, given everything he now knew about her life. But it was Pastor Benny who was ashamed when Shayla invited him to dinner.

Because of her counseling sessions, she was able to hold her head high during the meal. But it was hard for Benny to get over the fact that Shayla witnessed his transgressions.

He apologized so many times, she had to stop him and ask, "Didn't you say you repented, and God forgave you?"

"Yes. Many, many years ago. But still—"

"There is no *but*," she told him. "If you're at peace with it, and God has forgiven you, you shouldn't go back to feeling guilty just because I told you I saw it. It was a long time ago. It's in the past. We have to move on."

"I want to, very much," he replied.

"Then, it's done. I worked out my issues in counseling, so we don't have to talk about it anymore. I'd rather make up for the time we lost when I didn't like you."

"You didn't like me?"

"Not really," she admitted. "But I do now. I love you, Daddy."

The big man smiled for the first time that evening. "I love you too, baby."

"Great," she said and picked up her menu. "What do you want to eat?"

"I don't know," Pastor Benny said. He picked up his menu, but he continued to watch his daughter's eyes. "Did, did your counselor do anything to restore your faith in Jesus?"

Shayla chuckled. "No, she didn't. She had other things to work on."

"Is she planning to get started on Jesus now?"

"*Noooo*," Shayla hummed, still grinning. "Friday was my last day with her. She thinks I'm a certifiable success."

"I don't know if it's a success, if you don't believe in God," her dad said with a frown.

"My counselor isn't a pastor. I probably need someone with a lot of knowledge of the bible, someone I'm very close to, to help restore my faith in God..."

Her father grinned. "Someone, like me?"

"If you're volunteering."

"I am," he said. "We can get started right now." He reached across the table and took her hand. "Let's say grace..."

Shayla spent the next few months getting to know her father, which was something she hadn't cared to do since her mother died. She didn't know that he wrote poetry, mostly love poems for his beautiful wife. She didn't know Pastor Benny started building model airplanes ten years ago. His favorite was a

Ford Tri-motor plane that took more than four months to complete.

She invited him to a couple of shows at the Jubilee Theatre. In turn, Pastor Benny invited Shayla to barbecues, church picnics, and dinner at his home, at least once a week. She spent a lot of time around her stepmom and gradually let go of the grudge she'd been holding onto from the day her father brought Melinda home to meet her and Carla.

Pastor Benny appreciated the time he and Shayla were sharing, but restoring her faith was at the forefront of his mind. He didn't want to push too hard, so he didn't invite her to church *every time* the doors opened, but he pointed out the glory and the life-changing powers of God each time an opportunity presented itself.

Fortunately, he wasn't starting with a clean slate. Unlike her atheist friend, Shayla had a strong foundation in Christ already embedded. The more she spent time with her father, she came to see that his marriage with Melinda was rock solid. His adulterous ways of the past were truly in the past. Pastor Benny introduced her to the leaders of his church, and she saw that they weren't horny devils. She understood that it was wrong to stereotype all deacons and pastors based on the few bad apples she was called on to expose.

As far as the seemingly unsuccessful rehab program Pastor Benny was running, he invited Shayla to spend more time at the car washes, home remodeling and other activities his former addicts took part in. He showed her that even though the majority of them gave in to the temptation of drugs when they left his home, during the six months to a year they spent in his program, they truly lived their lives for God.

After a few months of special time with her daddy, Shayla gave him the wonderful news that she was ready to return to God's good graces. She asked Pastor Benny if he would baptize her again. Teary-eyed, he said he'd be honored.

With her mind and soul finally at peace, and more than six months between her new life and the ugly incident at Midwest Media, Shayla set out to look for a job. She wanted to stay in Overbrook Meadows, but there were only four marketing firms in the area. They were competitors, but they occasionally employed the same professionals. Some of the folks at Midwest had left the firm to work for one of the other three and vice versa.

Shayla was almost positive she wouldn't run into any of her old colleagues at the other firms, but when it comes to someone seeing your body and secrets laid bare, *almost positive* was not good enough.

She decided to look elsewhere. Her job search took her to the state capital. Austin was nearly 200 miles away. She never dreamed of relocating, but she was excited rather than intimidated about starting over.

Carla married her boyfriend Jimmy around the time Shayla completed her counseling with Mrs. Webb. The newlyweds moved into Jimmy's apartment on the east side. Shayla was willing to leave the home to Lisa, but her best friend surprised her by refusing the house.

"I don't wanna live here all by myself. I wanna go to Austin with you."

Shayla was thrilled but also shocked by the request. "Why do you want to leave Overbrook Meadows? Your whole life is here."

"Your whole life is here too," Lisa told her. "If you can start over, I can too."

"I'm not starting over because I want to. I'm running away from my problems."

"You want to go to a new city all by yourself?"

"No, but I don't want to drag you to Austin when you have no reason to go."

"Maybe I wanna go," Lisa said.

"You never said anything about leaving before."

"Maybe I wanna go 'cause you're going," Lisa clarified.

"I know, but *why*?"

"Look, we've been friends since high school. We've been living together since college. You're a nutcase, but I honestly don't know what I'd do without you around, Shay. Can I go to Austin with you? *Please*?"

Shayla laughed. "Of course you can go! I would love that. I was gonna ask you, but it sounded selfish."

"It's not selfish. I wanna be with my best friend. What's wrong with that?"

Shayla smiled, but she thought about something Carla accused them of on more than one occasion. "People might *really* start to think we're gay now," she kidded.

"We should make-out, just to mess with their heads," Lisa offered.

Shayla narrowed her eyes, not sure what to make of her friend's sense of humor.

"Yeah, let's *not* do that."

"Spoil sport," Lisa said, and they both laughed.

The hardest part about moving to Austin was saying goodbye to friends and family. Pastor Benny didn't like the idea. He was just getting used to having Shayla back in his life, and he didn't want to lose her again. She assured him the distance between them wouldn't diminish her love for him. Plus, Austin was only thirty minutes away by plane. She promised to visit as often as possible.

Pastor Benny shed a tear when he took Lisa and Shayla to the airport, but he understood that in order for his little girl to become completely whole, it was necessary to go somewhere she could have a clean slate. This was the same advice he gave some of the addicts who graduated his program.

At the new firm, Shayla's starting salary was almost as much as she was making at Midwest Media, and her benefits were a whole lot better. They offered her a company car and were even helpful when she told them she needed to find a job for her friend who moved to Austin with her.

"What kind of work does she do?" her new director asked.

"She has four years experience in Human Resources."

"That department is a mess," the director said. "I know they're looking for a supervisor. Could you ask your friend to apply for the position?"

"Absolutely!" Shayla said with a smile. Lisa had never been a supervisor, but she was a natural leader. "I'll make sure she does it today..."

After three months in a new city and two and a half months at her new job, Shayla was comfortable enough to declare her transformation a success. She went to a tattoo parlor one breezy Saturday afternoon and told the artist she wanted a phoenix on her back. He showed her a few pictures, and she picked the one that looked the most beautiful, majestic and powerful.

When she left the tattoo parlor, she stopped at a downtown boutique and bought a new dress. She put it on the next morning and asked Lisa if she wanted to go to church with her.

"*Church*?" Lisa gave her a knowing look. "Are we backsliding already?"

Shayla laughed. "Girl, you must not know what backsliding means."

"I know exactly what it means. It's when people go back to their old, *ugly* ways. Your ugly ways happened in church, so you can totally backslide by going back."

"Okay, so you do know what it means," Shayla noticed. "But, no. That's not what I'm doing. It's Easter, and Christians have to go to church on Easter. It's a rule."

"It ain't no rule."

"If you were a Christian, you'd know that it *is* a rule," Shayla said. "No matter what kind of sinning you've been doing all year, you'd better have your ass at church on Easter."

"I can tell this is a real *spiritual* experience," Lisa said sarcastically.

"Whatever. Do you want to go or not?"

"Shit no."

Shayla walked away giggling. It was probably better that her friend stayed home. If she took Lisa with her, they'd end up cracking jokes throughout the service, like the *bad* old days.

Shayla arrived at the Greater Missionary Baptist church at ten a.m., which was right on time for praise and worship. The choir director was a tall, skinny man with a large afro. Shayla watched in appreciation as he marched back and forth, working his arms and shaking his fists, encouraging his choir to be as lively as possible.

The enthusiasm quickly spread throughout the church. Everyone rose to their feet and made a joyous sound as they worshipped the Lord. Within seconds of locating a seat, Shayla found herself clapping and rocking too.

Her face was bright, her dress was beautiful, and she didn't notice any of the glances she was accumulating from some of the *less than Christ-like* men in the pews around her. She wasn't aware that a handsome gentleman wearing a powder blue suit had approached her until he tapped lightly on her shoulder.

"Hello, sister. How are you this morning?"

She turned, grinning broadly. "Good morning. I'm doing fine."

"That's good," he said, "I'm Jason Turner, an assistant pastor. I wanted to offer you a New Visitor's card to fill out, if you don't mind." He pulled the card from his jacket pocket. "This is your first time here, isn't it?"

"Yes." She took the card but didn't look at it.

"How you liking it so far?"

"I love praise and worship," she replied. "Your choir director is awesome."

The stranger couldn't hear her, because the band was going strong. He leaned closer and said, "What's that?"

Up close, Shayla thought he smelled nice. But she frowned as she was struck with a strong sense of déjà vu. Pastor Turner was tall and dark-skinned. His hair was short and neatly cropped. His suit was a little flashy, but that was to be expected because of the holiday. She thought he might be getting fresh, but it was possible he really didn't hear her. She gave him the benefit of the doubt.

"Yes, I like the church so far."

"That's good," he said. He backed away, and he wasn't looking Shayla in the eyes – not right away. His gaze swam from her breasts, up her slender neck, and finally to her face again. "That's real good. What's your name?"

"I'm Nicole." The lie came before she was aware of what she was doing. She reached to shake his hand. She reached with her left hand, and Mr. Turner had to do the same. She glanced down and noticed his wedding ring as their palms touched.

"I sure hope you visit us again," he said.

Shayla thought his grin was mischievous, but she tried not to read anything into it. Still smiling, she told him, "I might come back."

"That's great. I'll come and get that card at the end of service."

"Do you want me to leave it somewhere?" she asked.

"No," he said right away. "I'll come get it myself."

"You don't want me to give it to *nobody but you*?" she clarified.

"That's right," he said and began to back away.

Shayla thought his smile was definitely perverted now. She waved for him to come back, unaware that she had crumpled her New Visitor card in her fist, squeezing so tightly her fingertips were white.

"Yes," the pastor said when he returned.

Shayla reached for him with her free hand. The pastor continued to smile devilishly. When he was close enough, she placed a hand on his shoulder. Her fingers slid towards his tie, and then they clamped closed like an eagle's claw, a couple of inches under his Windsor knot. She squeezed hard and pulled. The man nearly lost his balance as he stumbled forward. He placed a hand on the back of the pew to steady himself.

His eyes widened. Shayla's sweet lips, that were making such joyful noise for the Lord a moment ago, were frozen in a sneer. Pastor Turner was stooped over and nearly panicked. Sweat blossomed on his forehead. He looked around wildly as she pulled his face closer to hers.

"I could ruin your whole life," she growled. Her voice was low, but not quiet enough. A few nearby parishioners turned to see what the commotion was.

"What are you, I didn't..." He tried to pull away, but her grip was true. He couldn't believe such a delicate woman had so much strength. Shayla watched the veins bulge in his neck as he struggled to free himself. "Let, let me go." He spoke more forcibly this time. He was getting upset, but Shayla didn't care. He had a lot more to lose than she did. She never had to return to this church, if she didn't want to.

"I know you," she said, her voice low and guttural. "I see the snake in your eyes. You're sick with sin."

"Let me go," he said again. He reached to pry her hand away, but there were more than a dozen people watching in stunned silence now. Maybe some of them were glad someone was finally standing up to him. Pastor Turner looked around and forced a smile. He lowered his hands. "Sister, you got the wrong idea."

"No, I don't," she said. "I know the beast when I see him. Now, I want you to crawl your disgusting self back to the nasty hole you crept out of. And leave these women alone. You got a wife."

"I didn't, I didn't do nothing," he pleaded.

"You heard what I said," Shayla spat. She released him and shoved him away at the same time. The pastor wasn't handsome at all anymore. In fact, he was the ugliest creature Shayla had ever seen. "If I have to tell you again, you won't like it," she promised.

The pastor didn't bother to deny his intentions again. He was free from the crazy woman's clutches, and that was all that mattered. He straightened himself and wiped the sweat from his brow. He adjusted his tie as he backed away. Many eyes were on him now. He offered them a smile that cracked and faded under the pressure. He took a few more steps backwards and then turned and made a hasty retreat.

When he was out of sight, Shayla turned back to the altar, just in time to see the praise and worship team exit the stage. She was hot and frustrated, but she was also proud of herself for putting Satan in his place. Someone standing on her left whispered, "Good job, sister," and that felt good too.

She closed her eyes and took a deep breath, and when she blew it out, she felt the stress leave her body.

"Amen!" the pastor said as he took his place behind the podium. "If you feel Jesus in the church this morning, let me hear somebody say *Amen!*"

"*Amen!*" Shayla said, and the beautiful smile returned to her face. And her heart was at peace.

And it was good.

KEITH THOMAS WALKER

ABOUT THE AUTHOR

Keith Thomas Walker, known as the Master of Romantic Suspense and Urban Fiction, is the author of more than two dozen novels, including *Fixin' Tyrone, Life After, The Realest Ever,* the *Backslide* series, the *Brick House* series and the *Finley High* series. Keith's books transcend all genres. He has published romance, urban fiction, mystery/thriller, teen/young adult, Christian, poetry and erotica. Originally from Fort Worth, he is a graduate of Texas Wesleyan University. Keith has won numerous awards in the categories of "Best Male Author," "Best Romance," "Best Urban Fiction," "Best Young Adult Romance," "Best Duo," "Book of the Year," and "Author of the Year," from several book clubs and organizations. Visit him at www.keithwalkerbooks.com.